THE SAN FRANCISCO

CLIFF HOUSE

THE SAN FRANCISCO
CLIFF HOUSE

MARY GERMAIN HOUNTALAS

WITH SHARON SILVA

TEN SPEED PRESS

BERKELEY

Published in the United States by Ten Speed Press,
an imprint of the Crown Publishing Group,
a division of Random House, Inc., New York.
www.crownpublishing.com
www.tenspeed.com

Ten Speed Press and the Ten Speed Press colophon
are registered trademarks of Random House, Inc.

Cover photo: View of the 1896 Cliff House. Courtesy of Jim Bell

Back cover photo: The Cliff House, March 31, 2005.
Photo by Ed Schuster, Cliff House Collection

Photo page 2: The Cliff House, September 29, 1943. Courtesy of the
San Francisco History Center, San Francisco Public Library

Opposite page: View of the 1896 Cliff House
from the Sutro Heights parapet. Courtesy of Jim Bell

Page 6: (Top) postcard, 1896-1907. Cliff House Collection
(Middle) postcard, circa 1920. From the collection of Glenn D. Koch
(Bottom) postcard, circa 1960. Cliff House Collection

Library of Congress Cataloging-in-Publication Data

Hountalas, Mary Germain.
The San Francisco Cliff House / Mary Germain Hountalas, Sharon Silva.
p. cm.
Includes bibliographical references and index.
ISBN-13: 978-1-58008-995-1
ISBN-10: 1-58008-995-X
ISBN-13: 978-1-58008-996-8
ISBN-10: 1-58008-996-8
1. Cliff House (San Francisco, Calif.) 2. Golden Gate National
Recreation Area (Calif.) 3. San Francisco (Calif.)—Buildings,
structures, etc. 4. Recreation areas—California—San Francisco Bay
Area—History. 5. Sutro, Adolph, 1830-1898. I. Silva, Sharon. II.
Title.
F869.S38C554 2009
979.4'61—dc22
2008053127

Printed in China
Cover and text design by theBookDesigners

1 2 3 4 5 6 7 8 9 10

First Edition

To my parents, Estelle and Howard Germain

&

To my best friend, business partner, and husband, Dan

CONTENTS

A HISTORY OF HOSPITALITY

LOCAL HISTORIANS routinely disagree on how many Cliff Houses have been built on the wind-beaten northwestern edge of San Francisco. Three is the most common answer, some argue that four is correct, and even five has its partisans. But everyone does agree that the city wouldn't be the same without its legendary Cliff House, a destination for the young and the old, the wealthy and the modest, presidents and plumbers, for a century and a half.

San Francisco natives and out-of-towners alike enjoy recalling the first time they spotted sea lions from the windows of the spacious Cliff House dining rooms. Most know at least a little of the landmark building's long history, its various owners, its connection to the Sutro Baths—now a ghostly ruin—and Playland—today blocks of condominiums. Many Cliff House regulars can even recount its many illustrious and occasionally notorious visitors, as well as its varied architectural styles, from showy château to neoclassical "shoebox."

Some observers insist that the first Cliff House was built by gold rush tycoon Samuel Brannan in 1858, who used lumber recovered from a nearby shipwreck. But his building stood a short distance south of the rocky promontory where the Cliff House stands today and where the second Cliff House—indeed, most maintain the first—was built in 1863 by local real-estate speculator Charles Butler. His clapboard structure offered peerless ocean views and its fashionable, high-priced dining room kept the carriage trade well fueled. Simply put, the Cliff House was the place to be.

Within five years, Butler's structure had tripled in size, an expansion that some call the second Cliff House. Others, who consider Brannan's building the first, have dubbed it the third. Still others insist Butler's was the first but with growing pains. These changes meant that more and more people—the masses along with the moneyed—were making their way to what was then the distant seaside for recreation. In time, the respectable nature of the

Cliff House clientele began to fade, as gamblers, grifters, and their girls slowly replaced the city's first families as regular visitors.

Adolph Sutro, a mining engineer who had made a fortune by modernizing the tunnels of the silver-rich Comstock Lode, decided to save the formerly respectable establishment from its descent into tawdriness and bought it in 1883. He quickly set about ousting the riff-raff and refashioning the Cliff House into a family destination. But little more than a decade later, the rambling structure was destroyed by fire.

By 1896, Sutro, who owned more than a thousand acres of the surrounding oceanfront property, had replaced the burned-out remains with a monumental, multiturreted edifice that was reminiscent of a French château, with facilities as grand as the architecture. The new Cliff House was a truly opulent sight, yet Sutro was intent on making it a destination for working-class and wealthy families. He succeeded by offering a menu with affordable prices—a dime got you a seat on the porch and a drink—and a rail line that only cost a nickel and ended at the beach.

Eleven years later, fire once again roared through the Cliff House, burning Sutro's "gingerbread palace" to the ground. A "giant gray shoebox" of concrete and steel rose in its place, opening in 1909. Although in the decades that followed, the building was regularly refurbished, refitted, and remodeled, shuttered and reopened, bought and sold, that 1909 "shoebox" is the Cliff House of today. In its lifetime, it has boasted everything from the largest gift shop in the world to an employee roster that included Rudolf Valentino as a dance instructor.

Today, the Cliff House remains an iconic destination and a beacon of hospitality at the westernmost edge of the city. Indeed, no visit to San Francisco is complete without a stop at the Cliff House. This book tells its story.

HIS CLAPBOARD STRUCTURE OFFERED PEERLESS OCEAN VIEWS AND ITS FASHIONABLE, HIGH-PRICED DINING ROOM KEPT THE CARRIAGE TRADE WELL FUELED.

SIMPLY PUT, THE CLIFF HOUSE WAS THE PLACE TO BE.

PART ONE

PART ONE

THE EARLY YEARS

IN EARLY JULY 1846, the sleepy pueblo of Yerba Buena, a small enclave of pine-wood shacks and adobes jumbled around a gently curved cove, changed hands. The Mexican flag was replaced by the Stars and Stripes on the plaza that was soon to be renamed Portsmouth Square, after the warship that delivered the conquering Americans. Of course, the Mexicans and the Americans were not the first to settle in this picturesque landscape. They had been preceded by the Ohlone Indians, hunter-gatherers who migrated here probably in the sixth century.

The Ohlones' world was first interrupted by the arrival of an overland expedition led by Spaniard Gaspar de Portolà in 1769. Five years later, another Spanish explorer, Fernando de Rivera y Moncada, accompanied by a handful of soldiers and a Franciscan priest, made his way to the top of a craggy outcropping (today's Point Lobos) overlooking present-day San Francisco Bay, and planted a cross in the soil. Only two years would pass before Captain Juan Bautista de Anza and a small company of men that included yet another Franciscan priest arrived at a spot nearby. In their role as representatives of the viceroy of New Spain, de Anza's group raised their own cross at the rocky, windblown tip of the peninsula (today's Fort Point) and declared it the future home of the Spanish presidio. Next, they headed inland a short distance, where they chose a more temperate location for what would become Mission Dolores de Asis, named after Saint Francis of Assisi, founder of the Franciscan order.

Spain's vast empire was already beginning to unravel, however, and in 1821, Mexico achieved its independence, ending three centuries of colonial rule. But the new rulers would hold the mission and presidio sites for just twenty-five years, before ceding them, without resistance, to the Americans on that July day in 1846. Sources disagree on the size of the settlement at the time, with some putting it at fewer than two hundred souls and others at as many as one thousand. Within a year, the backwater trading post would be renamed San Francisco, and within a dozen years, its population would balloon to nearly fifty-six thousand, a growth triggered by the discovery of gold roughly one hundred miles to the northeast.

THE FIRST CLIFF HOUSE

SAMUEL BRANNAN, who had sailed into Yerba Buena cove in 1846, helped fuel that growth. He had arrived a devout Mormon, but in the end proved to be more entrepreneurial than religious. Brannan would eventually launch San Francisco's first newspaper, open a general store at Sutter's Fort, in the heart of what would soon become California's gold country, and buy up large tracts of city real estate.

One piece of land that Brannan "acquired" (no evidence exists that he actually paid for it) was a windy bluff that overlooked Seal Rocks and the Pacific, not far from where the Spanish had planted their cross and near the station that signaled the arrival of ships—originally by semaphore and later telegraph—to the Merchants' Exchange downtown. The savvy tycoon negotiated a bargain price for the entire cargo of a lumber ship that had broken up on the notoriously rocky shoreline below his land. The salvaged

PAGE 12
"California Scenery,"
Hanover & Allen colored
print, circa 1863. Cliff
House Collection

14 THE SAN FRANCISCO CLIFF HOUSE

Yerba Buena, 1846, duotone print. Courtesy of Veronica Randall

timber was hauled up the cliff and a hotel and restaurant were erected. Brannan named his new establishment Seal Rock House, and most historians put its opening at 1858, though a few push it back to between 1854 and 1857. The primary disagreement is not over the date, however, but rather over the claim that this was the first Cliff House. Those who believe it wasn't point to the fact that it rose not on the rocky promontory where the Cliff House now stands, but on a site nearby. Those who claim it was insist the distance was not great enough to disqualify it from the legacy. (The Cliff House owners of the 1950s seemed to have favored the latter argument, boldly proclaiming "Since 1858" above the entrance.) Further history of this sprawling scrap-wood hostelry has been lost, except to know that it failed to attract a regular clientele in its early days, possibly because getting there meant traveling over

unending sand dunes by horse or mule, and at one point was dubbed the House of Mystery. A circa 1890 photograph taken looking south from the Cliff House identifies the Seal Rock House, and photographs of Ocean Beach from the second decade of the twentieth century continue to show it, albeit much remodeled.

Local real-estate mogul Charles Butler viewed Brannan's idea of acquiring land on the city's remote western edge as good business, so in the late 1850s, he purchased the spectacular headland that lay just south of Point Lobos and just north of Ocean Beach, a transaction that was not without difficulty. A potato farmer named Chambers had title to the bluffs and had cultivated them for a number of years, but when Butler tried to buy the 160 acres known as Chambers' Potato Patch, the farmer was not to be found. Butler discovered that Chambers had gone to Oregon, so

Seal Rock House and Ocean Beach from the Cliff House, circa 1865.
Courtesy of the San Francisco History Center, San Francisco Public Library

Only known photograph showing this small structure, which stood where the road left the beach. Watkins stereoview, date unknown. Courtesy of Dennis O'Rourke

he dispatched an agent north to arrange the purchase. The agent proved both a good sleuth and a good negotiator: Chambers reportedly agreed to let his land go for less than the fee Butler paid the agent to make the trip.

Butler's original plan was to hang on to the land until it could be sold for a handsome profit. But the presence of Brannan's Seal Rock House and of a second way station, the Ocean House, some four miles south along Ocean Beach, likely jettisoned that plan in favor of a seaside resort for the city's swells. On October 15, 1863, Butler opened a long, low, white clapboard structure—a writer of the day described it as "looking something like a barracks"—that offered drink, food, rooms, and peerless ocean views. He named it the Cliff House, and he pictured a fashionable neighborhood of pricey villas springing up around it.

Business was slow in the beginning because getting to it from downtown had not changed since the earlier days of the Seal Rock House. Visitors required equal parts fortitude and expert horsemanship along a six-mile route that rose and plunged like a carnival ride. Only the most adventurous day-trippers made the journey, and the earliest Cliff House receipts reflected that limited clientele.

Not surprisingly, it was Butler himself who came up with the solution to that rough ride out to the beach. In 1862, he had formed the Point Lobos Road Company with Senator John P. Buckley, who also became his partner in the Cliff House property, an arrangement stipulated by the state legislature in exchange for granting the road franchise. By spring 1863, several months before the first drink was served, work had begun on a toll road that would deliver travelers efficiently from the western end of Bush Street to the sands of Ocean Beach, passing near the Cliff House. On its completion—reportedly signaled by the detonation of hundreds of kegs of dynamite in the

dunes nearby—the one-hundred-ten-foot-wide Point Lobos Avenue proved itself a worthy rival to the roadway that carried visitors from Seventeenth Street, near Mission Dolores, to the Ocean House. The city's horse fanciers were particularly happy: one stretch of the new thoroughfare boasted a parallel, nearly two-mile, high-speed clay track—the perfect testing ground for their fast-moving trotters. A February 15, 1866 *New York Times* article describes the macadam surface as being "as smooth as a dollar. . . . At any stable in town you can get a pair of horses that will carry you out there in a half hour . . . my first drive was behind a livery team that brought three of us and a rockaway in twenty-four minutes." Point Lobos Avenue cost its backers $175,000, which they hoped to recoup quickly at the toll box where they were charging the steep round-trip fare of $1.00.

Point Lobos toll road, circa 1865, was the only direct route between the city and the Cliff House. Courtesy of the San Francisco History Center, San Francisco Public Library

"A SORT OF FAMILY GATHERING"

BUTLER'S STATE-OF-THE-ART road provided the city's most prominent families a comfortable ride to his new establishment. Keeping his rarefied clientele happy once they arrived was his next challenge. Toward that end, he wisely leased the Cliff House to Captain Junius Foster, a seasoned hotel man and former purser on the steamship *Orizaba*, which had ferried men to the gold-fields from Panama. Foster was the guiding hand behind the service at the well-regarded International Hotel on Jackson Street, where Butler was living when he purchased the headland. A guest of the time recalled, "meals . . . were on 'the American plan,' and not at all bad. Long tables were each adorned with a center line of pies, the line

View from the road leading up from the beach with the carriage barn clearly visible to the north of the main building. Houseworth stereoview, circa 1865 Courtesy of Bob Schlesinger

View from the road leading up from the beach. Watkins stereoview, circa 1865. Courtesy of Bob Schlesinger

broken by an occasional jelly cake in a high glass dish with glass cover. Facing me sat a stout elderly woman in a . . . red velvet dress with a diamond necklace and fingers literally covered with rings set with every variety of precious stone." Simply put, Foster knew how to keep a moneyed crowd spending their money.

Just as Butler and Foster had hoped, the best families—the Crockers, the Hearsts, the Stanfords, the Lathams, the Vandewaters—flocked to the broad veranda of the road-house, where they sipped refreshments and watched the sea lions cavort on the nearby rocks. Gentlemen arrived astride their stylish trotters, while their wives, friends, and children rolled along more slowly by carriage on the wide macadam drive. Robert O'Brien describes this lively scene in *This Is San Francisco*: "Almost daily adding crust and elegance to this procession were the Vandewaters in their rockaway, Mrs. S. J. Hensley and friends in her blue, sea-shell carriage that was drawn by four horses, Mrs. Milton Latham in her brown, yellow-wheeled barouche with the blue satin lining, and various additional matrons of fashion sitting in their neat broughams or basket phaetons with the inevitable Dalmatians trotting docilely along between the rear wheels." The Cliff House road also saw the West's first four-in-hand coach imported from England, the property of the clever, colorful Lucky Baldwin, a former horse trader who made millions in the silver rush. Kentucky-born James Ben Ali Haggin, a lawyer who had migrated west and made a fortune investing in the goldfields, "drove the second with a pair of bays and a pair of iron-grays."

"Everybody knew everybody, so it was a sort of family gathering," Foster recalled years later when asked about his days at the Cliff House. En route "there was

Front entry and carriage shed. Houseworth stereoview, 1868–81.
Courtesy of cliffhouseproject.com

a continual nodding and buzzing from one carriage to another, while there was a constant succession of spins on the track between the flyers. These matches . . . were generally just for the fun of the thing, or for champagne all around for the speeders."

The road to the Cliff House was always busy. The city's power brokers took to it in the early morning, before they were bound to their desks for the rest of the day. Their wives and children were driven out along it in the afternoons, happy to breathe in the fresh sea air, and moonlit nights brought out spooning lovers. When the sky was clear and the sea was calm, it seemed as if everybody headed to the beach. Newspaper accounts of the time report as many as twelve hundred teams tying up at the Cliff House hitching posts on a sunny day, with still more visitors forced to go farther down the coast in search of a place to tether their horses.

Front entry, 1865–81. Courtesy of cliffhouseproject.com

The "Cliff House," engraving, circa 1863. Cliff House Collection

In the *San Francisco Daily Morning Call* of June 25, 1864, Mark Twain sang the praises of a trip to the Cliff House: "If one tires of the drudgeries and scenes of the city, and would breathe the fresh air of the sea, let him take the cars and omnibuses, or, better still, a buggy and pleasant steed, and, ere the sea breeze sets in, glide out to the Cliff House. . . . Away you go over paved, or planked, or Macadamized roads, out to the cities of the dead, pass between Lone Mountain and Calvary, and make a straight due west course for the ocean. Along the way are many things to please and entertain . . . the little homesteads . . . Dr. Rowell's arena castle, and Zeke Wilson's Bleak House in the sand. Splendid road, ocean air that swells the lungs and strengthens the limbs. Then there's the Cliff House, perched on the very brink of the ocean, like a castle by the Rhine."

In another account little more than a week later, Twain describes a second and decidedly less successful trip to the Cliff House, this one in the predawn hours: "The wind was cold and benumbing, and blew with such force that we could hardly make headway against it. It came straight from the ocean, and I think there are icebergs out there somewhere. True, there was not much dust, because the gale blew it all to Oregon in two minutes. . . . From the moment we left the stable, almost, the fog was so thick that we could scarcely see fifty yards behind or before, or overhead; and for a while, as we approached the Cliff House, we could not see the horse at all, and were obliged to steer by his ears. . . . But for those friendly beacons, we must have been cast away and lost. . . ." Strong winds and dense fog—San Franciscans of every era can easily imagine Twain's journey.

In an article in the *Californian*, Twain was no more complimentary about what the Cliff House offered indoors than he was about his predawn trip. "There was

nothing in sight but an ordinary counter, and behind it a long row of bottles with Old Bourbon, and Old Rye, and Old Tom, and the old, old story of man's falter and woman's fall, in them."

Amelia Ransome Neville, who settled in San Francisco as a young newlywed in the 1850s, provided a somewhat sunnier account of the early days of the Cliff House in her 1932 memoir, *The Fantastic City*: "From its balcony high above the breakers one gazed through binoculars at the seals or sighted ships beyond the Farallones. . . . There was an excellent cuisine at the Cliff House, specializing in fried Eastern oysters, and a bar famous for its mixed drinks. Mixed spirits, however, were never served to ladies. On cold afternoons we sipped port or sherry on the balcony while men drank high-balls, cocktails, or Tom-and-Jerry at the brass rail indoors." In an 1894 interview, Charles Butler seconded Neville's assessment of Foster's table: He "would have the finest sea fish right out of the ocean and crabs within ten minutes after they were caught. Mushrooms he grew himself. . . . Some of his suppers cost $50 for each person."

Watkins stereoview, 1868–82. Cliff House Collection

Foster knew that even society people would sometimes try to skip out on those high tabs. On one occasion, two young stockbrokers and their ladies arrived in a carriage, enjoyed several bottles of wine along with plates of duck and frog's legs, and then the men told the waiter to "charge it" as they headed for their carriage. Foster, overhearing them, quickly invited them all back to the table for another bottle of wine, relieving the women of their sealskin wraps just as they were seated. When that final bottle was finished, the sealskin wraps were nowhere to be found until the gentlemen paid the bill.

But people gathered at the Cliff House for more than fine food and wine. The balcony and big windows on the ocean side afforded guests a front-row seat for watching scores of sea lions climb and gambol on the sheer, craggy rocks just offshore. Occasionally, the visitors were treated to a considerably more dramatic performance. In 1865, aerialist James Cooke, a veteran circus performer, stretched a rope from the Cliff House to Seal Rocks and slowly made the journey before a cheering gallery of fifteen hundred. The following year, Miss Rosa Celeste matched Cooke's feat before an equally enthusiastic—and even larger—audience.

As the crowds grew, the Cliff House did, as well. An article in the April 26, 1868 issue of the *Daily Alta California* announced the near completion of a pair of extension wings, tripling the original size of the building. The area between the new structures, on the land side, was transformed into an open seating area for visitors who wanted to enjoy the sun but escape the wind. On the seaward side, the balcony was widened into a veranda that could double as a dance floor when the need arose. The new south wing would eventually include "a ladies' parlor and accessories," while the north wing housed "a bar-room, reading-room, restaurant, card room, and other conveniences for gentleman's use." Although the increased space meant that more visitors could be accommodated, Captain Foster was intent on keeping the Cliff House an exclusive address. He carefully crafted the menu for his newly expanded operation, listing terrapin and guinea hen, quail, and duck, all served in luxurious surroundings at prices that only the elite could afford.

A CHANGING SCENE

BUT FOSTER could not keep one of city's most famous excursions off of the calendar of everyday San Franciscans and out-of-towners forever. In the early 1870s, the sand dunes that made such a rough ride from the city to the seashore until Point Lobos Avenue was built were being transformed into Golden Gate Park. In 1877, the city opened the first public road through the park to the beach, improving access for everyone. Hotels and freshly minted tour operators were selling full-day trips to city visitors who had read about the dramatic views and the "loud talking surges and doleful intonations of the seals." At the same time, new and old establishments farther down the beach, such as the Ocean House and the Ingleside Inn, were delivering a heavy dose of competition to what had been an exclusively privileged location.

As more people of modest means made their way to the seaside, Foster began losing his hold on the city's elite families, who were tiring of the crowds and longing for what they remembered as the good times. Gone were the days described by social observer Benjamin E. Lloyd, in his 1876 *Lights and Shades in San Francisco*: "A drive to the 'Cliff' . . . a hearty welcome from Captain Foster, and an hour passed over his hospitable board discussing the choice contents of his larder, and a return to the city through the charming scenery of Golden Gate Park, tends to place man about as near to Elysian bliss as he may hope for in this world."

But a free road and growing competition were not the only reasons behind Foster's disappearing client list of leading citizens. The goldfields of the Sierras had helped to build Brannan's Seal Rock House in the 1850s, and the 1859 discovery of a bountiful vein of silver ore in the hardscrabble ground of western Nevada paid for plates of eastern oysters and bottles of French Champagne on Cliff House dining tables throughout the 1860s and into the 1870s. The discovery also guaranteed a busy city port and funded a building boom and a bonanza in retail sales of food, equipment, and clothing to miners. However, banking on mineral wealth proved a seesaw proposition, with stock shares skyrocketing on news of a newly found vein and crashing on news of a once-productive mine petering out.

By the mid-1870s, the silver mines were waning, and the boom was turning into a bust. Families that once boasted "a $10,000 team of Kentucky grays, . . . and a gold-mounted four-in-hand [coach] and the uniformed livery to go with [it]" could no longer afford them. Carriages for hire, at about ten dollars a day, were replacing family coaches on Point Lobos Avenue, forcing Captain Foster to rethink his market.

The competition offered later hours, serious gaming tables, and a generally more boisterous atmosphere, and Foster, who was desperate to keep the Cliff House doors open and till full, decided he should, too. He turned first to the young men of the moneyed class who were interested in high-stakes poker, high-proof liquor, and high-class call girls, and who wanted to enjoy themselves far from the judgmental eyes of their families. He offered private rooms for both dining and trysting and employed waiters who knew how to keep their mouths shut. Soon, Foster proved to be even more broadminded. In *This Is San Francisco*, Robert O'Brien describes the sea change from the "Nob Hill and tallyho set" to a new kind of heavy spender: "Society matrons sipping imported sherry vanished from the imposing galleries, and in their place swaggered flashy, generous, good-natured demimondaines who took their whisky straight, and wore golden double eagles for heelpieces on their slippers. And as long as they were buying champagne, Captain Foster let the parties go on a little longer and a little more loudly in the . . . [private] rooms; if they were miners and their wenches from the Barbary Coast dance halls, what difference did it make as long as they paid their bills, and settled for the breakage?"

CLIFF HOUSE

Stage Busses connect with the Central (or Bush Street) and the
Sutter Street Cars, at their Terminus at Lone
Mountain, every fifteen minutes.

This is the pleasantest ride of twenty-five minutes outside the city, and the
most enchanting view in the world.

HUNDREDS OF SEA LIONS!

Sporting in the water, and basking on the rocks, and

*Vessels and Steamers from all parts of the world, entering and
leaving the Golden Gate.*

Elegant Breakfasts, Lunches and Refreshments of all kinds.

HOTEL ACCOMMODATIONS ON THE EUROPEAN PLAN.

FOSTER & CO., - - - - Proprietors.

Bacon & Company, Steam Printers, corner Clay and Sansome Streets.

Promotional bill encouraged San Franciscans to journey out
to the Cliff House by horse-drawn stage "busses," 1865–81.
Cliff House Collection

Although evenings at the Cliff House had become a wild mix of drinking contests, gamblers winning bundles of cash or losing their shirts, and dining and more in the private rooms, Foster attempted to maintain enough decorum during the day to welcome families, who still came to watch the sea lions and sip cool drinks on the veranda. But cool drinks didn't pay the bills. One afternoon, a group of one hundred seventy tourists from Massachusetts visited the Cliff House and ordered just "two hundred glasses of water and three glasses of lemonade." As they left, Foster was heard to remark, "Hell, two prospectors and their girls spend more money for one dinner than the whole state of Massachusetts does in an entire day."

In 1881, the Cliff House got a new neighbor, who was soon unhappy with the raucous atmosphere and sordid reputation of what had gone from being a meeting place for San Francisco society to a tawdry roadhouse that hosted more fistfights than families. The newcomer's solution was simple: he bought the Cliff House.

The Cliff House and Seal Rocks from the beach, taken by Bartholomew Ogilvie, circa 1868. This photograph was identified by Ogilvie's great-granddaughter Barbara Newman. Cliff House Collection

HIGH-FLYING DAREDEVILS
AT THE SEASIDE

ON JUNE 30, 1859, the Great Blondin became the first person to cross the chasm below Niagara Falls on a tightrope. He followed that remarkable feat by adding a degree of difficulty to each subsequent trip: a blindfold, a man sitting on his shoulders, running backwards, pushing a wheelbarrow. Not surprisingly, tightrope walkers soon became a nationwide fad—a fad that first arrived at the Cliff House in 1865. According to the *Circus Scrap Book*, on September 28, James Cooke, an accomplished acrobat and contortionist, strung a rope between the Cliff House and Seal Rocks and, though he needed to pause and sit on the rope several times to rest his aching muscles, succeeded in completing the four-hundred-foot crossing, his first public appearance as a rope walker. (Five years later, he placed a one-hundred-pound live bear in an open box, strapped the box to his back, mounted a tightrope that had been set up in one of San Francisco's parks, and, after one failed attempt due to the fidgety bear, finished the stunt.)

The one-hundred-sixty-foot bridge to Flag Rock, prior to its collapse in 1884.
Courtesy of the Golden Gate National Recreation Area Archives

A year later, on June 17, eighteen-year-old Miss Rosa Celeste was set to duplicate Cooke's achievement. She had arrived in the city two years earlier, and prepared herself for the perilous feat by completing six tightrope crossings in a variety of locations, including Oakland, Alameda, and at least two sites in San Francisco: downtown at Platt's Hall at Bush and Montgomery streets and at sand-strewn Hayes Park. But, as reported in the *Circus Scrap Book*, June 17 was "disagreeable," being both "cloudy and blowing a perfect hurricane." When the wind failed to die down by noon, Miss Celeste decided against the walk, and promised to return in a week. (To the delight of the crowd, Mr. Eugene Lee, a talented gymnast, stepped in to take her place, and though he began with grace and some ease, by the time he reached the midpoint of his journey, the high wind tossed him from the rope. Fortunately, his training saved him: he grabbed the rope before the sea grabbed him and maneuvered himself to safety.)

On June 24, Miss Celeste returned to the Cliff House as promised. Thousands had gathered to watch at the seaside, and the Cliff House veranda was packed with people who had each paid a dollar for a prime seat. At noon, with the sun shining, Miss Celeste "stepped on the rope, cast a quick glance 'round on the assembled multitude, and amidst loud applause started on her dangerous journey." By the time she was two-thirds of the way to her goal, the fog "sprang up from the sea . . . [and] enveloped [her] in its misty folds. . . . Now all eyes were attracted toward Seal Rock. See! The flag is waved." Miss Celeste had made it safely, and without stopping to rest as Cooke had. Cliff House manager Captain Junius Foster sent a message insisting that, because of the fog, the young daredevil return by boat, not by rope, and she wisely heeded his advice. On the following Sunday, she succeeded in completing a round trip above the crashing waves.

The distance between the Cliff House and Seal Rocks continued to prove irresistible, and the following year, the strong-jawed Miss Millie Lavelle rigged

April 6, 1884, the day the bridge to Flag Rock collapsed. Courtesy of the San Francisco History Center, San Francisco Public Library

up a wire cable between the two points, attached a trolley to the cable, and fixed a bit to the trolley. Then, with her teeth firmly gripping the bit, she slid along the cable, arriving without incident at her sheer rock destination.

Gary Stark, who has preserved a wealth of Cliff House history on his Cliff House Project Web site, provides more evidence of the thrill of being above the sea at the Cliff House. His source is a newspaper account of an incident that took place on April 6, 1884, and this time it is the people, not the professionals, who are making the trip. A one-hundred-sixty-foot-long, four-foot-wide suspension bridge fashioned from two wire cables and a series of wooden slats had been stretched between the Cliff House and Flag Rock (later known as Fisherman's Rock or Fishing Rock). According to the article, some young boys, looking for fun, began swinging both ends of the bridge, which caused the folks who were strolling its length to panic and move immediately to the higher side. That sudden shift turned the bridge upside down, spilling the strollers onto the beach below—the tide was out—where they were doused by incoming waves. No one died, but many broke bones, and the nearly five dozen people who had already crossed to Flag Rock were forced to make their way back on the bridge that no longer had a secure hand railing.

The final daredevil is Thomas Baldwin, who took to the air near the Pacific in a feat that was hosted by the Cliff House. In January 1885, Baldwin strapped on a parachute, climbed into the basket of a hot-air balloon, and took off above a cheering crowd that included President Benjamin Harrison. Once he was high in the sky, Baldwin exited from the basket, safely parachuting one thousand feet into Golden Gate Park, a trip for which he was paid a dollar a foot.

Crowds gathered on Ocean Beach for the January 1885 balloon
ascension by Thomas Baldwin. Courtesy of the Golden Gate
National Recreation Area Archives

ALL ROADS LEAD TO
THE CLIFF HOUSE

BEFORE CHARLES BUTLER and his partners built the toll road from the terminus of Bush Street to the front door of the Cliff House, a rough ride on horseback was the only direct route. Pony-express-rider-turned-poet Joaquin Miller described the six-mile track as "tossing, terrible, moving mountains of sand. . . . At one place a little mountain [threw] itself right in the road . . . [and] our horses plunged and wallowed belly deep." The main competition for the new byway was the Ocean House Road (the equivalent of today's Ocean Avenue), which began near Seventeenth Street and Mission Dolores and ended about four miles south of the Cliff House, at the rival Ocean House.

Carriages and horse-drawn eighteen-passenger omnibuses transported picnikers to the beach along the Point Lobos toll road for about a decade and half, until the owners' fortunes turned and the road fell into disrepair, at which point it was sold to the city for a fraction of what it cost to build. During the 1870s, winding roadways appeared through the slowly developing Golden Gate Park, and in 1877, the city completed a public road through the park to the Cliff House. The era of the toll road was finished.

In the early 1880s, the Park and Ocean Railroad launched a steam-train line that carried people along the southern edge of the park to the foot of Cabrillo Street, just south of the Cliff House, at a cost of twenty cents for a round trip. But when Adolph Sutro opened the grounds of his Sutro Heights estate to the public in 1885, he declared the fare too high for the common man, and he and his cousin soon backed the building of a second steam railway to Sutro Heights and the Cliff House. In 1887, before the line was finished, the Sutros sold their interest to the Powell Street Railroad Company. The agreement included a provision that prevented the new owner from charging more than ten cents for a round trip when the line was completed. Opened in 1888, the Ferries & Cliff House Rail Road had a depot opposite the entrance to Sutro Heights, and the fare included transfers to other transit lines. In 1892, the Ferries & Cliff House Rail Road was snapped up by the big, brash Southern Pacific Railroad, which stopped handing out transfers. That move angered Adolph Sutro, who knew that the absence of transfers effectively doubled the fare, so he went back into the railway business, completing the electric Sutro Railroad in 1896 and setting the fare at a nickel, transfer included. By the turn of the century, both the Ferries & Cliff House Rail Road and the Sutro Railroad had been gobbled up by United Railroads, along with most of the city's other transit lines.

In the first decade of the twentieth century, corruption in the city's privately held transportation and other utilities companies generated a fiercely populist campaign for public ownership. On a 1909 ballot, San Francisco voters passed two bonds to finance the purchase of the privately owned Geary Street cable car line and to convert it to an electric streetcar line that extended to the Ferry Building at the foot of Market Street. In 1912, the Municipal Railway of San Francisco, one of the first municipal railways in the United States, christened the new line. Not long after, three streetcar lines were humming along Geary Street. The B line began at the Ferry Building, proceeded along Geary to today's Presidio Avenue, and then along Point Lobos Avenue, today's Geary Boulevard, terminating at the foot of Cabrillo Street, a short walk from the Cliff House.

Electric Sutro Railroad car. The line was installed by Adolph Sutro in 1896 to compete with the Ferries & Cliff House Rail Road that had been launched in 1888. Courtesy of Dennis O'Rourke

Like his comrades frolicking in the surf, Ben Butler was not a true seal but a sea lion. Postcard, circa 1890. Courtesy of cliffhouseproject.com

VISITORS HAVE PATRONIZED the Cliff House not only for the food, drink, and ocean views, but also for the chance to watch the large community of sea lions frolic—and sometimes fight—on the nearby Seal Rocks. Wagering on how long it would take a particular sea lion to scramble from the rocks into the water became a popular pastime. With everyone's binoculars firmly focused on the subject, bets were placed. The stakes were so high and heated that some gamblers rigged the results by hiring men to hide near the rocks and shoot air guns at the prescribed time. The sea lions' shenanigans even

1011 Seals on the Rocks at the Cliff House, showing old Ben Butler, the famous King of the Seals, now deceased

drew the delight of their famous neighbor, Adolph Sutro, who, in an effort to ensure they were well protected, saw to it that Congress passed an act in 1887 granting Seal Rocks to San Francisco "in trust for the people of the United States."

But since the mid-nineteenth century, there has been only one star on those crowded rocks: Ben Butler, named after General Benjamin Franklin Butler, a Massachusetts politician who oversaw the occupation of New Orleans during the Civil War. This very large sea lion enjoyed a dedicated following, primarily due to his grand physique that was easily identified among his fellow rock dwellers. According to a July 14, 1895 obituary in the *New York Times* headlined "The Biggest of the Sea Lions Dead," Ben "weighed 4,800 pounds, and was over 15 feet long and 8 feet 9 inches around the body." He had floated in on the tide, and settled in the soft sand near the Cliff House, where he took his last breath, succumbing to injuries incurred in a pitched battle on the rocks. Just before he passed, he raised his head and "bellowed pitifully," a sound that was answered with a giant roar from his fellow sea lions.

It took "twelve men and four horses to remove the body" from the shore. Adolph Sutro, mayor of San Francisco at the time, assured everyone that Ben would be prepared by the best taxidermist in the city, and then put on display in the museum of the Sutro Baths for everyone to see. Proof that the promise was kept appears in a photograph taken later the same year.

Ben was not forgotten. Nearly eighty years later, the Ben Butler Bar opened in the Cliff House, where it remained a popular seaside halt for twenty-seven years. Folks who stopped in at the bar could also order the open-faced Ben Butler crab salad sandwich.

DINING OUT
IN SAN FRANCISCO

IN HIS *Eldorado, or Adventures in the Path of Empire*, journalist Bayard Taylor attested to the diversity of dining choices already available in San Francisco by 1849: "The tastes of all nations can be gratified here. There are French restaurants on the plaza and on Dupont Street [today's Grant Avenue]; an extensive German establishment on Pacific Street; the Fonda Peruana; the Italian Confectionery; and three Chinese houses denoted by their long three-cornered flags of yellow silk." The city's first Chinese restaurant, the Canton, had opened in the previous year at Jackson and Kearny streets, close to the heart of what Taylor describes as the French quarter, and according to San Francisco archivist Gladys Hansen, at least some of the French stoves were manned by Chinese cooks, not unlike today. That early scene would blossom, and just twenty-five years later, *Scribner's Monthly* reported that San Francisco had more restaurants per capita than any city in America. "They number between two and three hundred . . . and at least thirty thousand people take their meals at them. They are of all grades and prices, from . . . Martin's and Maison Dorée, where a meal costs from $1.50 to $20—down to the Miners' Restaurant, where it costs only forty cents."

Writer Frank Marryat, who arrived in San Francisco in 1850 and spent time in both the Sierras and the city for the next two years, provides a colorful picture of dining out in the heady days of gold fever in Malcolm E. Barker's delightful *More San Francisco Memoirs 1852–1899*: "It is eight o'clock now, and, in an instinctive search for breakfast, I enter the Jackson House. Here are a hundred small tables nearly all occupied, I secure one and peruse the bill of fare. . . . 'Fricassee de Lapin,' that sounded well, so I ordered it; I didn't tell the waiter, when he brought it, that it

was not rabbit but gray squirrel . . . [which] I knew from experience . . . It was very good, however . . . ." Marryat goes on to praise the city's diverse, seasonal menus, from which diners could choose "bear, elk, deer, antelope, turtle, hares, partridges, quails, wild geese, . . . snipe, plover, curlew, cranes, salmon, trout," and more.

Barker also treats readers to the reminiscences of French writer Louis Laurent Simonin, who visited the city in 1859 (he found a room at the International Hotel, where Captain Junius Foster was looking after guests) and describes it as "crisscrossed with beautiful streets, some of which are quite grandiose, like Montgomery Street, . . . [and remind him] of the Rue de la Paix in Paris." He dines at the Barnum Restaurant, run by a fellow countryman, and says it holds "its own against the most famous restaurants in Paris." But Simonin's most interesting description is of lunchtime on a Montgomery Street corner, site of "the most famous bar in California." The food is laid out on a table—"oyster soup, pork and beans, roast beef and potatoes, . . . [and] thinly sliced bread"— diners fill up their plates with as much as they want, and eat standing up. Then they make their way to the bar and pay a quarter for "a glass of claret or sherry." If you don't drink you don't pay, and so the hungry can fill their stomachs for free. Years later, Victor Pollack, who was the orchestra leader at the popular Techau Tavern on Powell Street from 1915 to 1921, recalled similar "free lunches" in the 1890s: "You could go into any saloon and get a 2-ounce glass of whiskey. . . for 10 cents and Steam or Lager beer for 5 cents, with all the free lunch you could eat. In the better places like the Waldorf on Market Street opposite the Palace Hotel, you bought a mixed

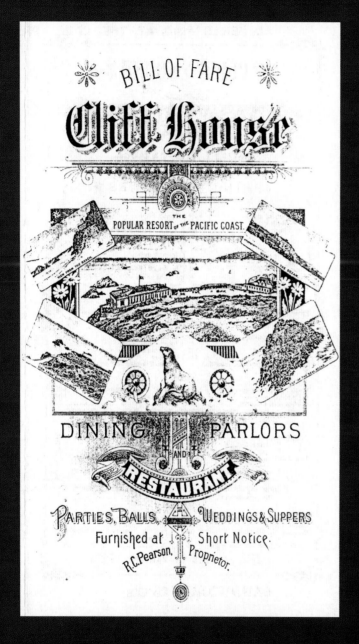

BILL OF FARE

Cliff House

THE POPULAR RESORT OF THE PACIFIC COAST.

DINING PARLORS
AND
RESTAURANT

PARTIES, BALLS, WEDDINGS & SUPPERS Furnished at Short Notice.

R.C. Pearson, Proprietor.

drink for 15 cents, [made from] the finest liquor, . . . [and were] served a hot baked ham sandwich free. In Newman's College Inn at Eddy and Powell you got a hot enchilada and all the free lunch with a 10 cent glass of beer, which was high priced then."

The presence of oyster soup on Simonin's free-lunch menu—or oysters in any form on any menu—was not surprising. Indeed, oysters seemed to be in every restaurant kitchen, prepared in every way imaginable—raw, steamed, stewed, sautéed, fried, baked—and eaten at every time of day. Gobey's Ladies and Gents Oyster Parlor, on Sutter Street, is credited with serving the city's first oyster cocktail. Clarence Edgar Edwords, in *Bohemian San Francisco*, reports that women sitting down to breakfast in the Palace Hotel's Ladies' Grill invariably ordered "an omelet of California oysters, toast, and coffee." The Palace kitchen also originated oysters Kirkpatrick, named for the hotel's general manager, Colonel John C. Kirkpatrick. The bivalves were topped with cheese and bacon and baked, a preparation that purportedly helped the high-living Kirkpatrick tame his frequent hangovers. To make the popular dish once known as The Squarer and nowadays called an oyster loaf, cooks filled a buttered loaf of bread with fried oysters. It, too, promised to help cure folks who had drunk too much.

French restaurants remained a draw after Simonin's days, in large part because of Raphael Weill, who emigrated from France as a teenager in the 1850s. Weill, who went to work in a dry-goods store and then later bought it and renamed it the White House Department Store in 1870, after the famous Grande Maison de Blanche in Paris, was a key figure in promoting everything French in the city, from the imported stock that filled his high-class emporium to the haute cuisine served in the best restaurants. Dishes were even created in his honor, such as chicken Raphael Weill, which called for cooking the bird in butter with shallots, brandy, white wine, and tarragon and serving it with a cream sauce. In

The Fantastic City, Amelia Ransome Neville attests to Weill's success in keeping French cuisine in fashion, recalling when locals and visitors "from the Old World . . . could dine as well as in Paris for but slightly higher tariff. Seventy-five cents paid for the *table d'hôte* at the Old Poodle Dog, an eminently epicurean feast served with wine."

According to California historian James R. Smith, the Old Poodle Dog, originally called Le Poulet D'Or, opened in 1849, in a rickety structure at the corner of today's Washington Street and Grant Avenue, where it offered a five-course prix-fixe menu of fine French food for only fifteen cents, with a large coffee for just a nickel more. In 1868, the restaurant moved to Bush Street, changed its name to the Old Poodle Dog, and kept its patrons satiated for decades, until it was destroyed in the 1906 earthquake. It rose again, only to be shuttered during Prohibition. Reopened in the mid-1930s following the repeal of the Volstead Act, it experienced a series of ups and downs and name changes over the years, until it closed a final time in the mid-1980s.

But other nineteenth-century San Francisco restaurants have lasted to this day, through a host of name changes, location shifts, natural disasters, and manmade disruptions. Among them are Tadich Grill, which opened in 1849 and has been serving its seafood menu on California Street since 1967; Jack's, founded in 1864 on Sacramento Street and now called Jeanty at Jack's, in the same location; Sam's Grill, which dates from 1867 and has been on Bush Street since 1946; Fior d'Italia, opened in 1886 on Broadway and now in the San Remo Hotel on Mason Street; Schroeder's, which started on the south side of Market Street in 1893 and now, under a banner proclaiming it the oldest German restaurant on the West Coast, operates on Front Street, on the north side of Market Street; and finally, of course, the Cliff House, which has fallen down, burned down, and been shut down but still stands on the same rocky promontory facing the Pacific.

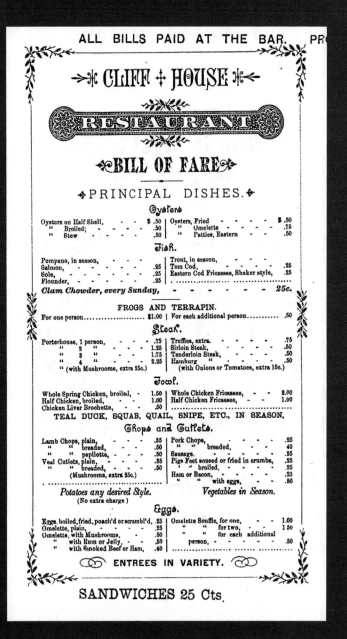

THE EGG WAR

WHEN FRANK MARRYAT went in search of breakfast at the Jackson House, he "wished for fresh eggs, but these were two shillings each, and in the then uncertain state of the mine considered economy a duty." As the population of San Francisco ballooned—official sources show about twenty-five thousand people in 1850 and about fifty-six thousand in 1860—its appetite swelled along with its numbers, and such everyday items as fresh eggs were in short supply, making them a costly commodity—as Marryat described, they were pricier than "rabbit."

San Francisco was a beehive of entrepreneurs, and in no time some resourceful souls found an answer to the egg shortage about twenty-five miles off the western edge of the city: the Farallon Islands. The islands were thick with sea lions and seabirds, especially the common murre, which laid eggs that tasted very much like chicken eggs. Several companies sprang up to gather the eggs, a seasonal business that ran from May until July. Collecting the eggs wasn't easy on the islands' craggy cliffs, nor did the choppy waters of the Pacific make it easy to get them back safely to the restaurants, bakeries, and shops of San Francisco.

Murre eggs proved to be good business—one company alone reported delivering three million eggs annually to the city's tables—and competition was lively. The Pacific Egg Company, founded in 1849 and later known simply as the Egg Company, became not only the biggest player, but also the biggest bully, threatening smaller contenders, including the lighthouse keepers, who not only made sure the beacon was glowing, but also collected and sold eggs. In 1859, the U.S. government claimed the Farallon Islands as federal property so it could maintain the lighthouse that had been built a few years earlier. The new landlord did not halt the egg collectors.

Then, on June 4, 1863, just four months before Charles Butler opened the new Cliff House, with its balcony view of the islands, the Egg War broke out between the Egg Company, which was backed by the government-employed lighthouse superintendent, and a rival operation. Gunfire was exchanged, with one or two men killed (reports varied) and several others wounded. The war was finished in an afternoon, and the "peace" awarded the Egg Company the sole right to collect the eggs, although the lighthouse keepers kept their hand in the business on a small scale. The arrangement lasted until 1881, when the government ended commercial egg collection on the Farallon Islands forever.

Egg robbers, Farallon Islands, date unknown. Courtesy of the San Francisco History Center, San Francisco Public Library

OYSTER LOAF

THIS NO-FRILLS oyster preparation, also known as The Squarer, was a big seller in San Francisco in the final decades of the nineteenth century. Street vendors fried the mollusks, packed them into hollowed-out bread loaves, wrapped the loaves in paper, and then sold them piping hot to passersby, typically gents who had just stumbled out of a nearby saloon. The tidy takeaway package was also known as The Peacemaker, carried home by tardy husbands to placate their angry wives. The natural tanginess of an authentic San Francisco sourdough loaf perfectly balances the richness of the fried oysters.

4 round sourdough bread loaves, 8 ounces each
½ cup (4 ounces) butter, at room temperature
I cup all-purpose flour
½ cup cornstarch
½ teaspoon kosher salt
½ teaspoon paprika

Pinch of white pepper
2 eggs
5 cups water
20 extra-large oysters, shucked
Canola oil for deep-frying

WITH A SHARP, serrated knife, cut off the top ½ inch from each bread loaf. Set the tops aside. Using your fingers, gently hollow out the center of each loaf, creating a pocket for the oysters. (Reserve the removed interior for making bread crumbs.) Spread the interior of each loaf and the underside of its top with 2 tablespoons of the butter. Set the buttered loaves and tops aside.

Preheat the oven to 350 degrees F. In a bowl, combine the flour, cornstarch, salt, paprika, and pepper. (The cornstarch creates a batter that produces a particularly crispy finish.) In a separate bowl, whisk together the eggs and 1 cup of the water. Set the flour and egg mixtures aside.

In a small saucepan, bring the remaining 4 cups water to a boil. Working in 5 batches of 4 oysters each, add the oysters to the boiling water and boil for 10 seconds. As each batch is ready, quickly scoop out the oysters with a slotted spoon and drain well on paper towels. Discard the water.

In a wide, heavy saucepan, pour the oil to a depth of 2 to 3 inches and heat to 350 degrees F on a deep-frying thermometer. While the oil is heating, lightly dust the oysters with the flour mixture, dip them in the beaten eggs, coating them lightly, and then dust again with the flour mixture, shaking off the excess. When the oil is ready, carefully slide 4 oysters into the hot oil and fry until golden brown and crisp, about 2 minutes. Using the slotted spoon, transfer to paper towels to drain briefly. Repeat with the remaining oysters in 4 more batches.

Place 5 hot fried oysters in each bread loaf and replace the top. Place the loaves on a baking sheet and slip the sheet into the oven until the loaves are heated through, about 10 minutes. Serve at once.

Serves 4

HANGTOWN FRY

INVENTED IN 1849 in the hamlet of Hangtown—so-called for an oak tree that hosted numerous hangings, but renamed Placerville in 1854—this dish boasts several theories on its origin. One insists it was the last meal requested by a condemned man who hoped that gathering the expensive ingredients would take time, thus delaying his fate. Another theory suggests it was created by an exhausted miner trying to cook his supper in the dark. But the most widely accepted tale describes an exuberant prospector just back from the goldfields and anxious to celebrate his newfound wealth. The story goes that he asked the local barkeep to prepare the most expensive meal possible. The three main ingredients came all the way from San Francisco and all were costly: eggs, which had been carefully wrapped for transport over the rough roads; bacon, which had been shipped around Cape Horn from the East Coast; and oysters, which had been pulled from the cold waters of the Pacific and packed on ice for the trip. Eventually, the recipe traveled from the Sierras to San Francisco, where it quickly developed a dedicated following.

---

2 cups water
4 to 6 small oysters, shucked
About ¾ cup all-purpose flour
Pinch each salt and freshly ground black pepper

Pinch of cayenne pepper
3 eggs
2 slices apple wood–smoked bacon
1 tablespoon butter

IN A SMALL saucepan, bring the water to a boil. Add the oysters and boil for no more than 5 or 6 seconds. Quickly scoop out the oysters with a slotted spoon and drain on paper towels. Discard the water.

In a small bowl, stir together the flour, salt, black pepper, and cayenne pepper. In another small bowl, beat the eggs just until blended. Set the flour mixture and eggs aside.

Heat an 8-inch nonstick sauté pan over medium heat. Add the bacon and cook, turning once, until crisp, about 5 minutes. Transfer the bacon to paper towels to drain. Reserve the bacon fat in the pan. When the bacon is cool, cut it into large pieces and reserve.

Add the butter to the fat in the pan and place over high heat. While the pan is heating, one at a time, dip the oysters into the beaten eggs, coating them lightly, and then dust them lightly with the seasoned flour, shaking off the excess. Set aside on a small plate. Set the remaining beaten eggs aside.

When the fat in the pan is hot, add the oysters, tilting the pan as needed so the hot fat flows over the oysters. Fry, turning once, until golden brown on both sides, about 1 minute on each side. Transfer the oysters to a small plate.

Pour off the fat from the pan into a small bowl, and wipe out the pan with a paper towel. Return the pan to medium heat and pour half of the fat back into the pan (discard the remaining fat or reserve for another use). Pour in the reserved eggs, then add the reserved oysters and bacon. Using a rubber spatula, stir the eggs gently just until set, about 2 minutes. Serve at once.

Serves 1

PISCO PUNCH

SCOTSMAN DUNCAN NICOL, who bought the popular Financial District saloon, the Bank Exchange, in the 1870s, is credited with the invention of this iconic—and highly potent—beverage. Once he realized he had a hit on his hands, he kept the recipe a closely guarded secret—mixing the drinks himself in the cellar and sending them up by dumbwaiter—until his death in 1926. In time, his bar manager revealed the formula, and the recipe was published by the California Historical Society in 1973. The drink takes its name from the high-octane yet delicate Pisco brandy, which first arrived in California in the 1830s, with traders from the Peruvian port of the same name.

---

1 ripe pineapple
2 cups gum syrup (see note)
2 ounces Pisco brandy
1 ounce water, preferably distilled

⅔ ounce reserved pineapple-flavored syrup
¾ ounce fresh lemon juice
Cracked ice
1 pineapple chunk

TO MAKE the garnish, peel and core the pineapple, then cut into chunks about 1½ inches square by ½ inch thick. Place the pineapple chunks in a large bowl, and pour the gum syrup over the chunks to immerse completely. Cover and let soak overnight at room temperature.

The next day, drain the pineapple chunks in a large sieve lined with cheesecloth, reserving both the pineapple and the syrup. You will need only 1 pineapple chunk and a little of the syrup for each serving. The remaining pineapple will keep in a tightly covered container in the freezer for up to 2 months. The syrup will keep in a tightly capped jar in the refrigerator for up to

3 months. Use them both to flavor other cocktails or nonalcoholic drinks.

Fill a 4-ounce punch glass with cracked ice. Measure the brandy, water, syrup, and lemon juice into a cocktail shaker, cover, and shake well. Strain into the punch glass and garnish with the pineapple chunk on a cocktail pick. Serve at once.

Note: Gum (or gomme) syrup, a mixture of gum arabic and sugar, is a traditional bar ingredient that contributes sweetness and body. Visit www.smallhandfoods.com for more information.

Serves 1

TOM AND JERRY

JERRY THOMAS was the author of the 1862 *The Bartender's Guide*, which codified dozens of mixed drinks for the first time and put the stamp of professionalism on bartending in America. Thomas is also often credited with giving his name to this drink. But that honor actually goes to Pierce Egan, a London writer in the 1820s who penned both the book *Life in London, or The Day and Night Scenes of Jerry Hawthorn Esq. and his Elegant Friend Corinthian Tom* and the play *Tom and Jerry, Life in London*. Thomas reportedly did serve the Tom and Jerry wherever he worked, however, including San Francisco's El Dorado gambling saloon in the 1850s. When he bartended in New York, he was adamant that the egg-rich rum-laced libation was a wintertime drink, and would serve it only after the first snowfall of the season, a rule he obviously broke in San Francisco. By the turn of the twentieth century, the drink had become so popular that Tom and Jerry punch bowl and cup sets were being marketed to homemakers all over America.

2 eggs, separated
2½ tablespoons sugar
1 tablespoon plus 1 cup (8½ ounces) dark rum
⅛ teaspoon ground allspice
⅛ teaspoon ground cloves

½ teaspoon ground cinnamon
⅛ teaspoon cream of tartar
1⅓ cups whole milk
1⅓ cups water
Freshly grated nutmeg for dusting

IN A SMALL BOWL, whisk the egg yolks briefly to blend. Add the sugar, 1 tablespoon (½ ounce) of the rum, and the allspice, cloves, and cinnamon and whisk until smooth and thick. Set aside.

In a bowl, using an electric mixer, beat together the egg whites and cream of tartar until stiff, glossy peaks form. Fold the beaten whites into the yolk mixture, mixing just until the consistency of a light batter. Set aside.

Have 4 warmed mugs ready. In a saucepan, combine the milk and water and bring to a simmer over low heat. Remove from the heat. Briefly stir the egg batter, then divide it evenly among the 4 mugs (about 1½ tablespoons for each mug). Slowly add ¼ cup (2 ounces) of the rum to each mug, stirring constantly to prevent curdling. Divide the hot milk-water mixture evenly among the mugs, and stir to mix. Dust the tops with nutmeg. Serve at once.

Serves 4

MOONLIGHT AT THE CLIFF

REVERIE

By

50 cts

S. SEILER

PUBLISHED BY

S. SEILER

1977 SANTEE ST.   LOS ANGELES, CAL.

PART TWO

THE SUTRO YEARS

PART TWO
THE SUTRO YEARS

Portrait of Adolph Sutro, oil on canvas, artist and date unknown.
Photo by Ed Schuster, Cliff House Collection

ADOLPH SUTRO SET SAIL for San Francisco from New York on October 12, 1850, traveling first aboard the steamship *Cherokee*, and then, following a mosquito-infested journey up the Chagres River and across the lawless isthmus to the port of Panama City, aboard the *California*, finally steaming through the Golden Gate on November 21. Sutro was born in the Prussian city of Aachen (Aix-la-Chapelle) twenty years earlier, where he had seriously pursued interests in science and engineering. At sixteen, following the death of his father, he was forced to leave school to help run the family textile factory. Four years later, with military conscription on the rise, his mother decided America, where her son Sali was already living, was her family's future. Steamer passage was purchased and the family headed to New York, along with bales of cloth and crates of notions to sell in Sali's Baltimore store.

In New York, young Adolph was immediately seduced by the scores of handbills announcing ships sailing around Cape Horn to the goldfields of California. After just two weeks, he convinced his mother that their merchandise would fetch higher prices in the Sierras than on the East Coast and joined the "young men from every nation . . . in rough woolen trousers tucked in high boots and pistols hung from their belts" headed for "the new Promised Land." The *California* could not accommodate his bales of cloth, but he did manage to get his boxes of notions onboard and sold them soon after his arrival in San Francisco. That early retail success was followed by almost a decade of operating three shops that traded primarily in fine Turkish tobacco, cigars, and meerschaum pipes. Sutro married in the mid-1850s, and within about five years, his wife, Leah, was caring for their three children and running a pair of first-class lodges—rooms only, no dining—in the heart of downtown to supplement the family income.

In 1860, Sutro decided to sell off the stock in his tobacco shops and put his early studies to work developing an efficient means of processing the silver ore,

PAGE 42
Sheet music cover is a testament to the popularity of the Cliff House as a romantic dining spot at the turn of the century. Cliff House Collection

and especially the tailings, from the mines of Nevada's recently discovered Comstock Lode. A year later, he established a reducing mill at Dayton, just south of Silver City, and within two years was making a monthly profit of about $10,000.

From his first days in Nevada, Sutro was focused on how to rid the mining shafts of subterranean water: as miners dug deeper into the mountainside in search of silver, the shafts flooded with water, which both imperiled the workers and made the ore more difficult and more expensive to remove. A solution would save lives—and make Adolph Sutro a wealthy man. He proposed blasting a four-mile-long, nearly seventeen-hundred-foot-deep tunnel through solid rock that would drain the water, create much needed ventilation, and employ gravity in place of costly machinery for ore removal. Although the plan was sound, it took a decade to sell the idea to the government and investors and then more than eight years to complete the tunnel. It opened in June 1879, and news of its success traveled around the world.

But it was too late for the Comstock Lode. The only ore that remained was of such a poor grade that mining it was not profitable. Sutro prudently sold his shares in the Sutro Tunnel Company before nearly everyone realized that the silver bonanza had turned into a bust.

THE CLIFF HOUSE CHANGES HANDS

AFTER NEARLY TWO decades away, Sutro and his family returned to San Francisco in fall 1879 with the money from the sale of his shares. He would not be staying with Leah and the children, however. Just before leaving Nevada, Leah discovered that her husband was seeing a diamond-bedecked widow, a scandal that hit newspapers from San Francisco to New York. Leah and the children took up residence in a large house with extensive gardens in a quiet neighborhood at Hayes and Fillmore streets, while Adolph moved into the monumental Baldwin Hotel on bustling Market and Powell streets, built by Lucky Baldwin in 1877, with money made speculating on the Nevada mines.

Land values in the city were somewhat depressed, so Sutro shrewdly began buying up not only prime downtown blocks of the city but also large tracts in what was known as the Outside Lands, which roughly included the swath west from Divisadero Street to the ocean and the Mission and Potrero districts. By the time he finished shopping, he owned about one-twelfth of the city.

In March 1881, while enjoying a carriage ride with his daughter Emma through Golden Gate Park to the city's westernmost edge, Adolph spotted a small, white cottage on a bluff overlooking the Cliff House and the Pacific. When the Sutros knocked on the door, they were greeted by Samuel Tetlow, the longtime operator of the wildly successful Bella Union music hall at Washington and Kearny streets, who had purchased the cottage and its grounds from Charles Butler in 1860, just three years before Butler opened the Cliff House. Tetlow had shot and killed his business partner and been acquitted on a plea of self-defense only a few months before the knock on the door, and was anxious to sell the property and move on. An agreement was drawn up that very day that transferred title to the cottage and the 1.65 acres around it to Sutro for $15,000.

But Sutro didn't stop there. According to Robert E. Stewart and Mary Frances Stewart, in their book, *Adolph Sutro, A Biography*, "The surrounding land was for sale and bit by bit Adolph acquired not only 21.21 acres for an estate, but the shore lands north and east for 1½ miles with 80 acres bordering Fort Miley and part of the future Lincoln Park. Cliff House was directly west of his little cottage and had an unsavory reputation. He solved that problem with ease. He purchased [the] Cliff House. . . ."

UNDER NEW MANAGEMENT

YEARS LATER, CHARLES BUTLER recalled the circumstances of that 1883 Cliff House sale: "Foster was the only tenant from the time the house was built until I sold the property to Adolph Sutro. The Cliff House cost me about six times as much as a building like it would cost now, but it paid for itself a hundred times over. [But] I finally got tired of the property, and when Sutro wanted to buy it I asked him such a price that when he agreed to pay it I concluded he wanted the place more than I did."

Once the Cliff House was in Adolph Sutro's hands, Captain Junius Foster's days as the lessee were numbered. Sutro wanted the reputation of his new acquisition as a raucous destination for the "garter-snapping set" to end, and that meant the end of Foster's lease.

After evicting Foster, Sutro tried to operate the Cliff House himself with the help of two managers, Colonel Little and William Anderson. But after just seven months, he decided that his attention was better focused elsewhere, and he leased it to Sroufe & McCrum, a local wholesale liquor company. Then, in 1885, the lease passed to the "genial" James M. Wilkins, who remained the proprietor for more than two decades. He later recalled that when Sutro handed him the keys, he told him he

View from the beach with Sutro's Norman castle-style addition clearly visible on the south side of the building, 1882-94. Courtesy of Jim Bell

wanted the Cliff House to be "a respectable resort with no bolts on the doors or beds in the house," and from all reports, Wilkins met Sutro's standard. According to James R. Smith, in *San Francisco's Lost Landmarks*, with Wilkins at the helm, the Cliff House "again drew crowds of local people with its renewed focus on families, good food and entertainment."

Meanwhile, Sutro named the acreage surrounding his cottage Sutro Heights and hired workers to expand and beautify the gardens, add some rooms and a "rambling porch" to the house, and install a grand, palm-lined driveway up to the entrance. In 1883, on a trip to Europe, he commissioned more than two hundred sculptures, "copies of masterpieces," for the grounds, which were shipped from Antwerp around Cape Horn to San Francisco the following year. He had a large, ornate glass-paned conservatory erected to house his massive collection of palms, ferns, and other tropical plants, and in 1885, the Dolce far Niente Balcony was completed, a 250-foot-long railing-lined terrace anchored to the cliff

face overlooking the Cliff House and Ocean Beach. The same year, a wood-frame well house, with grillwork and decorative carvings, was built, the only structure from the Sutro era still standing. Sutro Heights opened to the public that same year, and San Franciscans flocked to the grounds. By 1889, records indicate a staff of seventeen full-time workers was needed to maintain the elaborate site for the steady stream of visitors.

The projects undertaken on Sutro Heights in the late 1880s are well documented, but information is sparse on changes made to the Cliff House during Wilkins's early years. We do know that he made it a more family-friendly environment by reducing the cost of meals and beverages, and planning a new railway that would carry passengers from downtown almost to the front door for just half the fare of other transports. There is evidence that Sutro was looking ahead, however. An April 8, 1887 article in the *Reno Evening Gazette* describes his intention to build a four-story Gothic-style "pavilion" next to the Cliff House. It would

View from Sutro Heights overlooking the Cliff House, circa 1882, prior to the addition of the imported statues to the parapet. Courtesy of Jim Bell

Enjoying the view from the parapet, Sutro Heights, June 19, 1894. Courtesy of the Golden Gate National Recreation Area Archives

include a large lower floor where a dance band would play twice weekly; several dining rooms, refreshment areas, and seating areas; and a roof promenade that could accommodate three thousand people. According to the reporter, upon the pavilion's completion, the old Cliff House would be demolished.

THE CLIFF HOUSE AGAIN DREW CROWDS OF LOCAL PEOPLE WITH ITS RENEWED FOCUS ON

FAMILIES, GOOD FOOD AND ENTERTAINMENT.

Parapet Observatory, Sutro Heights, near the Cliff House, San Francisco
On the Road of a Thousand Wonders

The parapet observatory, Sutro Heights, "On the Road of a Thousand Wonders." Postcard. Cliff House Collection

The Parapet, Sutro Heights, San Francisco, California.

The parapet, Sutro Heights. Postcard. Cliff House Collection

Garden and grounds, Sutro Heights. Postcard. Cliff House Collection

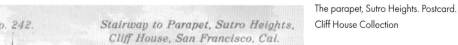

No. 242. Stairway to Parapet, Sutro Heights, Cliff House, San Francisco, Cal.

262 – PALM AVENUE, SUTRO HEIGHTS, SAN FRANCISCO, CALIFORNIA.

Palm Avenue, Sutro Heights. Postcard. Cliff House Collection

View of Ocean Beach from Sutro Heights. Postcard. Cliff House Collection

Stairway to the parapet, Sutro Heights. Postcard. Cliff House Collection

Entrance to Sutro Heights. San Francisco, California.

Grand entrance to Sutro Heights. Postcard. Cliff House Collection

"A TERRIFIC EXPLOSION"

BUT SUTRO'S GOTHIC DREAM was never built, and any physical changes to the Cliff House during Sutro's early tenure were lost on a January evening in 1887, when the one-hundred-foot schooner *Parallel*, loaded with kerosene, dynamite caps, and forty-two tons of black powder, crashed into the rocks at Point Lobos, just north of the clapboard structure. According to a January 17 *New York Times* article, marine reporter John Hyslop saw the *Parallel* come ashore at 9:30 p.m. in the rocky inlet just below the Cliff House. Hyslop "immediately gave the alarm and hastened to the cove. J. M. Wilkins of the Cliff House also hurried down to the cove." Then, while Hyslop, who had been joined by Sutro and several of his employees, lowered ropes to the schooner in the hope of rescuing the crew, Wilkins went for help to the lifesaving station. Within little more than an hour, the lifesaving crew had reached the Cliff House and were met with Hyslop's news that no crew members appeared to be on board. With nothing more to do, everyone went home to bed and the Cliff House closed for the night.

"At [about] 1 o'clock the sleepers were thrown from their beds by a terrific explosion [that] made them think that a great earthquake had upheaved the cliff. . . . An enormous wave dashed up and vaulted over the Cliff House. Pieces of the [schooner] were found more than a mile away." The Cliff House was in shambles. Every window was smashed, the heavy front doors were wrenched from their hinges, the balconies were punctuated with huge gaps, liquor glasses littered the barroom floor, overturned tables and fallen plaster and paintings covered the

View of Flag Rock from the observation terrace, 1887-94. Courtesy of cliffhouseproject.com

dining room floor, and the kitchen was ripped to pieces. "Had the explosion been a trifle more severe, the building would have certainly fallen down the cliff into the sea."

The north wing of the Cliff House was the hardest hit, and Wilkins estimated his losses at not less than $20,000. Sutro Heights was not spared, either. At the main house, the windows were shattered, the front doors were lifted from their hinges, and statues both inside and outside had tumbled from their pedestals. The panes of the conservatory were a sea of tiny fragments, and ironwork and wood were scattered over the grounds. No definitive reports on the number or seriousness of injuries or number of deaths brought about by the *Parallel* disaster have survived, though most accounts mention relatively few injuries and no deaths.

According to historian Robert O'Brien, "that morning, a Sunday, many of the town's ministers faced row upon row of empty pews, for most of the citizens were on their way to the beach." The first train pulled into the wrecked depot at 8:00 a.m., followed throughout the day by as many packed trains as the rails could handle. Carriages and buggies jockeyed for space on the Point Lobos road, and by one o'clock that afternoon, a low estimate put the crowd on the bluffs above the *Parallel* explosion at fifty thousand. Many of the curious gathered souvenirs—scraps of wood, bits of sailcloth—of the catastrophe, finding real ones on the ground or naïvely purchasing fakes from grifters who had stopped by junk shops on their way to the disaster site.

O'Brien points out that Wilkins recognized a good business opportunity, too. He "had the bar swept out and nailed up signs scrawled in charcoal 'House Open for Business.'" The action prompted a reporter of the time to quip, "It is safe to say that the Cliff House has sold more spirituous consolation since its encounter with villainous saltpeter than during any period since its bar was set up."

That same afternoon, Wilkins put men to work repairing the Cliff House, a job that would take only a few weeks to complete. Just two years later, in 1889, the exterior of the building was treated to a new paint job and the interior received modern water closets and a new kitchen closer to the dining room.

A GINGERBREAD PALACE

FEW CHANGES WERE MADE to the Cliff House during the next five years. People continued to rent telescopes and field glasses to watch the sea lions from the balcony, to admire the large sea shell collection

"Yours truly as he appeared on the beach at Seal Rock July 89."
Cliff House Collection

View from Ocean Beach, 1882-94. Courtesy of
cliffhouseproject.com

in the lower rooms, to eat in the dining room and drink in the bar, and to watch Johnnie-the-Birdman, who set up shop nearby and put his family of trained canaries, parakeets, and lovebirds through their paces. Other visitors waded in the shallow waters of the Pacific, ate picnics on the sand, and strolled through the gardens at Sutro Heights. But when the Panic of 1893 hit the nation, a depression brought on by the collapse of overextended railroad companies and a subsequent run on the banks, business cooled down everywhere. Even Adolph Sutro, who at the beginning of the downturn had purchased an estimated ten thousand meal and bed tickets from the Salvation Army to distribute to the newly unemployed, was eventually forced to borrow a huge sum of money at a high interest rate to keep both his property holdings and his myriad projects financed, including Sutro Baths.

The following year, the populist People's Party recruited Sutro to run for mayor, and he won the November election—a surprise victory that would lead to a disappointing two-year term in which he was constantly at odds with the Board of Supervisors. Just a month later, a fire started in the chimney of the Cliff House in the early evening on Christmas Day and, as reported in the *San Francisco Examiner* on December 26, in "half an hour everything was wrapped in flames. . . . It was a magnificent spectacle that filled the eye as the whirling flames were carried seaward on the breeze and the building shriveled visibly and sank."

Wilkins, who had returned to his nearby cottage just before the first signs of the fire, rushed back to the Cliff House and tried to put out the flames, first with an extinguisher and then with a hose from the nearby reservoir, but his efforts fell short. The fire patrol, though on the scene quickly, proved equally ineffective. Wilkins, speaking to an *Examiner* reporter, estimated his loss "at perhaps $25,000—at the outside $30,000. Of that, $10,000

View looking north from the Cliff House over the roofed carriage barn, circa 1894.
Courtesy of the Golden Gate National Recreation Area Archives

was about the value of the house. . . . Wilkins owned the furniture and had some valuable jewelry and a fine stock of liquors . . . worth fully $15,000." Just months earlier, "feeling times were hard and money scarce," he had lowered his insurance coverage to $8,000, just about half of what he needed now.

While Wilkins was wringing his hands, Sutro calmly watched the fire for a while and finally, when it was clear that no hope remained of saving more than "a little furniture and a few fixtures," went home to bed. Before he left, he said he was sorry to see it burn because it "had become one of the landmarks of the Pacific Coast." He then immediately added that he had been planning to build a hotel farther out on the point, nearer to the Golden Gate, and "now it may go on the site of the old Cliff House."

The day after the fire, Wilkins attempted to dissuade Sutro from that plan, insisting it was better to build a bar and restaurant on the old site and go forward with his idea of a hotel on Point Lobos. He argued that the last few years had confirmed that combining a clubhouse and a hotel was not workable. But Sutro disagreed. The Cliff House was famous, the sea lions were a draw, and Sutro Baths, which had just opened, were bringing people to the seaside. That same day, he set his architects, Emile S. Lemme and C. J. Colley, to work designing a new building that would rise from the ashes of the old.

Lemme and Colley quickly came up with a design, and within six months, the site had been leveled and a new foundation, consisting of some two dozen iron rods cemented into the cliff face, had been laid. The new

Cliff House, dubbed "a gingerbread palace" by one catty observer, was going up. An 1895 advertising brochure put out by Taber Photography describes the nearly completed structure: "Looking from the ocean, the building consists of four stories and an attic, while from Point Lobos Road, beside the attic, there are only two clear stories. The lowest one is devoted to the polishing of shells, manufacture of curios, and the electric plant for the lighting of the house and the running of the elevator, and contains sleeping rooms for the necessary attendants. On the second floor refreshments will be sold at the price of city restaurants. There are twenty dining rooms on this floor, also shell and curios rooms. The third floor doors can be enlarged or diminished at pleasure. The attic is used chiefly as a means of approach to the rooms in the turrets, three of them fitted up as private dining rooms, and the fourth containing the largest camera obscura west of Chicago [acquired with the closing of the 1894 Midwinter Fair]. Springing from the main roof, in its center, rises the handsome square tower, which, according to present plans, is to be used as an observatory room . . . [where] visitors may enjoy the magnificent and extensive view of the sea and shore, of plains and lofty mountain chains. A verandah, sixteen feet wide, open at the fourth but enclosed by glass on the lower three floors, runs around the ocean side. . . . The inside fittings and furniture have been chosen by Wilkins and Pearson, and are in keeping with the style and beauty of the building." In the end, although the building had many rooms, none of them were hotel rooms, despite what Sutro had told Wilkins.

Construction of the Sutro Cliff House nearing completion, 1895. Courtesy of Jim Bell

Even the statue seems to be enjoying the view of the 1896 Cliff House from the Sutro Heights parapet. Courtesy of Jim Bell

Cliff House manager James Wilkins at the wheel of the autobus he had built in 1895 from his own plans. The vehicle transported guests through Golden Gate Park to the Cliff House until 1906. Courtesy of the Golden Gate National Recreation Area Archives

On February 1, 1896, Mayor Adolph Sutro formally opened both his "château with spiraling towers" and his new Sutro Railroad, treating members of the city Board of Supervisors to a lavish banquet and a concert. He undoubtedly showed off his large gallery, where he displayed gems from his extensive art collection; the third floor's elaborate reception rooms, comfortable parlors, and panoramic vistas; and how the second floor duplicated the same good lunches, seashell-packed curio shop, and glorious views of sprawling sea lions and soaring pelicans of the previous Cliff House.

The public was wildly enthusiastic about Sutro's fanciful new structure, and crowds flocked to the rebuilt

Electric Sutro Railroad car, date unknown.
Courtesy of Jim Bell

Approach to the Cliff House from Ocean Beach, 1896–1907.
Courtesy of Jim Bell

seaside resort. But Sutro would not enjoy this heightened popularity for long. Early on the morning of August 8, 1898, just two and a half years after he had welcomed everyone to the new Cliff House, and about a year and a half after finishing his disappointing stint as mayor, Sutro died, reportedly from diabetes, at the home of his daughter, Dr. Emma Sutro Merritt. About six months earlier, when his mind had begun to deteriorate, she had moved him from his house on Sutro Heights to her apartment on Van Ness Avenue near downtown and had herself named his guardian by the court. Her two brothers and three sisters fought her strongly on both actions, but to no avail.

Calm winds and low tide allow for a family portrait, horse and buggy included, on Ocean Beach. Courtesy of cliffhouseproject.com

Keystone stereoview, circa 1896.
Cliff House Collection

Pastor Wooten, Miss Priest, and an unidentified companion enjoy the beach north of the Cliff House. Courtesy of cliffhouseproject.com

Sutro Heights, 1886. Adolph Sutro is the gentleman on the far left. Courtesy of the Golden Gate National Recreation Area Archives

At the end, Adolph Sutro did return to Sutro Heights. His body was taken there a few hours after his death. A simple funeral followed the next day, with just the family and a few friends present. He had hoped to be cremated and buried on his beloved Heights, but, according to newspapers of the time, his ashes were placed in a niche at the Columbarium at the Odd Fellows Cemetery. Some eighty years later, two boys clambering on the cliff face below Sutro Heights discovered a cement urn anchored to a rocky outcropping with a perfect view of the sea, and reported it to the National Park Service, which had purchased the Heights in the 1970s. When a park ranger checked the Sutro niche at the Columbarium, it was empty, prompting speculation that Sutro had been buried, as he had wished, overlooking the Pacific.

In a 1993 article in the *San Francisco Chronicle*, Donald Dale Jackson explains that two park rangers returned to the cliff, wrenched the urn from its perch, and took it to a funeral home for safekeeping, never knowing if it contained Sutro's ashes or not. A few days later, a self-identified Sutro descendant showed up at the funeral home and collected the urn. What happened to the vessel next is unknown.

However, Cynthia Soyster, great-granddaughter of Adolph Sutro, explained the boys' discovery in a 1998 address she delivered on her great-grandfather's life to the Daughters of the California Pioneers. In 1938, not long before her death, Emma Sutro Merritt, who was living in her father's house on Sutro Heights at the time, enlisted the help of her nephew Carlo, the son of

Emma's sister Rosa and Count Pio Alberto de Morbio, to remove the urn of ashes from its niche and bury it on the cliff.

MONEY TROUBLES

EMMA SUTRO MERRITT, in her role first as guardian of her father's property and then executrix of his estate, discovered a financial world in serious disarray and debt. Before his dementia had taken its toll, Sutro had spent a year trying to put his business and personal matters in order, but his daughter would be left with that task, including dealing with a claim made on his holdings by a Mrs. Clara Kluge, whom Sutro visited daily during his years as mayor.

Dr. Merritt also found that the Cliff House was in trouble financially. Wilkins, who was paying just $1,000 a month, had failed to make a success of the business, and was behind on the rent. A search for another tenant proved fruitless. A September 24, 1898 article in the *San Francisco Chronicle* reported that "she was further embarrassed by the fact that Wilkins owned all the furniture and carpets in the house, subject to a heavy mortgage. . . . If she ejected Wilkins, the house would be left vacant on her hands." In the hope of keeping the resort running, Dr. Merritt decided to continue the lease with Wilkins and reduce the rent to $700.

A year later the Cliff House was once again in the headlines, this time for the role it played in relaying the return of the troopship *Sherman* to the port of San Francisco from the Philippines, despite the carrier being blocked from view by heavy fog. A local physics teacher had been experimenting with signaling by wireless transmission, and the *San Francisco Call* newspaper decided to sponsor his effort. The teacher rigged up a wireless transmitter aboard the lightship *San Francisco*, which was moored nine miles offshore on the path the *Sherman* would take. The receiver was placed first downtown on Telegraph Hill, but the trolley cars interfered with the signal. Then it was moved to the basement of the Cliff House, where news of the arrival could be relayed to the newspaper office by a telephone call.

When the crew of the *San Francisco* spotted the *Sherman* through the fog on the afternoon of August 23, 1899, the message was sent. In an article in the *San Francisco Call* the following day, the successful transmission was heralded as "beyond question the most thorough and successful application of wireless telegraphy ever made in the United States." Within a few minutes of the Cliff House phone call to the *Call* office, "cannon[s] were booming, whistles were sounding their shrill blasts and thousands of men and women . . . cheered in an ecstasy of honest goodness."

Some three and a half years later, the Cliff House would host an even more important event in the history of communications. On December 13, 1902, the first section of the trans-Pacific telegraph cable, reaching from Ocean Beach, near the Cliff House, to Honolulu, was completed, an accomplishment celebrated with a brass band and a symphony of popping Champagne corks. In subsequent months, the cable route to the Philippines was finished, and people on the West Coast were at last able to send messages to the Far East directly, rather than via the Atlantic cable.

But such notable events typically boosted the Cliff House bottom line only briefly. Business generally remained slow for Wilkins in the months following the arrival of the *Sherman*. The exception was New Year's

Panoramic view from Sutro Heights of Sutro Baths, with the Cliff House at far left, December 21, 1895.
Courtesy of Jim Bell

Ocean side view of Sutro Baths, with the Cliff House in the background, 1896–1907.
Courtesy of Jim Bell

Visitors of all ages enjoying Ocean Beach, 1896–1907.
Courtesy of Jim Bell

Unusual view of the 1896 Cliff House.
Courtesy of Jim Bell

Panorama of Sutro Baths, Sutro Heights, the Cliff House, and Seal Rocks
from the ocean, 1896–1907. Courtesy of Jim Bell

The 1896 Sutro Cliff House dominates the view, with Ocean Beach stretching off to the left, the pumping works for the saltwater baths in the foreground, the electric railroad at right, and Sutro Heights perched on the cliff top. Courtesy of the Golden Gate National Recreation Area Archives

Postcard commemorating the laying of the trans-Pacific telegraph cable near the Cliff House, December 13, 1902. Cliff House Collection

Wilson Mew (in the passenger seat) and friends enjoy a drive along Ocean Beach in a 1905 White Tonneau steam car. Courtesy of Jim Bell

The Cliff House was often used as a backdrop for product advertisements, including motorcars made by The Locomobile Company of America, which was in business from 1899 to 1929. Courtesy of cliffhouseproject.com

Eve of 1899, when pounds and pounds of lobster and magnums of Champagne were consumed to welcome the new century.

In March 1900, in yet another attempt at generating some buzz around the Cliff House, Wilkins hosted the first local meeting of people interested in starting a club in support of the automobile, though there were only a dozen motorcars in the city at the time. His invitation drew twenty-five men, and by the close of the meeting, eleven of them agreed to be charter members of the Auto Club of San Francisco, none of them car owners except for Wilkins. The organization's mission included campaigning for better roads; for lifting the horses-only restrictions in certain areas, including parts of Golden Gate Park; and for an end to the requirement that the fuel tanks of cars transported on local ferries be emptied before the cars could be boarded.

Wilkins's decision to host that first club meeting set the stage for the launch of the Automobile Club of California in August 1901, with Wilkins offering the club its own meeting room, complete with billiards tables, at the Cliff House. The prescient resort operator also installed a charging station for electric vehicles. Two years later, on July 6, 1903, Wilkins, still enamored of the automobile, watched as Lester L. Whitman and

Eugene E. Hammond climbed into their Curved Dash Oldsmobile, backed it to the edge of the surf below the Cliff House, and then set off for Portland, Maine, where they arrived seventy-five days later, delayed by mechanical problems, bad weather, and fun. Although they were not the first to cross the country by car, they did succeed in the same year that the feat was first accomplished.

Wilkins was no newcomer to the automobile, having designed one himself in 1876. It remained no more than a set of blueprints until 1895, when, faced with the need to transport guests through Golden Gate Park to the Cliff House, he dusted off the plans and had it built. It was actually a bus, with wheels as large as those on a "horse truck" and a powerful engine, and it ran through the park until 1906. Half a dozen years later, it was discovered in storage by Benjamin Briscoe, head of the U.S. Motor Company of New York, who bought it and had it

shipped to the East Coast, noting that "it was difficult for him to understand how auto makers overlooked . . . the Wilkins invention for so many years, as it was far ahead mechanically of all early models."

The perennially money-strapped Wilkins faced a stack of bills in early January 1901, when gale-force winds of up to eighty miles per hour struck the south and west sides of the Cliff House one evening. More than a dozen large windows were shattered, scattering glass throughout the rooms. Employees struggled to nail dining tables across blown-out windows to prevent more damage. "One large window in the northwest corner private dining-room was smashed in so suddenly and in such small fragments that a man and woman who were quietly dining in the middle of the room were showered with glass." Big patches of shingles were stripped from the roof, and snapped telephone and

View of the Cliff House from manager James Wilkins's cottage, April 6, 1900.
Courtesy of the Golden Gate National Recreation Area Archives

Peanut vendor on the road near a sign proclaiming "The Panorama of the World at Sutro Heights is one of the Most Interesting in America." 1896–1907.
Courtesy of Jim Bell

electrical wires hung loose across the porch. When the winds finally died down, Wilkins estimated the cost of repairs at $500.

The repairs were made and Wilkins, despite no lessening of his financial problems, managed to keep the doors open. But by November 1903, his situation was dire. Wholesale liquor dealer John Sroufe entered a claim of more than $30,000 against him—some sources put the figure as high as $38,000—labeling it primarily money loaned, and the sheriff assumed control over the establishment until Wilkins could satisfy Sroufe. The Pabst Brewing Company followed Sroufe with its own $10,000 claim, and others were owed as well. All of the creditors contended that Wilkins, rather than pay his bills, typically took the money he made at the Cliff House and invested it in speculative enterprises that invariably failed. A November 21 article in the *San Francisco Chronicle*

provides a sad snapshot of the Cliff House: "This once popular resort is no longer regarded as such. At one time, [it] . . . was noted for its cuisine and its cellars, but these are now but a memory." On December 29, Wilkins filed a bankruptcy petition in district court, stating that he owed nearly $40,000.

Despite the bankruptcy filing, Wilkins and the Cliff House continued to limp along together. In 1904, the gingerbread palace; the adjacent stables and tourist kiosks; and the surrounding seven acres were appraised at just under $160,000, but neither Wilkins nor the Sutro estate was investing in the property. Two years later, the Cliff House would make it through the 1906 earthquake, suffering only $300 in damages, despite one newspaper confidently reporting that it was "hurled from its rocky foundation into the sea." It did remain closed for two months, however, due to damage to the water system.

View from the Sutro Heights parapet, April 18, 1907. Courtesy of the Golden Gate National Recreation Area Archives

Finally, in June 1907, the Cliff House lease passed into the hands of local businessman John Tait and seven partners under the name the Cliff House Company (later the Cliff House Corporation), and they immediately began costly and elaborate renovations. Among the changes were the installation of a large dining parlor and foyer on the main floor, the outfitting of a series of elegant private dining rooms on the second floor, and the transformation of the third floor into a magnificent ballroom. The new operators also gained permission to widen and illuminate the Cliff House drive down to the beach, making it automobile friendly. But, within one month of the scheduled reopening, tragedy struck the Cliff House once again.

At four o'clock in the afternoon of September 7, Wilkins, still a presence though no longer the lessee, was standing with a watchman on the south balcony of the Cliff House enjoying the view of the beach. Suddenly, they spotted smoke emerging from a small hole in the balcony floor. The watchman ran to trip the fire alarm, and Wilkins ran to the north side of the building to telephone Tait. The fire had started on the bottom floor and "spread with frightful rapidity." As Wilkins placed the call, the north wall crashed in, enveloping him in smoke and flames. He escaped the building, only to collapse unconscious outside. Fortunately, he was pulled into the open air by a fireman. Within moments, the firemen were forced from the building by the ferocity of the fire, and as they turned their attention to saving Sutro Baths and the nearby stables, the statuesque gingerbread palace burned to the ground. The fire frightened even the sea lions, who scampered off Seal Rocks that night and headed for the Farallon Islands.

His work now a heap of ashes, Tait, like Sutro after the 1894 fire, quickly insisted that the city would not have to wait long for the return of its famed seaside resort. On September 8, the *San Francisco Examiner* reported Tait's promise, stating simply, "a new building will [rise] . . . on the rocky site of the old landmark as soon as the . . . ruins are swept into the sea."

HIS WORK NOW A HEAP OF ASHES, TAIT, LIKE SUTRO AFTER THE 1894 FIRE, QUICKLY INSISTED THAT THE CITY WOULD NOT HAVE TO WAIT LONG FOR

THE RETURN OF ITS FAMED SEASIDE RESORT.

Three renderings of the Cliff House fire, 1907. Postcards. Cliff House Collection

Spectators gather on Ocean Beach as the Cliff House burns, September 7, 1907. Courtesy of Jim Bell

Mrs. Brinsmead in Sydney, Australia, received this postcard in March 1908: "Dear Ma, This is a view of the ruins of the Cliff House showing Seal Rocks and H. Davidson. Love from Sharry." Cliff House Collection

View of Sutro Baths taken between the destruction by fire of the 1896 Cliff House in 1907 and completion of a new Cliff House in 1909. The Sutro Heights parapet is just discernible on the cliff top, above left. Cliff House Collection

Final stage of the fire that destroyed the Cliff House, September 7, 1907. Photo by T. E. Hecht. Cliff House Collection

JOHNNIE-THE-BIRDMAN

BEGINNING IN THE LATE 1880S, British-born John Williams (or David Williams, according to some accounts), sporting a bow tie, a bushy moustache, and a thick Cockney accent, was a well-known attraction at Ocean Beach. He would arrive each afternoon at one o'clock with a folding table, his flock of trained birds—canaries, parakeets, lovebirds—and the stock of miniature ladders, mirrors, toy cannons, and other props he used to show off the agility and intelligence of his feathered charges. In the earliest days, he positioned his table near the Park and Ocean Railroad depot, but later settled on a spot near the terminal of the Ferries & Cliff House Rail Road, closer to the Cliff House.

Within minutes of setting up shop, onlookers would gather, and Williams, who was affectionately known as Johnnie-the-Birdman, would begin addressing his chirping performers, calling each one by name. (Williams was also less affectionately known as Scarface because he was heavily pockmarked, reportedly due to an angry woman and a bottle of vitriol.) He would then encourage the women in the crowd to come a little closer so they could see better—and, hopefully, open their purses. John Freeman, in an article on the colorful bird trainer published in the fall 2006 issue of the Western Neighborhoods Project newsletter, includes a description of the scene by Cora Older in an 1897 article in the *San Francisco Bulletin*. She characterizes Williams as "cunning, perceptive . . . and droll," and then explains that he always engaged the women first because "they gave freely and with pleasure, while the men stood by and sulked." The moment the women were hooked on how clever the birds were, he would instruct his avian acrobats to stop, explaining to the crowd that they needed some sustenance before they could go on. The women gladly handed over coins for birdseed, the birds ate a bit, and the show continued.

The birds scurried up ladders, hoisted flags up poles, walked tightropes upside down, or primped in front of mirrors. For one of the most popular stunts, Williams directed a canary to fire a toy cannon, which was the signal for a second canary to keel over, feigning death. For another stunt, Williams ordered a bird to alight on the shoulder of an unmarried girl, and the bird would immediately perch on the sleeve of a young lady, startling her and impressing the crowd.

According to historian Robert O'Brien, Johnnie-the-Birdman even tried a stunt himself one day. After watching daredevil Tom Baldwin walk a tightrope between the balcony of the Cliff House and Seal Rocks in 1892, Williams reportedly said, "Damned if I won't do that myself." To steady his nerves, he quickly downed seven or eight shots of bourbon and then followed successfully in Baldwin's footsteps.

At the end of each show, Williams would ask for a few more coins in exchange for hearing one of his finest songbirds sing a sentimental ballad. With the workday over, Williams would pack up his table, props, and stars and head home at four o'clock. This routine continued for some twenty years, until the Cliff House burned to the ground in September 1907. After the fire, fewer people came to the beach, so Johnnie-the-Birdman and his talented flock stopped performing. In February 1909, Williams died, surrounded by his birds, in the Richmond District home he had bought a few years earlier with the coins he had collected each day in the shadow of the Cliff House.

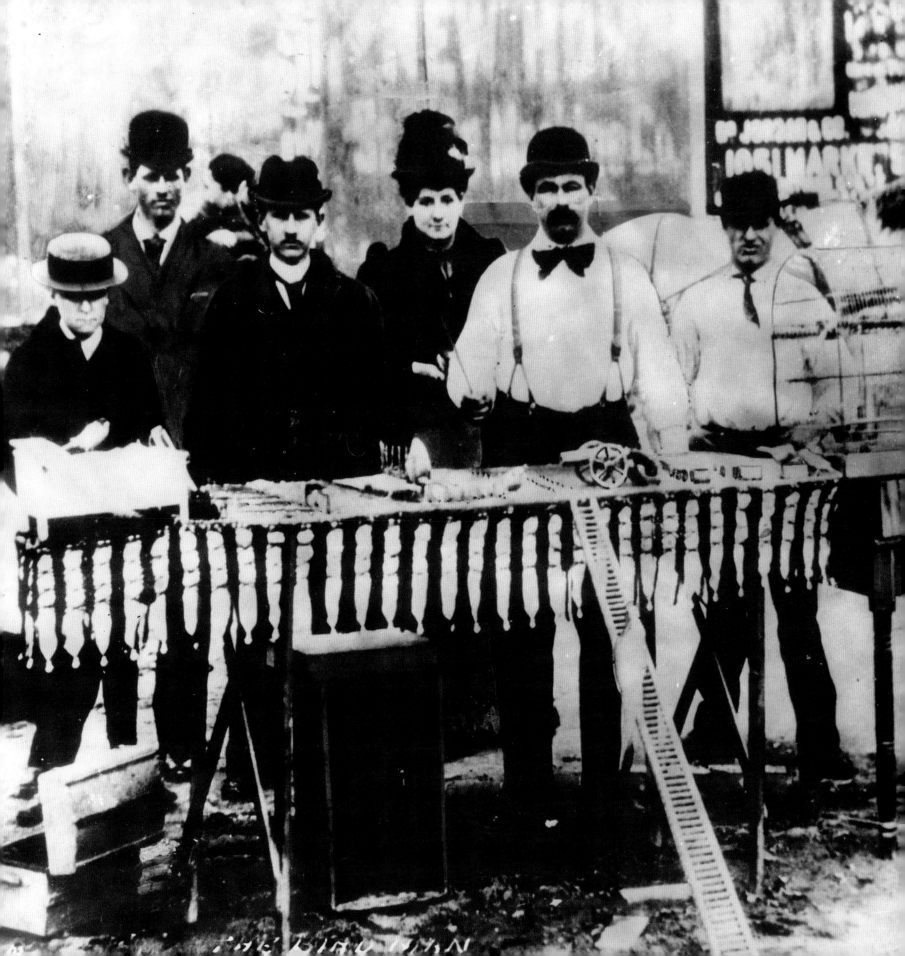

THE BIRD MAN

A WANDERING EYE

DEPSITE ADOLPH SUTRO'S glittering success in the silver bonanza and property market of San Francisco, a successful home life eluded him. From the time of their marriage in the mid-1850s, Adolph Sutro and Leah Harris were at odds. She craved a sedate life that focused on her children and her synagogue and its charitable works. He was a man who craved the limelight, whose business interests kept him on the move and who needed a hostess at his side when he was at home. In the early years of their marriage, Leah was both a mother and a businesswoman, renting elegantly outfitted rooms to elegantly outfitted patrons, while Adolph ran his elite tobacco shops. But their lives would change forever with Adolph Sutro's first visit to Washoe County, Nevada, in 1859.

Sutro came down with mining fever on that trip, which would take him away from San Francisco for years. Family finances were tight and the silver mines were a man's world, so Leah and the children remained in the city. Then, in 1869, Sutro swung the pick that struck the first blow to begin the Sutro Tunnel, and by 1872, he was overseeing the finishing touches on "a large, gracious home, devoid of frills, but well lighted, heated, and with lots of plumbing" near the tunnel entrance. According to *Adolph Sutro, A Biography*, he wanted a "place to entertain important visitors . . . large enough for him, Mrs. Sutro and their six children," and so the family moved to their Nevada home, which stood in yet another Sutro project, the slowly rising Sutro Town. But for the rest of the decade, Adolph's near constant traveling meant he would see relatively little of Leah or his children. And by the summer of 1879, Leah was ready to see even less of her husband.

The headline on a July 8, 1979 *San Francisco Chronicle* article tells the story: "Report Concerning Mr. Sutro and Wife." The "report" involved a Mrs. George Allen, who had arrived from Washington, D.C. and had taken up residence at the International Hotel in Virginia City, where she was dubbed "the $90,000 diamond widow" for the black dress and excessive sparklers she donned whenever she left her room. During her stay, the Sutros had traveled to Virginia City from their nearby home to attend a performance of Gilbert and Sullivan's *H.M.S. Pinafore* and were registered at the same hotel. One evening, the hotel guests were startled to hear a woman's piercing scream for help. Reaction was immediate, with a flood of people pouring into Mrs. Allen's room, where they found Mrs. Sutro about to break a Champagne bottle over the head of its diamond-clad occupant. The Champagne-wielding Leah Sutro was promptly hustled back to her room, where she "commenced accusing Mr. Sutro of infidelity." Adolph Sutro insisted that he and Mrs. Allen had only recently been introduced, and though they had dined together—on cold Champagne and quail on toast—in her room, nothing more than a meal had transpired. The *Chronicle* did not buy his story, bluntly stating, "Mr. Sutro has long been intimate with the woman, their relations having been established at the East; but, nevertheless, they were introduced recently as if they never met." Nor did Leah Sutro, who said she was not going to stand for her husband "sharing a bird and a bottle with that woman so close to home." Mrs. Allen, in her own defense, insisted that she had assumed a false name, that her real name was Miss Hattie Trundle, and that the rumors that she had engaged in an affair with Adolph Sutro on the East Coast were without merit, as she was newly out of finishing school and would never have been in the company of a gentleman without a chaperone at her side.

News of the scandal reached both coasts and places in between, and, not surprisingly, public sentiment favored Mrs. Sutro. She soon instructed an attorney to file for divorce, but then halted the action before it could be completed. There was no divorce, but there was no reconciliation either, so the Sutros lived apart until Leah's death in December 1893, with Sutro always providing generously for her ($500 a month) and their children ($200 a month for the girls and $150 a month for the boys). In the last months of her life, Adolf was by all accounts a considerate husband, visiting her often, and on her death, he had a "majestic marble tomb" built for her.

Although there is no record of Sutro and Mrs. George Allen, aka Miss Hattie Trundle, meeting again following the Nevada dustup, her name was linked with Sutro's once more many years later, following a similar scandal. During his two-year San Francisco mayoral term, which began in 1895, Sutro daily visited a grand house on the corner of Steiner and Clay streets, the home of Mrs. Clara Kluge, an attractive German woman, and her two young children, a ritual that kept neighborhood gossips watching and whispering. As a young woman, Mrs. Kluge had worked as a seamstress on staff at Sutro Heights, and later became a milliner. Sutro had not only provided Mrs. Kluge with her large home, but had also established the Golden Gate Ostrich Farm, near the foot of Sutro Heights, which ensured Mrs. Kluge a steady source of feathers for her own hats and, by selling the balance of the plumes to other milliners for their broad-brimmed chapeaus, an equally steady source of income.

On Sutro's death in August 1898, his daughter Emma filed his 1882 will with the courts. Mrs. Kluge immediately contested it, insisting she had married Sutro by contract and that she and her children, Adolph Newton Sutro (born in 1894) and Adolphine Charlotte Sutro (born in 1896), the legal offspring of the deceased, were entitled to a portion of his estate. She also contended that Sutro had written a later will, with two different executors named, that was being suppressed by Emma because it provided for Kluge and her children. The eighteenth clause of the

probated will returned to an earlier scandal: "Unto Miss Hattie Trundle of Washington, heretofore known as Mrs. George Allen, the sum of $50,000 as a reparation . . . for the injury done her by a scandalous charge, falsely and maliciously, at Virginia City . . . in the month of July, 1879, then and there brought against her." The presence of this clause only heightened the suspicion that a second will did indeed exist, since Mrs. Allen had been dead for a number of years.

About three years would pass before Mrs. Kluge-Sutro (who had by now attached his name to hers) would prevail. There are two differing accounts of the amount she and her children received. One account, by a Sutro descendant, puts the figure at $60,000 for Mrs. Kluge and $20,000 for each of the children. An April 1901 *Los Angeles Times* article states that Mrs. Kluge accepted an offer of $150,000 from the roughly $7 million estate. Either story proves that the Sutro heirs believed Mrs. Kluge-Sutro had a good case. On hearing of her victory, she reportedly remarked that she would "like to get the Cliff House as [part of] her share," though that was not to happen.

The Cliff House had also played a role in an earlier, equally famous contract-wife claim. In 1896, Mrs. Nettie Craven, on the death of millionaire James G. Fair, insisted she possessed an authentic document—a so-called pencil, or handwritten, will—signed by Fair that stated she was his "lawful wife." During the court battles with his heirs, Craven, besieged by the press and her health weakened by the fight, took refuge in a cottage adjoining the Cliff House, courtesy of Adolph Sutro. But unlike Mrs. Kluge a few years later, Mr. Fair's children were able to counter successfully the Craven claim—they produced proof that their father was a registered guest at the Parisian Hotel, in San Rafael, on the day she alleged he signed the paper—and Mrs. Craven left the court empty-handed and the Cliff House cottage soon after.

THE WHITE HOUSE
AT THE CLIFF HOUSE

IN THE LATE-NINETEENTH and early-twentieth centuries, U.S. presidents rarely passed up the chance to visit the Cliff House. Ulysses S. Grant was welcomed to San Francisco on September 29, 1879, and although his presidential days were already over—his 1876 bid for a third term had failed—the general was still treated like a president when he landed at the city wharves in the waning days of his round-the-world trip. His packed schedule included, among other events, a meeting at City Hall, a review of the local military installation, and a large procession to the Cliff House, where the sea lions reportedly greeted him with loud barks.

A year later, on September 20, President Rutherford B. Hayes arrived in the city, and the though his White House years were lackluster at best, he, too, was given a first-class welcome, with trips to Nob Hill, the main post office, the customs house, Golden Gate Park, the Bank of California (where he viewed forty-five tons of silver bars, holdovers from the Comstock Lode bonanza), and a formal lunch at the Cliff House. Little more than a decade later, on April 27, 1891, President Benjamin Harrison watched the sea lions from the balcony and likely even toured the dining room of the Cliff House, although he dined at the home of Adolph Sutro, just next door.

In mid-May 1901, President William McKinley, who was traveling with his wife and who would fall to an assassin's bullet less than four months later, put up in San Francisco for about a week while the first lady recuperated from an infection. Chef Zenovich had drawn up a luncheon menu for the presidential party at the Cliff House, but the meal had to be canceled because of Mrs. McKinley's illness.

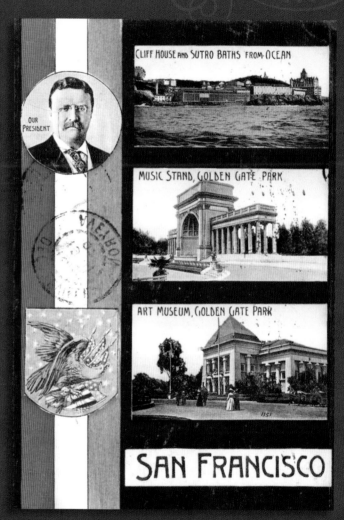

Postcard commemorating the 1903 visit of President Theodore Roosevelt to the Bay Area. Cliff House Collection

Cliff House menu served at the formal luncheon honoring President Theodore Roosevelt, May 13, 1903. Cliff House Collection

THE
SAN FRANCISCO
ROOSEVELT RECEPTION
COMMITTEES'

LUNCHEON TO
PRESIDENT ROOSEVELT

CLIFF HOUSE
SAN FRANCISCO, CAL.
WEDNESDAY, MAY THE THIRTEENTH
NINETEEN HUNDRED AND THREE

Menu

TOKE POINT OYSTERS   Roderick Dhu Scotch
                      Manhattan Cocktails

                      ALMONDS
OLIVES

ESSENCE OF CHICKEN IN CUP

FILET OF SOLE, A LA CLIFF HOUSE   Asti Sauterne

                                   Olivina Burgundy
LAMB CHOPS, PRINCESS

ROAST SQUAB CHICKEN

TOMATO AND ROMAINE SALAD

                      ICE CREAM
STRAWBERRIES   FANCY CAKES

                      Apollinaris
COFFEE   Henry Clay Perfectos

Luncheon for visiting President Theodore Roosevelt, May 13, 1903.
This is the only known photograph to show the interior of the 1896
Cliff House. Marilyn Blaisdell Collection

Two years later, in May 1903, President Theodore Roosevelt stopped in San Francisco, where, among a host of activities, he broke ground for a monument to the assassinated McKinley, whom he had served under as vice president and succeeded as president; and took lunch at the Cliff House. The luncheon guests numbered eighty-five, and the president arrived at the table about a half hour late, taking time first to greet the large crowds that had gathered outside and then attempting to view the Farallon Islands, which were unfortunately shrouded in fog, from the Cliff House's observation tower. According to a newspaper account, by the time he sat down to eat on the flower-and-bunting-decorated veranda, he was very hungry. "He began to munch the salted almonds, and when the oysters were served, he consumed them with an avidity that would have done justice to the heartiest rough riders." A cup of chicken bouillon, fillet of sole à la Cliff House, princess-style lamb chops, roast squab, and a tomato and romaine salad followed, capped off by strawberries and ice cream, "fancy" cakes, coffee, brandy, and cigars. The president announced that he especially enjoyed the fillet of sole, and then promptly asked for a second serving.

On a three-day trip to Northern California in October 1911, President William Howard Taft stopped in San Francisco for the groundbreaking ceremonies for the 1915 Panama-Pacific International Exposition. During the president's visit, there was a big parade, dinners at the Palace Hotel and the Bohemian Club, and other festivities, and on the final day, lunch at the Cliff House, though details of the menu are lost.

Most U.S. presidents since Taft have visited San Francisco, but any additional presidential trips to the Cliff House have remained strictly off the record.

THE WILD WEST
IN THE FAR WEST

IT TOOK A LONG TIME for William Frederick Cody—better known as Buffalo Bill—to bring his Wild West show to San Francisco. Beginning in the early 1880s, the show's exciting mix of acts—sharpshooters, bucking broncos, roping and other trick riding, battle reenactments between cowboys and Indians—played to large crowds nearly everywhere else in the country. In 1887, Cody took his troupe to England, where it drew huge audiences, and even performed before Queen Victoria as part of her Golden Jubilee celebration. After the show left England, it headed to France, Italy, Germany, and elsewhere on the continent. So

intrigued—and trusting—was Crown Prince Wilhelm of Germany, he reportedly let the famed Annie Oakley (who had been nicknamed Little Sure Shot by fellow performer Sitting Bull, the Lakota Sioux holy man and survivor at the Battle of the Little Bighorn) shoot a cigarette from his lips.

As the years passed, Cody's show grew, so that by the early 1900s, it boasted six hundred performers from all over the world, five hundred horses, several buffalo, and even a portable grandstand to seat twenty thousand, and had appeared everywhere from Buffalo to Birmingham to Bologna. Some say that

William "Buffalo Bill" Cody astride his horse on Ocean Beach during the San Francisco tour of his Wild West show, September 1902. Courtesy of the McCracken Research Library, Buffalo Bill Historical Center, William F. Cody Collection

with Indians playing the Spaniards. On September 13, the entire troupe sat down to a luncheon at the Cliff House, then remounted their horses and formed a long line at the edge of the surf—a moment caught in a stunning panoramic photograph.

In September 2008, Western artist Thom Ross surprised regular—and irregular—visitors to Ocean Beach. For one week, anyone who ventured to the seaside found themselves sharing the sand with one hundred brightly painted life-sized wooden cutouts of Indians on horseback in a line just below the Cliff House, a re-creation of the famous 1902 image.

Performers from the Wild West show gather on the observation terrace of the Cliff House to marvel at the Pacific, September 1902. Courtesy of the McCracken Research Library, Buffalo Bill Historical Center, William F. Cody Collection

Cody was reluctant to bring the show to San Francisco because he thought the residents would laugh at how the cowboys and Indians were depicted. After all, San Francisco was in the West, where people must know the difference. But in the end, Cody was convinced that real cowboys and Indians were as common in San Francisco as they were in Rome, and Buffalo Bill's Wild West show arrived in the city in September 1902 for a week of performances.

Tens of thousands of spectators gathered at a city racetrack to watch Cody's troupe stage its many stunts, including a re-creation of the Battle of San Juan Hill,

William "Buffalo Bill" Cody and five performers from the Wild West show pose at the front entrance of the Cliff House, September 1902. Courtesy of the McCracken Research Library, Buffalo Bill Historical Center, William F. Cody Collection

"AN INCOMPARABLE PLEASURE RESORT"

THE MID-1890S marked the beginning of a boom in the building of amusement parks in America, with George Tilyou's Coney Island leading the way. According to a March 8, 1896 story in the *New York Times*, Adolph Sutro wanted to be part of this new wave. He immediately planned to spend $200,000 to build Sutro's Pleasure Grounds, just north of the Cliff House, and he tapped Colonel T. P. Robinson, a San Francisco native known for his business acumen and his promotion of baseball, to operate the park as well as the amusements at the adjoining Sutro Baths. "The Colonel has already made arrangements for a host of popular shows, compared with which the brilliancy of the Chicago Midway would be as a candle in the sunlight. . . ." San Francisco, Sutro promised, would have an "incomparable pleasure resort" on Ocean Beach before summertime.

In January 1894, the six-month-long California Midwinter International Exposition, popularly known as the 1894 Midwinter Fair, which was put together with exhibits, rides, and midway booths shipped west from Chicago's much larger Columbian Exposition of 1893, opened in Golden Gate Park. When it closed down, Sutro bought up some of the best attractions for his future midway: a sixteen-carriage Ferris wheel called the Firth Wheel that would carry riders high enough to see far out into the Pacific; the Haunted Swing, which unsettled riders by giving them the impression the room was rotating around them as the swing glided slowly back and forth; and the Mystic Maze, a mirror-lined labyrinth that disoriented visitors with every step. He also purchased concession booths for food and souvenir vendors that would line the midway, which was named the Merrie Way when the park opened. The booths would cater not only to everyone who bought tickets for the carnival rides, but also to visitors to Sutro Heights, Sutro Baths, and the Cliff House.

Sutro's Pleasure Grounds opened in 1896 as planned, and within a couple of years had added, according to historian John Martini, a roller coaster, a "curiously named ride called 'Springs on Platform,' and a cluster of chowder stands." Excavations completed in the area in 2007 unearthed piles of oyster shells, plenty of liquor bottles and glasses, and various signage remnants, further evidence of a once-lively concession scene.

The pleasures would not last long, however. Martini reports that insurance maps dating from 1900 label all of the carnival attractions as no longer operational, and a 1901 newspaper account describes the sale of some of the Merrie Way properties to a new amusement park scheduled to go up nearby. That development, called Ocean Side Gardens, was set to rise between the Cliff House and Golden Gate Park, and it, too, threatened to rival Coney Island, promising thrilling rides, "goblets of 'steam' and 'lager,' and tamales and enchilados [sic]."

In April 1902, Charles Bundschu, director of the Merchants' Association, campaigned for including the purchase of Sutro Heights and some of the land below it (though the deal excluded both the Cliff House and Sutro Baths) in a city bond issue, taking sharp aim at some cliffside sites in his argument: "Let the city secure the [Heights and land] if it can. . . . Let us then exercise as speedily as possible the proud privilege of removing the awful monstrosities and eyesores that today disfigure and disgrace one of the natural beauty spots near our glorious Golden Gate. Let us clear the surroundings of the unsightly collection of Midwinter Fair eccentricities and rookeries that provoke so much charitable criticism and ridicule on the part of every American tourist or visitor from abroad."

A 1910 photograph, described by Martini as the last known image of Sutro's Pleasure Grounds, reveals a "weather-beaten Wheel and the Swing and Maze building overlooking the Baths bisected by a deserted midway." A March 14, 1911 newspaper article reports the dismantling of the heavily rusted Firth Wheel following a storm that left it spinning dangerously in the wind. Photographs from roughly a decade later reveal only a barren stretch of ground where people once queued patiently for a ticket on the Ferris wheel and bowls of hot soup.

But the Merrie Way did not disappear with the carnival rides and chowder stands. In the 1920s, the city officially named Sutro's long-abandoned roadway Merrie Way, though nothing would be done to merit the name for almost nine decades. Finally, in October 2008, the Merrie Way overlook, trailhead, and parking area was opened as part of the Golden Gate National Recreation Area, the first phase in an ongoing plan to restore the Lands End habitat. A park visitor center is slated to follow.

The Firth Wheel had been purchased and shipped west immediately upon the closure of Chicago's 1893 Columbian Exposition and erected in Golden Gate Park for the 1894 California Midwinter International Exposition. At the conclusion of that fair, it was snapped up by Adolph Sutro for the much-anticipated Sutro Pleasure Grounds, which opened in 1896. The venture, however, was not a success, and the Firth Wheel was dismantled in 1911. Cliff House Collection, restoration by Jim Bell

Map of Sutro Heights, the Cliff House, and Seal Rocks from *Album of Sutro Heights*, circa 1896. Cliff House Collection

ADOLPH SUTRO HAD ALWAYS loved books, but it wasn't until he began a year-long world tour in 1883 that he started buying them in huge quantities. Just before he returned home, he told his London buyer to continue the purchases, setting a budget for him of $2,000 a month. According to the State Library Foundation, on this trip and others, Sutro collected roughly 250,000 books and pamphlets, including almost 3,000 of the 20,000 books extant from the second half of the fifteenth century. Sutro's dream was to erect a library in San Francisco for scholars and stock it with his rare finds.

But settling on a location for his library proved more difficult than acquiring its contents. While he pondered a suitable site (his first choice was Sutro Heights, which he promptly rejected because of the damaging sea air), he packed his books away downtown, in twenty-four office suites in the fireproofed Montgomery Block, at 628 Montgomery near Washington, and in a warehouse on Battery Street, and turned his attention to another decision he made easily: to build a large indoor swimming pool for the people of San Francisco.

Deciding where to build his pool was no problem. It would be just north of the Cliff House, next door to the Aquarium, his tidal pool project that taught visitors about the many wonders of the ocean. In fact, he spoke of plans to construct a large "bathing station" nearly

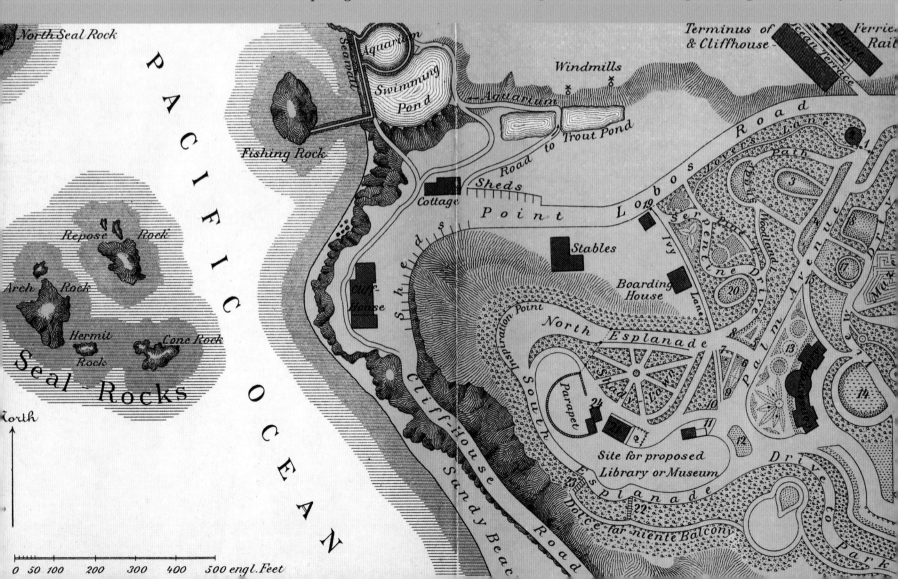

four months before the Aquarium was even finished in September 1887. Work would not begin until 1890, however, following completion of a large north-south seawall and a causeway. By then, the single tank had grown to six saltwater pools and one freshwater pool and the Aquarium had gone from an educational attraction to part of the supply system for the bathing pools.

Sutro handled the engineering side of the project, but launched an architectural competition for the structure to house the pools, with a $500 cash award. The winner, a large glass-enclosed pavilion with a main entrance reminiscent of a classical Greek temple, was completed in 1894 and covered nearly three acres. It was called Sutro Baths and was the world's largest public bath at the time.

As visitors entered the building, they could climb potted plant–lined stairways to a gallery area displaying selections from Sutro's large collection of treasures, including stuffed birds and animals, Egyptian and Peruvian mummies, oil paintings, Aztec pottery, Asian swords, Alaskan totems, Japanese and Chinese fans, and countless other curios and artifacts, including a trunk and clothing that once belonged to Tom Thumb, a popular circus performer of the mid-eighteenth century.

Visitors to the baths could descend by stairways or an elevator to the six saltwater pools—five small and one large—all heated to different temperatures, and one freshwater plunge pool. Bathers could create a splash by entering the water via one of seven slides or thirty swinging rings. There were bleachers to accommodate nearly fifty-five hundred spectators, more than five hundred dressing rooms, and a laundry that could handle forty thousand towels and twenty thousand bathing suits daily. Above the pools, alcoves on three levels held restaurants, cafés, a promenade, a series of viewing balconies, and an amphitheater.

This monumental structure had two formal debuts. The first was in May 1894, which introduced the public to the gallery of exhibits and the alcove attractions but not to the bathing pools. At the time, Sutro was embattled with Southern Pacific Railroad over the high fare it charged passengers to travel to Sutro Heights, the Cliff House, and now the baths. After two years of struggle, Sutro resolved the issue by opening his own Sutro Railroad in February 1896. While the

Entrance to Sutro Baths. On the reverse side of the postcard, the sender noted that "Sutro Baths are much advertised in San Francisco." July 7, 1914. Cliff House Collection

Swimming tanks of Sutro Baths. On the reverse side of the postcard, the sender remarked, "Had a big swim today in this pool." August 30, 1916. Cliff House Collection

The swimming tanks were encircled by a gracious promenade for anyone wishing to relax and observe the bathers below in comfort. Postcard, dated June 10, 1909. Cliff House Collection

new railway was under construction, finishing touches were put on the baths. The pools finally opened to the public on March 14, a stormy day that reduced the turnout to a disappointing seven thousand.

Not surprisingly, Sutro Baths, like the 1896 Cliff House, proved an expensive proposition. Historian John Martini, who has written extensively on the baths and the era, notes that Sutro told one reporter he had put more than $500,000 into realizing his dream of a grand public swimming pool. A later professional appraisal put the amount at about $650,000, not counting machinery. Following Sutro's death in 1898, his daughter Emma petitioned the court to allow the sale of both the Cliff House and Sutro Baths, to raise money to pay off some of the debts owed by her father's estate. Neither was saleable, however, because neither was a moneymaker. Martini cites a newspaper article from September 1900 that included information on the average number of daily bathers, putting the weekday figure at about five hundred and the Sunday and holiday figure at about eight thousand, obviously too few to produce big profits. Simply put, the baths were among the least viable properties in Sutro's estate in 1899, a situation that never improved. According to Martini, "The structure would always operate at a loss, and the family tried several times over the next four decades to sell it to the City of San Francisco or other investors." Replacing the largest pool with an ice skating rink in 1937 helped the building to limp along until 1952, when it was sold to George Whitney, who owned

the Cliff House at the time and ended up overseeing the final days of Sutro Baths.

Sutro saw his grand public bath built, but did not live to endure its rockiest days. He never saw even the first shovel of earth turned toward the building of his library. Not long before his death, he gave twenty-six acres in the center of the city to the University of California, half of which was designated for the library. But Sutro's health deteriorated and the library remained a dream. The books stayed in storage downtown until the earthquake of 1906, which, according to the *New York Times*, destroyed the Battery Street warehouse and left the Montgomery Block and its roughly one hundred thousand treasures unscathed, including early Shakespeare quartos, misprinted bibles, and Civil War–era pamphlets.

The collection eventually found a home when the Sutro family donated it to the state library system in 1913, stipulating that it must remain in the city of San Francisco. For the first decade, it was housed in the dank basement of a local medical library, and then for nearly four decades, it sat in the equally clammy basement of the main branch of the San Francisco Public Library. In 1960, it began sharing quarters with the collection at the University of San Francisco. Finally, in 1982, the San Francisco branch of the California State Library was transferred to its own building near San Francisco State University, where it continues to be recognized for its extensive genealogy collection and for the rare book and manuscript collection of bibliophile Adolph Sutro.

SUTRO BATHS

Monday Afternoon, May 31, 1897
Decoration-Day Festival

Special Attractions!!

Conlon and **Ryder**

Acrobatic Comedians and Pantomimists,
in their exceedingly funny act for
Ladies and Children.

MISS IRENE LYNCH
and
Master Wm. H. Rice

Juvenile Cornet Duetists and Soloists.

Grand Concert Afternoon and Evening

MAMMOTH OPENING
OF THE
SWIMMING SEASON
AT
Sutro Baths

SUNDAY, APRIL 18, 1897

Open from 7 A. M. until 11 P. M.
(And every day thereafter)

GRAND CONCERT BY SUTRO BATHS BAND

Chance to win Valuable Prizes

Charles Cavill

Champion Swimmer of the world, will swim
around Seal Rocks and also perform his wonderful
MONTE CHRISTO ACT

In **Sutro Baths**

Immense * Program

ADMISSION:
Adults 10 Cents.   Children 5c

LOUIS ROESCH CO., PRINTERS, S. F.

THE COCKTAIL ROUTE

FROM ITS EARLIEST DAYS, San Francisco has been a place where people work hard and play hard. During the gold rush, it was also a place where cocktails were drunk as morning eye-openers, rather than early-evening appetizers.

One of the city's most famous gambling halls was the El Dorado, which started as a canvas tent and grew into a four-story showplace at the corner of Washington and Kearny streets. For a time, the man pouring the libations at the El Dorado was the flamboyant Jerry Thomas, the self-described "Jupiter Olympus of the bar," who is credited with creating dozens of mixed drinks, including the Blue Blazer, which called for tossing a flaming mixture of scotch and boiling water between two silver mugs before finally smothering the fire and adding sugar and a twist. He is also mistakenly believed to have lent his name to the packs-a-wallop elixir known as the Tom and Jerry.

The era produced a long list of equally potent concoctions, including the White Tiger's Milk, a creamy blend of milk, brandy, apricot brandy, and bitters; the Black Velvet, cold stout topped with a Champagne float; the Stone Wall, a hot merger of rum and apple cider, and the Sazerac, an icy, well-shaken mix of absinthe, rye, and bitters that originated in New Orleans but was happily welcomed by San Franciscans. Locals imbibers also took to Pisco Punch, a brandy-based beverage "that went down as lightly as lemonade and came back with the kick of a roped steer." It was introduced by a Scotsman, Duncan Nicol, who arrived in the city in the early 1870s and not only put the Bank Exchange saloon, which stood near the El Dorado, on the map, but also gave women their own entrance and a seating area where they could sip their cocktails in peace without being bothered by male patrons.

By the 1880s, a formal Cocktail Route was in fashion, a pastime that grew out of the tradition of the free lunch, where the cost of a beverage afforded unlimited grazing at the buffet table. In *Sumptuous Dining in Gaslight San Francisco*, Frances de Talavera Berger and John Parke Custis describe a "near-sacred, never-varying 'Cocktail Route' that was pursued at a leisurely pace from bar to bar, by such notables as Senator William Sharon and his compatriots." The Palace of Art saloon and restaurant, on Post Street, was one of the best-known stops on the itinerary of the fancy set, delivering not only a lavish culinary spread and first-class beverages, but also a room decorated with enough paintings, statues, curios, and the like to fill a museum. The Cliff House was on the Cocktail Route, too, especially on Sundays, though the meals, while equally lavish, were not free.

According to Talavera Berger and Custis, by the 1890s, San Francisco boasted one licensed saloon for every ninety-six residents, plus more than two thousand unlicensed speakeasies to keep the competition sharp. In 1897, when the city's population was about three hundred thousand, "it was rumored that at least a hundred thousand residents . . . were outright public nuisances. . . . Between the nuisances and the nabobs, it is safe to say that half the population must have functioned, if it functioned at all, only during the night. . . . The cocktail hour was their breakfast time, and late supper at three o'clock in the morning signaled the end of a typically decadent evening"—a devil-may-care style that the City by the Bay has never completely surrendered.

SOLE VÉRONIQUE

THIS DISH OWES ITS popularity to two factors: the longstanding American love affair with French cuisine and the arrival of seedless green grapes in California in the 1870s. The variety, the Thompson Seedless, was an instant hit—ideal for table grapes and raisins. This sole preparation was equally popular in the late-nineteenth century, and was likely the dish that President Roosevelt requested a second serving of during his Cliff House lunch in 1903.

2 tablespoons butter, at room temperature
12 skinned English sole fillets, about 2 ounces each
Kosher salt
I pound Thompson Seedless grapes
I cup dry white wine
I small onion, thinly sliced
2 celery ribs, chopped
2 bay leaves
4 cups water

SAUCE
3 tablespoons butter
3 tablespoons all-purpose flour
I cup heavy cream
¾ cup dry sherry
I tablespoon Worcestershire sauce
Pinch of white pepper

PREHEAT THE OVEN to 350 degrees F. Generously grease a 6-by-10-inch baking dish with the butter. Lightly season the sole fillets on both sides with salt. Starting at the narrow end, and with the skinned side up, gently roll up each fillet. Arrange the rolled fillets, seam side down and in rows of 3 fillets each, in the prepared dish. Set aside.

Cut 20 grapes in half crosswise and set them aside. Place the remaining grapes in a small stockpot or a saucepan and add the wine, onion, celery, bay leaves, and water. Bring to a boil over high heat and boil until the liquid is reduced by half, about 10 minutes. Remove from the heat and pass the mixture through a fine-mesh sieve, pressing against the contents of the sieve with the back of a spoon to force through as much liquid as possible.

Pour the hot strained liquid evenly over the rolled fillets, then cover the dish with parchment paper or aluminum foil. Bake the fish until it is just opaque throughout, about 10 minutes.

While the sole is baking, make the sauce. In a small saucepan, melt the butter over medium heat. Stir in the flour and cook, stirring, until frothy and the mixture turns a light golden brown, about 1 minute. Slowly pour in the cream while stirring constantly, then continue to stir until the sauce thickens, about 1 minute. Season with the sherry, Worcestershire sauce, and pepper, simmer briefly to cook off some of the alcohol, and then remove from the heat and keep warm. Don't worry if the sauce is too thick at this point, as you will be adding some of the liquid from the baking dish.

Remove the fish from the oven. Using a slotted spatula, divide the sole fillets evenly among 4 warmed dinner plates. Return the sauce to low heat and add as much of the poaching liquid from the baking dish as needed to thin to a nice sauce consistency. Add the reserved grape halves to the sauce and heat for a minute or two to warm through.

Spoon the sauce over the rolled fillets, dividing it evenly. Serve at once.

Serves 4

SAND DABS
WITH MEUNIÈRE BUTTER

NEARLY EVERYTHING in the world of dining is cyclical. Today's preference for simple preparations, pure flavors, and the freshest ingredients possible was common fare at many dinner tables in gold rush San Francisco. These sand dabs, straight from the Pacific and sauced with only fresh lemon juice, butter, and parsley, are a perfect example of how the best cooking styles never go out of style.

---

12 whole sand dabs, about 6 ounces each, cleaned
Salt and freshly ground black pepper
½ cup all-purpose flour

1 cup (8 ounces) butter
Juice of 1 large lemon
¼ cup chopped fresh parsley

TRIM OFF THE HEAD, tail, and fins from each sand dab. Then trim away the feather bones, the line of fine bones that runs the length of the body on both sides. This is relatively easy to do, but if you haven't done it before, ask your fishmonger to trim the sand dabs this first time, so that you can see how it is done. Rinse the sand dabs and pat dry.

Just before you are ready to begin cooking, season the fish on both sides with salt and pepper. Salt draws out moisture, so you don't want to salt the fish in advance. Spread the flour on a plate, then lightly dust each fish with the flour, coating evenly and shaking off the excess.

Have ready 4 warmed dinner plates. Place a large sauté pan over medium-high heat. When the pan is hot, add ½ cup (4 ounces) of the butter. When the butter melts and begins to foam, working in batches to avoid crowding, add the sand dabs, dark-skin side down, and cook until golden brown on the first side, 3 to 4 minutes. Flip the fish over and cook on the second side until lightly browned, about 2 minutes. (There is more meat on the dark-skin side, so it takes longer to cook.) Diners will be able to separate the fillets easily from the skeleton if the fish are properly cooked. To test if a fish is done, slip a fork or knife tip between the fillet and the backbone; if the fillet lifts cleanly off the bone, the fish is ready. Transfer the fish to the warmed plates, placing 3 fish on each plate. Repeat until all of the fish are cooked.

Return the pan to high heat and melt the remaining ½ cup (4 ounces) butter. When the butter begins to brown and smell faintly nutty, after about 1 minute, immediately add the lemon juice and parsley, working carefully to avoid spatters that can burn you. Stir briefly, then pour the sizzling butter sauce evenly over the fish. Serve at once.

Serves 4

FRIED CREAM FLAMBÉ

THIS DELICIOUSLY DECADENT Italian dessert was served in all of the best restaurants and hotel dining rooms in early San Francisco, and continued to appear on the city's menus until the 1960s.

2 cups (1 pint) heavy cream
5 tablespoons cornstarch
¼ cup whole milk
2 tablespoons dark rum
⅛ teaspoon salt
2 tablespoons sugar
Pinch of ground cinnamon
3 egg yolks, plus 1 whole egg
3 tablespoons water

¼ cup all-purpose flour
1 cup finely ground graham cracker crumbs
Canola oil for deep-frying

FOR SERVING
¼ cup sliced almonds, toasted
¼ cup dark rum
Whipped cream flavored with vanilla extract (optional)

LINE A SHALLOW 6-inch square pan with plastic wrap, allowing the wrap to overhang 2 opposite sides by at least 3½ inches. To make the custard, in a small saucepan, scald the cream over high heat (about 170 degrees F on an instant-read thermometer). Meanwhile, in a small bowl, stir together the cornstarch and milk. When the cream is ready, stir in the rum, salt, sugar, and cinnamon, and then stir in the cornstarch paste. Cook over medium heat, stirring frequently, for a few minutes to cook away the raw taste of the cornstarch.

In a small bowl, lightly beat the egg yolks until blended. Whisk in a little of the hot cream mixture, then slowly add the yolk mixture to the cream mixture, stirring constantly. Continue to cook over medium heat, stirring constantly, until the mixture coats the back of the spoon, about 2 minutes. Remove from the heat, let cool slightly, and pour into the prepared pan. The custard should be ¾ inch deep. Fold the overhanging plastic wrap over the custard, pressing it gently onto the surface. Let cool, then refrigerate overnight until firm.

The next day, to fry the custard, combine the whole egg and water in a small bowl and beat lightly until blended. Place the flour in a second small bowl, and the graham cracker crumbs in a third small bowl. Remove the custard from the refrigerator. Using the plastic wrap, lift the custard out of the pan and cut into 3 strips each 2 inches wide and 6 inches long. Then cut each strip crosswise into 6 equal pieces. Using your hands, form each piece into a 2-inch-long log. One at a time, dust the pieces with the flour, dip into the egg mixture, and then finally dust with the cracker crumbs.

Have ready 6 small dessert bowls. In a deep saucepan, pour the oil to a depth of about 2 inches and heat to 375 degrees F on a deep-frying thermometer. Add 6 custard pieces and fry until dark brown, about 2 minutes. Using a slotted spoon, transfer to the bowls, dividing them evenly. Fry the remaining pieces in 2 batches.

Sprinkle each serving with the almonds. Warm the rum in a small saucepan until tiny bubbles appear and ignite with a long-handled match. Spoon the flaming rum over each serving. Serve at once, topped with the whipped cream, if desired.

Serves 6

Cliff House
SAN FRANCISCO

PART THREE

THE WHITNEY YEARS

PART THREE
THE WHITNEY YEARS

JOHN TAIT KEPT HIS PROMISE: within two years, a new Cliff House rose on the same site where its predecessors had burned to the ground. A year after the fire, in 1908, Dr. Emma Sutro Merritt, blueprints in hand, had applied to the city for a permit to build a steel-reinforced, poured-concrete structure on the cliff overlooking Seal Rocks, listing the cost at about $43,000. Dr. Merritt had retained the Reid Brothers, who had drawn up plans for a rectangular, neoclassical building that, because of the materials, was less likely to burn than either of the previous structures. She approached James and Merritt Reid fully aware of their credentials. The brothers were already well known for designing the first steel-frame building in the West, in Portland, Oregon; the Hotel Del Coronado in San Diego; the Call Building, San Francisco's first skyscraper (now, minus its original dome, the Central Tower, at 703 Market); the city's famed Fairmont Hotel; and a number of classical-revival mansions in Pacific Heights.

The permit was issued and work began immediately. The fact that the design was a dramatic departure from the previous Cliff House suited the many observers who had disliked the tall, sprawling French château–style structure. The new building was dubbed a "giant gray shoebox" by one disparaging critic, though others appreciated both its clean, classic looks and its modest scale,

especially because the latter allowed unobstructed views of the headlands that lay to the north. The final price tag for the three-story building was $75,000.

On July 1, 1909, the new Cliff House opened its doors with a first-class celebration. The *San Francisco Chronicle*'s report on the event led off with a popular saying of the time—"San Francisco without a Cliff House is like Venice without the Campanile"—and then went on to describe the layout of the new building: The first floor, which stood below the road level, included a large foyer, a café, and a bar. Banquet rooms and a cedar-floored ballroom were on the second floor, and the main dining room and a spacious lounge occupied the top floor. (Another newspaper article of the time, the reporter perhaps heady with the opening's festivities, reversed the layouts of the two top floors.) On the ocean side, windows on all three stories looked out to the Pacific, and

Sand sculptures on Ocean Beach titled "Cast Up By The Sea" featuring portraits of poet Henry Wadsworth Longfellow, President Ulysses S. Grant, President Howard Taft, and other notable Americans. December 1909. Courtesy of cliffhouseproject.com

THE NEW CLIFF HOUSE AND ITS PREDECESSORS

SOUVENIR MENU
OPENING
OF THE NEW
CLIFF HOUSE
SAN FRANCISCO

JULY 1ST, 1909

Menu cover and menu for the Cliff House July 1, 1909 opening dinner. From the collection of Glenn D. Koch

Menu

Hors D'Oeuvres a la Russe

Bisque of Terrapin

Almonds   Ripe Olives

Vol au Vent of Crab

...sed Celery and Beef Marrow

...ne of Chicken, Artichoke Heart

New Potatoes   Romain Salad

...spberry Meringue

Coffee

the lower floor opened onto a wide, iron-railing-ringed terrace on the brow of the cliff that offered an appealing promenade and plenty of room for tables in good weather. Tait and his partners were intent on keeping the worldwide reputation of the Pacific Coast landmark intact, outfitting it with only the best furnishings.

The new operators were also determined to assure guests that getting to the seaside would be convenient and affordable. They had made arrangements with the Auto Livery Company, known for its handsome touring cars, to offer a fixed rate of $4.00 to ferry four to seven passengers from any address in the city out to the Cliff House. At the end of the visit, the car could be summoned for the return trip for the same price, with no waiting expenses incurred. The same trip for two passengers was priced at $3.50 each way. Guests interested in booking a taxi could take advantage of the special rates offered by Pacific Taximeter Company: One or two passengers could travel to the Cliff House at the rate of 50 cents for the first half mile and 10 cents for each subsequent quarter mile, plus a charge of $1.50 per hour for waiting. The average journey cost $7.50, which included an hour at the Cliff House. Three or four people could make the same trip by taxi with only a small increase in the rates. And visitors watching their pocketbooks could make the trip by streetcar.

The city's top families attended the opening, and though some celebrants worried before the gala that exchanging Gothic turrets and towers for concrete walls and steel bars would dampen the traditional gaiety of the Cliff House, their worries were over that evening. According to the *Chronicle*, "while many referred to the pleasures of the Hotel Ritz of Territet and the world-famed hotels on the Riviera, the consensus of opinion

The Cliff House was a popular backdrop for studio portraits, 1909-14. Cliff House Collection

was that here by the Golden Gate was to be found something which surpassed them all." The exuberant crowd also saw the reappearance of the Cliff House as an important step in the rehabilitation of a city that had been devastated by the 1906 earthquake and fire. Even the sea lions that had fled Seal Rocks the night of the 1907 fire and resettled on the Farallon Islands must have approved, for they returned to their old home just as the new building was finished, to the delight of the Cliff House staff and guests. To keep interest high, the

Early touring buses, 1910–16.
Cliff House Collection

about the night Sarah Bernhardt "swept magnificently" into the dining room of the Cliff House to eat a bowl of the turtle soup for which the kitchen was famous.

For nearly a decade, the Cliff House would enjoy success much as it had in the 1890s, though one still heard the occasional complaint from visitors who longed for the grandeur of the old "Sutro castle" they had seen on so many postcards. In fact, the entire five-mile stretch of Ocean Beach, with the Cliff House at the north end, was a wildly popular destination in these years. Allan Dunn, writing in 1912, described a nighttime dash along "the boulevard that borders the sea, with throbbing engines and shafts of headlights all about, the surf pounding on one hand . . . and on the other the electric signs and gay windows of half a dozen roadhouses. . . . Each has its separate bar, the inevitable [dance] floor, . . . its fireplace and its corps of entertainers. . . . At most of the places you can eat, at all of them drink and be merry. . . . The music is supposed to stop at one o'clock, and sometimes does, as the eye of the law happens to glance that way. . . . By day, . . . motorcars take their owners out for a taste of salty, tonic breeze along the boulevard. . . . Horse-women and their escorts come out of the Park . . . to wet fetlocks in the surf. Lovers sit on the outward rampart of the dunes and watch for their ships to come home. Children paddle in the seafoam, and parents out of tide reach boast about them. . . . [At one end] stands the famous Cliff House. . . . Here one can revel in sunset dinners, looking out between courses to where the day dies like a dolphin, radiant in the west."

One of the most memorable events of that year was the Champagne-laden flight of Captain Roy N. Francis. The captain had rented space in an auto repair shop on

management ran a newspaper ad later in July announcing that a brass band would play on the terrace for two hours every afternoon.

The well-known modernist painter Otis Oldfield, who moved to San Francisco in 1909 to attend art school, worked as a hat-check boy at the new Cliff House. Years later he recalled that no formal system existed for linking hats to their owners. Instead, the hat-check boys were required to remember which derby or stovepipe went to which gentleman. He also delighted in telling the story

Van Ness Avenue near Sacramento Street, where he set a couple of men to work building "a twin-tractor, outrigger-type" airplane that would fly at a top speed of about sixty miles per hour. When the plane was ready, Francis made a couple of test flights and then took the actress Dorothy Lane, who was starring at the Alcazar Theater downtown, for a ride that started across the bay in Alameda, circled around San Francisco, and landed on the Great Highway, just below the Cliff House. Francis had no sooner turned off the engine, when

Ned Greenway, one of local society's leading playboys, sprinted out of a nearby tavern and made a beeline for the craft. Catching his breath, Greenway told Francis he wanted "to see Champagne sprinkled from the sky." Francis, up for the challenge, packed three bottles of bubbly into the cockpit, restarted the motor, taxied down the Great Highway, and soared out over the water. Guiding his craft back toward the shoreline, he uncorked two of the bottles, and from a height of about one hundred feet, he sent a stream of golden bubbles splashing down on

Harp concert in one of the several opulently decorated rooms of the Cliff House, 1909–16. Courtesy of the Golden Gate National Recreation Area Archives

the Cliff House, where magnums of Champagne had been drunk with abandon for nearly five decades. Then, sweeping down along the highway at a height of about fifty feet, he uncorked the final bottle and, with great precision, sprinkled the expensive contents at the feet of a very happy Greenway.

Such stunts only added to the appeal of the Cliff House, for both the public and investors. In February 1912, after a two-week negotiation, a trio of prominent local clubmen, Bill Lange, Sam Rucker, and Roy Carruthers, acquired the stock of Cliff House Corporation partner John Farley. (According to some accounts, a fourth clubman, Dr. E. G. McConnell, may also have been one of the buyers.) Farley, one of San Francisco's leading café men, had been serving as manager of the famed landmark, and was not particularly anxious to sell, but the price must have been right. The fact that the buyers were well connected—they all belonged to the socially exclusive Olympic, Bohemian, and/or Family clubs—gave observers confidence that

Formal banquet in one of the Cliff House dining rooms, 1909–15. Marilyn Blaisdell Collection

40 - CLIFF HOUSE AND BEACH, SAN FRANCISCO, CALIFORNIA.

Promenade Overlooking the Ocean. Cliff House. San Francisco, Californ

2702 - Cliff House from Ocean Boulevard, San Francisco, California.

The Cliff House and Beach, San Francisco, Cal.

Colorful postcards featuring the Cliff House, 1909–10. Cliff House Collection

2893 A Moonlight Night at the Cliff House, San Francisco, Cal.

John Hogan of Philadelphia received this postcard from a disenchanted visitor: "I leave here after March 30. I wish I were back in Philadelphia. I don't care for this country out here." March 11, 1911. Cliff House Collection

2083 — ON THE OCEAN BEACH BELOW CLIFF HOUSE, SAN FRANCISCO, CALIFORNIA.

Dan McQuarrie of Missoula, Montana, received this postcard from a friend in San Francisco: "This is the way I'm passing the time now. I pity you fellows tramping the snow. It is just like summer here." January 30, 1913. Cliff House Collection

TELEPHONE
PACIFIC
3040

THE NEW
CLIFF HOUSE
SAN FRANCISCO

the Cliff House would not lose its luster with the arrival of the new group. Carruthers, who had made his name as a purveyor of fine French Champagne, was tapped as Farley's successor as manager and announced the group's goal on the eve of the sale: "It is our intention to make the Cliff House the most widely advertised point of interest in the city. . . . We'll make [it] the most attractive place on the beach, and at the same time maintain its present high standard of conduct."

Carruthers, who was both debonair and ambitious, quickly went to work. San Franciscans were beginning to spend money again after several tough years and tourists were continuing to flock to the beach, and the new manager wanted to entertain both groups. The local social elite gave high points to Carruthers's food and wine, and were soon filling the tables for Sunday breakfast and organizing horseback parties to the beach, much as their counterparts had done in the 1880s. Just four months after assuming his role, Carruthers allowed the public onto the terrace free of charge, opened a new wing where men could smoke, drink, and watch the sea lions, and made plans for a glass-enclosed tea garden. He also instituted dancing nightly, and nearly every evening the sons and daughters of the city's elite climbed into their automobiles and headed out to the beach to spin around the Cliff House floor.

Downtown at the Hotel St. Francis, manager James Wood had convinced the New York–based dance team of Ivy and Douglas Crane to come to California and, with the help of the Art Hickman Orchestra, introduce tea dancing to the hotel's guests. Dubbed The Castles of the West (after the famed ballroom-dancing couple of the day, Irene and Vernon Castle), the Cranes did just that, but were soon convinced by the genial Carruthers to move their act to the Cliff House, where they appeared nightly before an appreciative audience. The Cranes eventually separated and Ivy, minus her dance partner, became the manager of the Cliff House when Carruthers left to head up the luxury Palace and Fairmont hotels downtown and later a handful of celebrated East Coast hostelries, including Chicago's Blackstone and Drake and New York's Waldorf-Astoria.

In 1917, Ivy Crane employed a good-looking young Italian to give dance lessons at the Cliff House. The talented teacher's name was Rudolph Valentino, and he arrived with a résumé that included stints as a gardener on Long Island and a taxi dancer at Maxim's in New York, and with a front-page scandal that linked him to a Chilean heiress who killed her husband, the event that prompted him to flee west. Valentino found similar work at other seaside operations, but was soon looking to better himself, enrolling in classes to become a security bonds salesman. History records the sale of only two bonds, one of them to the head waiter at the Cliff House, and then Valentino moved on, first to Utah with an operetta company and then to Hollywood. There he continued his dancing career—partnering wealthy older women—until he finally struck it rich in the movies, only to die at a youthful thirty-one.

CLIFF HOUSE LUNCH ROOM

THE Tourists who are often limited as to the length of their stay, and for that reason are not able to partake of the hospitality as dispensed in the main dining room, are also well cared for.

The management have arranged a commodious Lunch Room which is on a level with the Terrace floor and accessible from any part of the Terrace and where refreshments are daintily served at very moderate prices.

We make a charge of ten cents for admission to the Terrace, but the admission card is redeemable in trade.

A copy of our Lunch Room Bill of Fare is herewith submitted.

MENU

California Oyster Cocktail 20c
Consomme 15c   Clam Chowder 15c
(with Bread and Butter)

SANDWICHES
Ham 15c   Cheese 15c   Beef 15c
Chicken 25c

COLD MEATS
Ham 25c   Corned Beef 25c   Beef 25c
Potato Salad with all Cold Meats

Frankfurter Sausage and Sauerkraut
with Glass of Beer 25c
Cut of Pie 10c   Cake 10c
Ice Cream with Cake 15c
Coffee, Tea or Milk   -   -   10c
Wieland's Pale Lager Beer -   -   10c
Wieland's Brown Lager Beer   -   10c
Plain Drinks   -   -   -   -   10c
Mixed Drinks and Case Goods - 12½c

THE DARK YEARS

JUST A YEAR LATER, no one was dancing at the Cliff House. World War I had broken out in Europe in 1914, and munitions orders brought an economic boon to the United States for the first years of the fighting. But in April 1917, the United States joined the Entente Powers, and in July 1918, President Wilson signed an order instructing all establishments within a half mile of a military installation to halt the sale of liquor. The Cliff House and Fort Miley met the description, and the operating partners decided to close their doors, rather than try to make it without pouring spirits.

Once the war was over, Charles Sutro, who now owned the Cliff House property following a family battle over the estate of his father, Adolph, began looking for a new lessee for the Cliff House. A New York restaurateur attempted to reopen the landmark, but failed to attract sufficient investors. The Cliff House had been closed for more than two years when on December 8, 1920, the *San Francisco Chronicle* carried a display ad announcing the opening that evening of the "redecorated, magnificent Cliff House." The message was simple: "In returning to the peoples of Our City the spot they have always cherished, it shall be my ambition to maintain by every standard the high regard in which men and women all over

the world have held this historic landmark; and in this I ask your cooperation." The advertisement was signed Richard P. Roberts, better known as Shorty Roberts, and it included an easy-to-remember phone number for reservations, Pacific 123. A San Francisco native, Roberts was a successful operator of local cafés and restaurants, among them the nearby Roberts' at the Beach (also known as the Sea Breeze Resort), which dated from 1897 and was described in promotional materials as "a landmark for the connoisseur, fastidious imbiber, and gourmet who [likes] to dine royally."

Roberts had signed a ten-year lease on the Cliff House, and proceeded to pour thousands of dollars into renovating and redecorating the space to create a first-class restaurant and entertainment destination. He was especially proud of the new Doric-columned entrance portico, named the Pompeian Court, which included terra-cotta floors, lattice-paneled stone walls, and a large central fountain. Beyond the portico, the lobby was decorated in blue and gold, and the main dining room was done in ivory and gold, with draperies from light peach to deep rose and valances of Italian cut velvet. The wallpaper copied the chinoiserie style popular during the reign of Louis XVI of France, and the wall brackets for the electrical candles in the ballroom were shielded with parchment covers in a French design.

CLIFF HOUSE
SAN FRANCISCO
OPENING DINNER
WEDNESDAY EVENING
DECEMBER EIGHTH 1920

Roberts also enlarged the building's footprint with a three-story addition at its north end.

The opening was a great success. Some four hundred and fifty people attended, and Roberts and his staff were careful to make sure each of them felt as if he or she was an honored guest of the evening. The meal was prepared by chef John Lane and "his corps of eight experts in cuisine" and served by seventy-five waiters. Dancing followed supper, and plenty of talented entertainers were on hand for those who were shy about their two-step.

The card rooms were not open on that first evening, but guests were assured they would be the following day, when the Cliff House began its regular daily service of lunch, afternoon tea, and "dinners with distinctive menus at $2.50 a plate." À la carte service would be offered throughout the day and evening so guests could order anything they fancied, and a six-piece orchestra would play for diners—and dancers—in the main dining hall.

Aware of the competitive dining atmosphere of San Francisco, and conscious of wanting to draw the first families of the city, Roberts introduced a unique feature to the Cliff House dinner hour: the menu included a stuffed "squab chicken" that featured a different stuffing each night. To ensure a proper presentation, Roberts retained a French chef, previously with New York's Waldorf-Astoria, to supervise preparations and create new dishes for his sophisticated customers. He also decided to refine the afternoon tea, offering a choice of two services. For 50 cents, guests were served hot muffins, assorted marmalades and jams, and a choice of tea, coffee, or chocolate; for 75 cents, patrons could choose either a mixed shellfish

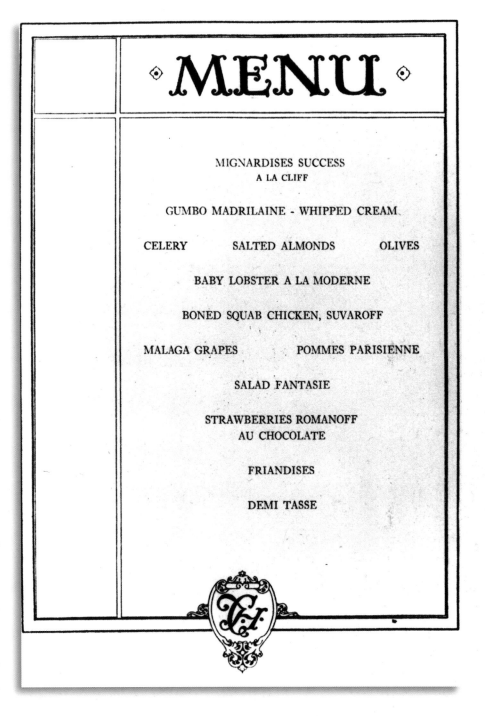

MENU

MIGNARDISES SUCCESS
A LA CLIFF

GUMBO MADRILAINE - WHIPPED CREAM

CELERY   SALTED ALMONDS   OLIVES

BABY LOBSTER A LA MODERNE

BONED SQUAB CHICKEN, SUVAROFF

MALAGA GRAPES   POMMES PARISIENNE

SALAD FANTASIE

STRAWBERRIES ROMANOFF
AU CHOCOLATE

FRIANDISES

DEMI TASSE

Strolling Ocean Beach, 1916–20. Courtesy of cliffhouseproject.com

salad or chicken à la king, served with muffins and jams; various ice creams, puddings, and cakes; and a choice of beverage. Roberts also continued the Cliff House tradition of Sunday breakfast at a reasonable price.

Ingredients were widely advertised to reassure guests that only the best was being used: extra pale ale from the local John Wieland Brewery, canned fruits and vegetables from the Del Monte company, meats from Clay Street's respected California Meat Company, oysters and shellfish—"cooked by a master chef and . . . served in one hundred and one various ways"—from Polk Street's Cable Oyster Depot, poultry from the locally respected O'Brien, Spotorno & Mitchell, and fruits and fruit syrups for fountain drinks from Howard Street's Magnus Fruit Company. Roberts bragged about his coffee, which he bought from the Van Winkle Company on Clay Street; his line of Gato cigars, "from fully matured Havana leaf"; and Jackson's Napa Soda Springs water, bottled at the source in the Napa Valley and "known around the world."

Shorty Roberts was off to a good start. Intent on keeping interest in the Cliff House high, he held the first

By the 1920s, motorcars had replaced horses and buggies on the beach. Courtesy of cliffhouseproject.com

of what he promised would be an annual long-distance swim around Seal Rocks in June 1921. The route began at the beach behind Sutro Baths and finished at the end of the Cliff House Road, and the event was open to women only. Roberts enlisted the aid of the South End Rowing Club to patrol the waters in case any swimmers encountered trouble, and the winner was awarded the R. P. Roberts perpetual trophy. After the inaugural event, no record of subsequent races exists.

Six months later, Charles Sutro announced that he would be making $50,000 in improvements to the Cliff House building, including the remodeling of the restaurant facilities, and that work would begin within a month. At the same time, the city revealed its plans to triple the width of the adjacent road, adding street-lights to ease nighttime passage, and installing a concrete sidewalk on the water side. Roberts was forced to close during the renovation, but hoped the Cliff House would be ready to reopen within about eight weeks. It took nearly twice as long, but on June 2, 1922, Roberts ran an ad in the *San Francisco Chronicle* heralding the reopening on June 7: "It has been completely remodeled—made much larger and more beautiful than ever before. All that remains of the old is the 'Cliff House Spirit.'" The opening-night dinner was priced at five dollars. A later ad promised breakfast, lunch, tea, dinner, and midnight specialties, all at "moderate prices," and, of course, dancing.

About three weeks after the opening, the Down Town Association, of which Roberts was a member, held a luncheon in the Cliff House ballroom. Most of the speakers that afternoon related stories about the previous Cliff Houses, and then encouraged members to patronize the new enterprise to ensure this important scenic spot of San Francisco's history would be preserved.

But the optimism that filled the Cliff House that day could not be sustained in the era of Prohibition, launched in 1919. Quite simply, a Cliff House without a bar did not draw enough guests to keep it going. Despite the government's enforcement of the Volstead Act, private production, sale, and consumption of black market alcohol flourished all across the country. Roberts tried to keep the doors open by turning the Cliff House into a nightclub—allegedly without liquor—but police raids convinced him to give up on the idea. According to an article in the January 30, 1925 issue of *The Evening Independent*, Roberts decided the Cliff House could be no more than a coffee house and posted a sign reading "Coffee and Doughtnuts [sic] 5 Cents." Later that year, he shut down the place completely.

Prohibition was finally repealed in 1933, but the Cliff House remained shuttered for another four years. Even the sea lions began to disappear. In a February 7, 1936 letter to the editor in the *San Francisco Chronicle*, a one-time Cliff House regular dubbed the empty building "the old box, dead box" and bemoaned the fact that no local citizen was coming forward to restore it to its former glory. Seven months later, the *San Francisco News* reported that the administrators of the estate of the late Charles Sutro, who had died the past April, were hearing offers from parties interested in purchasing the property.

The Cliff House remained a popular subject for postcards throughout the 1920s and 1930s. Cliff House Collection

THE CLIFF HOUSE WILL BE A REVELATION
TO YOU WHEN YOU VISIT IT.
YOU WILL BE PREPARED FOR SOMETHING FINE, BUT
YOU WILL BE STARTLED
WITH THE SHEER BEAUTY OF IT.

Reconstruction of Point Lobos Avenue gets underway, February 15, 1922.
Courtesy of the San Francisco History Center, San Francisco Public Library

Reconstruction of Point Lobos Avenue continues, March 15, 1922.
Courtesy of the San Francisco History Center, San Francisco Public Library

Reconstruction of Point Lobos Avenue progresses, April 4, 1922.
Courtesy of the San Francisco History Center, San Francisco Public Library

Reconstruction of Point Lobos Avenue almost reaches the beach, April 28, 1922.
Courtesy of the San Francisco History Center, San Francisco Public Library

Reconstruction of Point Lobos Avenue complete, June 23, 1922. Courtesy of the San Francisco History Center, San Francisco Public Library

Seal Rocks and the Cliff House observation terrace on a rainy day, circa 1910. This view was likely taken within a few years of the 1909 reopening. Clues are the absence of structures on the terrace, the "Admission to Terrace 10 cents" sign, the light globes visible in the foreground, and the rustic wooden benches. All of these features changed between 1915 and 1920. Photo courtesy of cliffhouseproject.com; analysis courtesy of John Martini

ENTER THE WHITNEYS

"THE FORLORN CLIFF HOUSE, which once specialized in cold bottles and hot birds, and where up to about ten years ago dandies could dine in private with their friends, may become a swanky nightclub," the *News* continued. "Many promoters are interested in it, for it has a romantic location." On December 1, following a ten-day submission period for sealed bids for the purchase of the Cliff House, Sutro estate attorney F. M. McAuliffe announced the bids would be reviewed and the most suitable one submitted to the court for approval.

Two weeks later, Judge Frank H. Dunne approved the sale. The Wells Fargo-Union Trust Company, acting on behalf of the Charles Sutro estate, handed the deed to the Cliff House and the property between it and Sutro Baths to brothers George and Leo Whitney for $200,000—$50,000 in cash and the balance in the form of a promissory note secured by a deed of trust.

In 1939, San Francisco would be hosting the Golden Gate International Exposition on Treasure Island, a celebration to commemorate the completion of the San Francisco–Oakland Bay Bridge in 1936 and the Golden Gate Bridge in 1937. The city would be flooded with visitors and the Whitneys intended to serve them. They promised a $75,000 interior renovation of the Cliff House that would include a first-class restaurant and an elegant cocktail lounge. They also announced their intention to tear down and rebuild the structures on the adjacent property. A week later, Mayor Angelo Rossi formally congratulated the Whitneys on their decision to undertake the reopening of the beloved landmark, citing its importance to San Franciscans: "Next to our city's name, people from near and far thought of the Cliff House. To it, the great of the world were taken and wined and dined. No like institution added such fame to any city."

George and Leo Whitney were already a commercial force in the city. In 1904, when Leo was nineteen and George was just fourteen, the brothers had opened a photography studio in Seattle, Washington, with only a white bedsheet for a backdrop and $35 for supplies. The innovative pair devised a speedy method for making prints, and soon had three studios and were clearing $600 a month. The brothers left Seattle for Melbourne, Australia, where they operated a successful amusement park, "complete with Ferris wheel and 150 penny arcade machines." After little more than a year, they had cleared $90,000 and were thinking about heading home.

But World War I changed their plans. The Australian government ordered all amusement parks closed, and the Whitneys returned to photography. When the fighting was over, they put together a traveling show of World War I mementos that toured large U.S. cities. By the early 1920s, they had opened a shooting gallery in San Francisco, on Market Street. Leo enrolled in art school for a time and then rejoined George, and together they bought a second shooting gallery at Ocean Beach, where Arthur Looff and John Friedle were operating amusement rides and overseeing an array of concessions, all under the name Chutes at the Beach.

The Whitneys opened three more shooting galleries, a photography concession that guaranteed customers could take their pictures home the same day, and a souvenir shop at Chutes at the Beach. Then, during the late 1920s and early 1930s, despite a battered national economy, the Whitneys gradually bought up most of the attractions assembled by Looff and Friedle and renamed the area Whitney's At the Beach, and less formally Playland. George was the financial mastermind of their endeavors and Leo was the creative force. In time, they purchased the land under the attractions as well, along with a number of adjacent lots, making the acquisition of the Cliff House the next natural step. Before the purchase was completed, George Whitney routinely borrowed the keys to the Cliff House from the Sutro estate so he could go into the empty restaurant, where he would plant himself at the southwest corner window and gaze down the beach, daydreaming of the potential the landscape held.

In mid-January 1937, journalist Carl T. Nunan, in his *Presidio Heights Press* column, "Strolling the Ocean Beach," reported that the Whitneys had big plans for the Cliff House gift shop. It would be rebuilt from the ground up, expanded to ten thousand square feet, and stocked with the biggest assortment of souvenirs of any gift shop in the West—an emporium that would one day be advertised as the world's largest gift shop. A month later, George and his Australian-born wife,

Eva, traveled to Australia to settle the estate of Eva's father, and then spent time hunting for unusual merchandise throughout the South Pacific for putting in the new shop.

As part of the renovation of the Cliff House itself, new plumbing and electrical systems were installed, along with a state-of-the-art kitchen that included, according to the April 1937 newsletter of Pacific Gas and Electric, three large ranges, a frying plate, a large oven, three walk-in refrigerators and two smaller refrigerators, a trio of coffee urns, a dishwasher, a sterilizer, and more. Every corner of the building was slated for a first-class makeover. For example, the walls

of the barroom and the cocktail lounge were paneled in natural-finish redwood, rafters and beams of split curly redwood were installed in their ceilings, and the original fireplace in each space was fully restored. Not surprisingly, as workers dismantled the old interior, they unearthed treasures from the past, including dusty Champagne flutes and ornate silver ice buckets, delicate sherry glasses and heavy highball tumblers, all reminders of the Cliff House's long history of hospitality.

For a time, Sadakichi Ihara stood in the way of progress. He had operated the Cliff House terrace tearoom, which had remained open despite the closure of the rest of the building, and refused to accept the Whitneys'

Sutro Heights, the Cliff House, and a billboard advertising the new gift shop, 1937. Courtesy of Dennis O'Rourke

eviction notice. Instead, Ihara launched a one-man sit-down strike, which prompted a municipal court trial in late February, with Judge Hugh L. Smith on the bench. Although it was Ihara who demanded the jury trial, he failed to appear in court, claiming that he spoke no English and sending his wife instead. Judge Smith dismissed the jury and found in favor of the Whitneys, who were awarded possession of the tearoom as of March 15.

With the final obstacle removed, the brothers stepped up the renovation in the hope of debuting the new Cliff House on opening day of the Golden Gate Bridge, May 27, around which a week-long celebration was planned.

But the work took longer than expected, and the Cliff House's official unveiling was delayed until August 4. Long lines were the rule that day, as visitors gathered throughout the afternoon and into the evening to marvel over the new interior.

Just beyond the lobby was the main dining room, decorated in a nautical theme of marine blue, ivory, and white, the work of the local firm of L. & E. Emanuel, and with a seating capacity of about two hundred and twenty. Guests who reserved a table for Sunday morning breakfast would be treated to a concert on a Hammond organ while enjoying their eggs Benedict or chicken

Aerial view of Sutro Heights, the Cliff House, and Sutro Baths, circa 1930.
Courtesy of Jim Bell

livers en brochette. The barroom and cocktail lounge on the floor below had their own entrance, flanked by two magnificent seventy-five-year-old Irish yew trees. In the bar, decorated with framed archival photographs, visitors typically paused in front of a built-in cabinet that held a variety of artifacts, including silverware, from the former Cliff Houses. In the cocktail lounge, known as the Sequoia Room, the steering wheel of the wrecked tanker *Frank H. Buck*, prominently displayed on the north wall, was another attraction.

To ensure the Cliff House would once again be a destination, the Whitneys announced it would operate continuously from eleven o'clock in the morning until two o'clock in the morning every day except Sunday, when it would open at seven-thirty for breakfast. No dance orchestra would be playing, but the organ in the dining room, a piano in the lounge, and a slate of top-drawer vocalists would provide ample musical entertainment throughout the week. The new owners also bragged about their air-conditioning system, which spoke more of the modernity of the renovation than the needs of the naturally air-conditioned ocean side location. They named Henry Geise, the manager of their popular Topsy's Roost, the maître d'hôtel, and A. C. Hines, formerly of Tait's at the Beach, the manager. The new Cliff House logo, which was used on menus, cocktail napkins, business cards, and the like, featured a sea lion balancing an ice bucket holding a bottle of Champagne and a tray with two glasses of bubbly, an homage to a time when the San Francisco landmark was a famed dispenser of the spirit. Carl T. Nunan summed up the excitement that surrounded opening day: "The Cliff House will be a revelation to you when you visit it. You will be prepared for something fine, but you will be startled with the sheer beauty of it."

SKATING INTO THE WAR YEARS

WITHIN LESS THAN FOUR months of the Cliff House reopening, another important attraction was added to the local scene, Sutro's Ice Arena. Sutro Baths had seen a drop in receipts in the 1920s and 1930s for several reasons: the 1925 closure of the coastal streetcar that had carried San Franciscans to the beach; the lack of household spending money for family outings during the Depression; the long-shuttered Cliff House and deterioration of Sutro Heights; and stricter municipal laws governing public swimming tanks. The baths had undergone only minor changes since their construction. In 1933, the main entrance was given a Coney Island–inspired facelift, two of the smaller tanks were transformed into volleyball courts, and the largest tank was divided into a diving tank, a swimming tank, and the Tropic Beach, where the water was replaced with a "sandy seashore," complete with thatched-roofed seating areas and a shuffleboard court.

Afternoon tea was offered every day but Sunday, 1937.
Cliff House Collection

The 1933 addition of an art deco façade to Tropic Beach was intended to give new life to the old Sutro Baths. This photo was taken August 27, 1952, four days before the baths closed. Courtesy of the San Francisco History Center, San Francisco Public Library

Interior of Tropic Beach at Sutro Baths, May 15, 1935. Courtesy of the San Francisco History Center, San Francisco Public Library

By 1937, it was clear that the Tropic Beach had not caught on, and the main tank was replaced with an ice rink for hockey, figure skating competitions, and recreational skating at a cost of about $100,000. On November 18, 1937, the ice rink opened to a large, enthusiastic crowd of skaters and spectators. Next door at the Cliff House, the Whitneys were happy to welcome anyone who couldn't squeeze onto the ice.

In January 1938, Mayor Rossi celebrated his birthday at the Cliff House, evidence the Whitneys were keeping the landmark in the best datebooks. During the same month, the Cliff House welcomed a group of professional models, who posed in bathing suits for a local photographer

in a famous shot that captured both the women and the legendary destination. Around this time, visitors enjoyed watching a pair of whales, nicknamed Mopey Dick and Mopey Mary by Cliff House patrons, who swam and frolicked together just offshore. But the big story of 1938 was undoubtedly the premiere of the film *Alexander's Ragtime Band*, set in San Francisco and the Cliff House and starring Tyrone Power and Alice Faye.

In August of the same year, Ruth Thompson, in her *San Francisco News* column "Eating Around," gave readers a sunny picture of business—and the kitchen—at the Cliff House, presided over by Frank A. Averill, by then the new maître d'hôtel. She revealed long-term plans for

Bathing beauties pose for a publicity photo at the Cliff House, January 1938. Courtesy of Zoe Heimdal, sanfranciscomemories.com

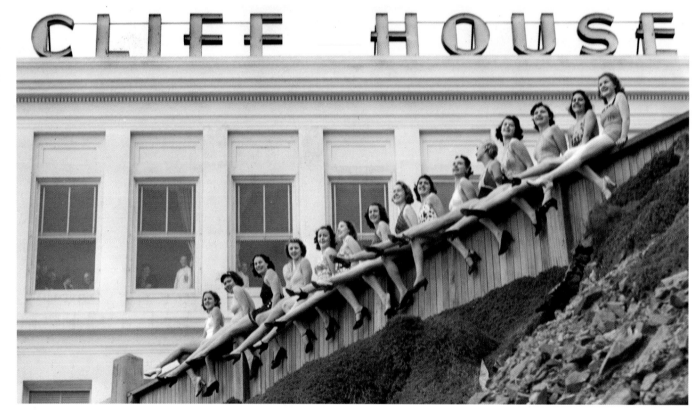

a new banquet room on the lower floor, and saluted the excellent staff, many of them "old-timers who know their food and beverages and who have catered to the public in San Francisco's best hotels. In all, twenty-one languages are spoken by this cosmopolitan group of courteous and interested attendants."

She also detailed some of the Cliff House's special culinary offerings, such as finnan haddie in cream and eggs à la Bercy for Sunday breakfast, fried spring chicken with corn fritters and grilled French lamb chops on pineapple offered at lunch, and baked oysters Kirkpatrick, lobster thermidor, frog's legs sautéed with mushrooms, and grilled sweetbreads with stuffed tomatoes on the dinner menu. Those looking for only a light bite were invited to head to the Sequoia Room, where a wide range of appetizers, such as caviar canapés and marinated Holland herring, and the kitchen's celebrated clam chowder and onion soup were served.

Thompson's glowing report leaves little doubt that the Cliff House remained a draw in the late 1930s. Visitors to the fair on Treasure Island in 1939 and 1940 typically included a stop at the Cliff House on their itinerary. When the fair closed, George Whitney purchased the models of all twenty-one California missions, a popular feature at the fair, and installed them at the Cliff House in a specially designed exhibit, where they remained a popular attraction for decades. (Today, thanks to vintner Nancy Cline, they are the centerpiece of the California

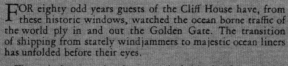

FOR eighty odd years guests of the Cliff House have, from these historic windows, watched the ocean borne traffic of the world ply in and out the Golden Gate. The transition of shipping from stately windjammers to majestic ocean liners has unfolded before their eyes.

Through the years they have watched ships head to sea with no more hazards to encounter than storms and reefs, and raging seas. But today, for those who sail towards the setting sun, danger lurks in a form more ruthless and sinister than nature ever conjured. Death and destruction at the hands of human wolves of the sea may be theirs.

Courageous men, undaunted by this new peril, take freighters, tankers, transports and fighting ships bravely over the horizon.

The inspiring sights you see from these windows, in comfort and comparative safety, are privileged to but few of the millions whose future and whose very lives are in the hands of these brave, heroic men.

When we leave here let us seal our lips that no untimely words of ours may lead to their destruction, to mass murder of our troops, our sons, bound over seas; to the sinking of precious ships and priceless cargoes; to the undoing of well laid plans; and in the end, perhaps, contribute to the loss of this war.

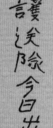

These few words, thoughtlessly spoken, short waved to the enemy, could do just that:

("CONVOY SAILED TODAY")

SILENCE IS A SMALL PRICE
TO PAY FOR VICTORY!

THE CLIFF HOUSE
SAN FRANCISCO

Your waiter will be pleased to supply additional copies of this card

Table card cautioned diners against inadvertently divulging information to an always-listening enemy, mid-1940s. Cliff House Collection

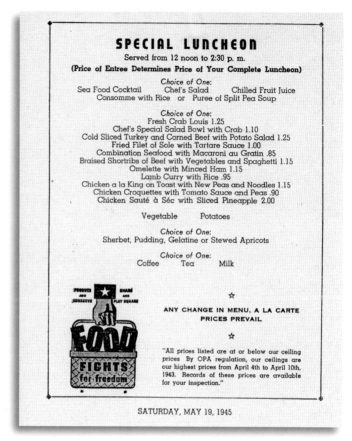

SPECIAL LUNCHEON

Served from 12 noon to 2:30 p. m.

(Price of Entree Determines Price of Your Complete Luncheon)

Choice of One:
Sea Food Cocktail   Chef's Salad   Chilled Fruit Juice
Consomme with Rice   or   Puree of Split Pea Soup

Choice of One:
Fresh Crab Louis 1.25
Chef's Special Salad Bowl with Crab 1.10
Cold Sliced Turkey and Corned Beef with Potato Salad 1.25
Fried Filet of Sole with Tartare Sauce 1.00
Combination Seafood with Macaroni au Gratin .85
Braised Shortribs of Beef with Vegetables and Spaghetti 1.15
Omelette with Minced Ham 1.15
Lamb Curry with Rice .95
Chicken a la King on Toast with New Peas and Noodles 1.15
Chicken Croquettes with Tomato Sauce and Peas .90
Chicken Sauté à Séc with Sliced Pineapple 2.00

Vegetable   Potatoes

Choice of One:
Sherbet, Pudding, Gelatine or Stewed Apricots

Choice of One:
Coffee   Tea   Milk

☆

ANY CHANGE IN MENU, A LA CARTE
PRICES PREVAIL

☆

"All prices listed are at or below our ceiling prices By OPA regulation, our ceilings are our highest prices from April 4th to April 10th, 1943. Records of these prices are available for your inspection."

SATURDAY, MAY 19, 1945

Food Fights for Freedom, special luncheon menu, May 18, 1945.
Cliff House Collection

Missions Museum on the grounds of the Cline Cellars winery in Sonoma, California.)

Just before the beginning of World War II, Leo Whitney retired and George bought him out of their joint operations, which by now extended from Fulton Street at the southern tip to a snack stand in the streetcar barn at Point Lobos on the northern end. In the early days of the Whitneys' tenure at the Cliff House, the brothers had disagreed on how best to run it. From the beginning, Leo had wanted to target the top-hat-and-tails trade and George had favored a more egalitarian profile. But business began slipping just a few months after the opening, so George had won the day and the Cliff House remained classy without being stuffy. With Leo's retirement, George would be making all the decisions.

When the war broke out, it was business as usual at the Cliff House, although two precautions were taken: the windows were blacked out after dark—the staff cleverly covered them with World War I posters—and a small printed card placed on each table reminded guests of the need for discretion: "These few words thoughtlessly spoken on short wave to the enemy could contribute to the loss of this war: 'Convoy sailed today.' Silence is a small price to play for victory."

Nearby, Playland had not seen a serious drop in business during the Depression because it offered good, clean family entertainment at low prices. Receipts remained fairly steady during the war, too, as soldiers and sailors in town on leave flooded the midway, where, according to Thompson, they enjoyed "wholesome games and thrills of many types . . . from chutes to shoots, from the merry-go-round to the various mirth houses." Although Playland was required to dim the bright lights of the midway after dark to satisfy the Office of Civilian Defense, all of the concessions remained open and busy.

After the war, George Whitney, Jr., his military service completed, joined the family business, primarily overseeing the arcades and rides. Up the road at the Cliff House, popular radio personality Dean Maddox, famous for his man-on-the-street interviews, was interviewing world travelers in the Sequoia Room and broadcasting their stories live on local station KFRC on Sunday

mornings. Maddox set the stage for future broadcasters at the Cliff House, including baseball announcer Russ Hodges, who hosted a Sunday morning talk show with ballplayers soon after relocating to San Francisco from New York with the Giants in 1958.

For a time in 1948, Dean Maddox shared the Cliff House spotlight with a sea lion nicknamed Buster, who somehow had managed to end up with a white toilet seat around his thick, wrinkled neck. Diners spotted him one day, and his fame spread. In no time, miniature paintings of Buster with his unique neck ornament were on sale at the Cliff House gift shop.

Postcard, circa 1949. Cliff House Collection

Menu cover, 1948. Cliff House Collection

Moderne design concept for a total remodel of the Cliff House, 1949. Courtesy of the Golden Gate National Recreation Area Archives

THE WHITNEYS EXTEND THEIR EMPIRE

THE COMICALLY COLLARED sea lion even made it into the *San Francisco Chronicle* column of Herb Caen, the local master of three-dot journalism, guaranteeing Buster citywide notoriety and giving the Cliff House some always-appreciated ink. But when Buster disappeared, the talk in 1949 turned to the installation of a camera obscura, with its slowly rotating periscope-like lens, on the terrace

below the Cliff House. Plenty of people came to see the new contraption, but the Whitneys realized they had to give them reasons to stay.

In 1950, the Whitneys spent $200,000 remodeling the Cliff House, which included an additional thirty-five hundred square feet to the overall floor plan. The kitchen was enlarged and updated, and a high-speed dumbwaiter was installed to ensure meals traveling from the kitchen to the new banquet room arrived piping hot. A canopy was hung over the main entrance; two huge neon signs were mounted, one facing south and one facing the Great Highway, making

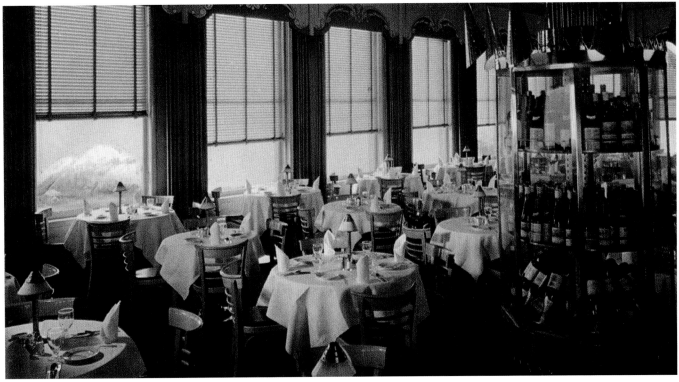

Cliff House dining room, early 1950s. Courtesy of Frank and Ruth Mitchell

Janet Pond of Portland, Oregon, received this review of the Cliff House: "Had dinner here, rented a car. Very foggy so can't see too much. Very good dinner." October 23, 1952. Cliff House Collection

the "Cliff House" visible from afar in two directions; and about one hundred and thirty lineal feet of windows were added on the ocean side. Finally, the entire exterior was sheathed in redwood to echo the extensive use of the locally milled wood in the bar and the Sequoia lounge (and to save the cost of painting). The new façade, which effectively hid the distinctive look of the 1909 original, was dubbed "modern rustic" by a local magazine. Whitney made one more addition: he put "Since 1858" in neon lights on one side of the building, throwing in with those who considered Samuel Brannan's slapped together Seal Rock House the first Cliff House.

Souvenir program cover for a 1951 San Francisco Forty Niners–Los Angeles Rams football game pictures Playland and the Cliff House. Used with permission of Lal Heneghan, Cliff House Collection

Next door, Sutro Baths continued to decline. By the early 1950s, the rink was drawing mostly children instead of hockey games; the swimming tanks, which still greeted visitors with the box-office sign "Five plunges in operation. Warmest temperature, 96," were facing tough competition from the city's public pools; and Adolph Sutro's wildly eclectic exhibits of artifacts were failing to attract visitors. The once-great attraction could no longer hold out against declining revenues and increasing maintenance costs.

In late August 1952, Adolph G. Sutro, a grandson of the Comstock Lode pioneer, announced the closure of the baths for September 1, with all of the equipment and museum exhibits—stuffed bears and monkeys, Egyptian mummies and cigar-store Indians, flip-card movie machines and funerary urns—going on the auction block shortly thereafter. Sutro went on to explain that the baths had failed to make money in decades, but the family had been content to keep the facility open because it contributed "to the city's life—particularly [the lives] . . . of the children." However, Sutro was nearing retirement and he could no longer shoulder the annual operating loss of $15,000. Once the building was emptied, it would be dismantled for salvage and the valuable shoreline property would be sold. Sutro had made the decision to close the previous spring, after failing to interest the city in purchasing the property, but he had delayed the padlocking until September 1 because he wanted the children of San Francisco to enjoy one more summer of swimming and skating before the arrival of the wrecking ball.

On September 2, George Whitney, Sr. stepped up and saved the day, offering to purchase the building for about $250,000 and promising to keep it open. Years later, George, Jr. recalled visiting the baths as a child, especially

Removal of the taxidermy collection from Sutro Baths, September 10, 1952. Courtesy of the San Francisco History Center, San Francisco Public Library

"the [pleasant] smells . . . of cedar wood and warm sea air." Despite the last-minute rescue, within a year, after discovering how much it cost to heat the swimming tanks, the Whitneys closed them. According to historian John Martini, from then on, "ice skating would be the only recreational activity at the baths. The drained tanks and their countless changing rooms were simply left to molder in the unused northern portion of the structure. . . ."

But the "museum" in Sutro Baths met a better fate. George, Sr. began adding his own acquisitions—George, Jr. once described his father as "a collector of other people's collections"—and even enlisted a curator from the de Young Museum to help bring order to the chaos. In time, the de Young loaned exhibits to Sutro Baths, and vice versa. George, Sr. did some housecleaning, too. He had Adolph Sutro's menagerie of

taxidermy, most of the pieces in sad condition, hauled off by an enterprising trash man, who sold many of them to interested parties on his way to the dump.

With the addition of Sutro Baths to his portfolio, Whitney found he was too busy to continue overseeing the day-to-day operation of the Cliff House. He was responsible for a number of other Ocean Beach properties nearby, including Louis' Sandwich Shop, the Golden Gate View Coffee Shop, and the Cliff Café, all of them rented to individual vendors but still requiring attention. In April 1953, he announced he would lease the Cliff House to the Foster's restaurant chain. At the time, Foster's, helmed by David Moar, was running Moar's Cafeteria, on Powell Street, and leasing The Pie Shop at Playland from Whitney. The ten-year agreement did not include an option to buy and the payments to Whitney

Dean Maddox, George Whitney, Sr., and Whitney's daughter, Mrs. Floyd Gilman, christening the new Sky Tram May 4, 1955. Courtesy of the San Francisco History Center, San Francisco Public Library

Sky Tram, mid-1950s. Courtesy of Frank and Ruth Mitchell

would be a percentage of the gross revenue. "Our policy," Moar said, "will be to maintain the traditions of the Cliff House, and to try to make it even more of a landmark than it already is—if that's possible."

In 1954, George Whitney, Sr. ordered work to begin on the final "modern attraction" he would introduce to the Cliff House area, the Sky Tram, an aerial cable car that would carry passengers about a thousand feet above the waves from the observation terrace at the rear of the Cliff House to Parallel Point, just beyond Sutro Baths. There they would alight on a newly constructed deck, where they could try to spot remnants of shipwrecks, weather and tides permitting; explore a pair of tunnels constructed for the baths; and see the old Aquarium. Two artificial waterfalls flowed down the cliff face, adding to the scenic views. It was an elaborate, costly project that Whitney believed would draw more guests to the dining tables and bars at the Cliff House, more kids to the ice rink and museum at Sutro Baths, and more dollars to the cash register at the "world's largest gift shop."

The Sky Tram opened on May 3, 1955, not quite a century after the tightrope walkers of 1865 had thrilled onlookers watching from the terrace of the Cliff House. The fare was just 25 cents, but the travel time was too slow (a stately four minutes one way) and the car was too small (it held just twenty passengers) for the tram to yield a profit. George Whitney might have been able to come up with a scheme to make the tram a moneymaker, but he passed away suddenly, following a brief illness, in January 1958. His obituary in the *San Francisco Call Bulletin* perfectly described this pivotal figure in Cliff House and Ocean Beach history: "a veteran showman who helped millions to have fun." The tram closed seven years later.

Postcards, circa 1955. Cliff House Collection

THE DUTIFUL DAUGHTER

EMMA LAURA SUTRO was born in 1856, the oldest of Adolph's seven children, and the child who would care for him in his final days. She was at Vassar College in 1872, and by 1877, she had studied medicine in San Francisco, become a doctor, and moved to Paris to continue her medical studies. In 1883, she married Dr. George Merritt in London and the two settled in San Francisco.

Following her father's death in 1898, Emma Sutro Merritt, hoping to fulfill his wishes, struggled to keep Sutro Heights open to the public. Adolph Sutro had been deeply in debt at the time of his death, and by 1904, the house, then occupied by a caretaker, and the twenty-one acres surrounding it had fallen into disrepair. Finally, in 1920, Emma Merritt, who had become the sole owner of Sutro Heights following a legal battle with the other heirs, deeded the cliff-top property to the city of San Francisco "under the condition that it be 'forever held and maintained as a free public resort or park under the name of Sutro Heights.'" At the same time, the estate tried to sell the Cliff House, Sutro Baths, and the land and buildings adjoining them to the city for $600,000 (Emma Merritt held a one-sixth interest in the properties), but the city declined.

Most sources describe the transfer of the property as a gift, but the November 19, 1933 issue of the *San Francisco Chronicle* reports otherwise. Thomas J. Bellows, who interviewed Emma Merritt for his article titled "Kin of Sutro Tells Tale of Heights' Sale," states that "on payment of $250,000, Mrs. Merritt and her husband, Dr. George W. Merritt, deeded the property to the city." The Merritts had been living in her father's house when the property changed hands, and Emma Merritt was intent on clearing up a misunderstanding that had existed since that time: "There is a mistaken notion that another condition of the transfer was that I should be permitted to keep my residence in the old home as long as I desired. This isn't true. I love the old home, but I could not stay if the Park Commissioners desired me to give up my residence."

Between 1920 and 1933, the public continued to visit Sutro Heights, and Emma Merritt dutifully maintain the grounds, with only one recorded exception. In 1924, the city was forced to step in and shore up the cliff face and the road leading to the entrance, both of which had been destabilized by work on the public road below. Finally, in 1933, Emma Merritt, perhaps faced with dwindling personal resources, persuaded the city to assume maintenance of the property. But short of funds itself, it initiated no improvements for the next four years. Then, in 1937, the city submitted a request to the Works Progress Administration (WPA), which resulted in the start of a rehabilitation program. Emma Merritt, who was in her early eighties at the time, was still regularly seen making her way down to Sutro Baths to collect the receipts.

But just a year later, in October 1938, Emma Merritt died in her father's famous cottage on Sutro Heights. Shortly after, WPA workers tore down the derelict house and what was left of the conservatory, the Dolce far Niente Balcony, the entrance gates, and other crumbling structures. However, they rebuilt some walls and paths, and they repaired some of the statues that remained from Adolph Sutro's 1883 European buying spree.

After World War II, the city considered rehabilitating Sutro Heights, but the plan foundered, and in 1976, the property was transferred to the National Park Service. Today, the site has been reduced to a handsome greensward with palm trees, shrubs, the restored well house, paths for quiet strolling, and a pair of stone lions, replicas of the originals, at the entrance. Although it lacks the one-time grandiosity, it still offers the same extraordinary views of the Cliff House and the ocean that Adolph Sutro and later Emma Sutro Merritt enjoyed in their time.

CONEY ISLAND
OF THE WEST

IN THE EARLY DECADES of San Francisco, the sandy stretch along the city's western edge offered only a trio of food-and-drink diversions, the Cliff House and the Seal Rock House at the north end and the Ocean House at the south end. In 1883, scores of out-of-work squatters took up residence just south of the Seal Rock House in a jerry-built settlement known as Mooneysville, after Con Mooney, a labor activist who was in a pitched battle against the "land-grabbing tactics" of local railroad barons. That same year, the Park and Ocean Railroad steam train was completed, linking the downtown cable car line to Ocean Beach. The entrepreneurial inhabitants of Mooneysville were ready with cracked crab, doughnuts, coffee, and liquor to sell to the day-trippers alighting from the train.

But Mooneysville would not be tolerated for long. On the last day of January 1884, two dozen Golden Gate Park employees and a small contingent of policeman rousted the squatters and flattened their makeshift community. Six months later, the grand Ocean Beach Pavilion, a combination dance hall and concert hall, opened next door to the Seal Rock House. A gravity roller coaster—modeled after one that had debuted at Coney Island the same year—was built soon after, the first amusement ride on Ocean Beach.

Four years after the new Cliff House opened in 1909, Arthur Looff assembled his beautiful sixty-five-horse merry-go-round on the beach and called it the Looff Hippodrome. The hand-carved horses "galloped" alongside John Friedle's shooting galleries and baseball throws. Looff and Friedle soon joined forces, and less than a decade later, they were operating dozens of concessions and ten different rides, including a Shoot the Chutes, in which passengers in flat-bottomed boats slid down a steep ramp into a large pool of water, a thrill that gave Looff and Friedle the name for their amusement park: Chutes at the Beach (other Chutes parks had preceded it in San Francisco, on Haight, Fulton, and Fillmore streets). The Bob Sled Dipper, the Big Dipper, the Aeroplane Swing, the Ship of Joy, Noah's Ark, and a Ferris wheel were among the other popular rides. In 1924, the Crazy House, later renamed the Fun House, opened. Inside, visitors got woozy in the maze of mirrors, tried not to get thrown off of a giant, spinning turntable, got tossed around in the topsy-turvy Barrels of Fun, stumbled along slinky catwalks, and flew down, a burlap sack protecting their backsides, the "longest indoor slide in the world."

George and Leo Whitney began running their own concessions at the park in the early 1920s, and took

Ocean Beach, early 1900s. Cliff House Collection

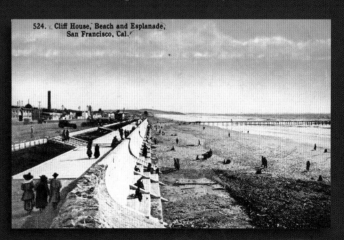

The Chutes, San Francisco, Cal.

S. F. 399. The Chutes, San Francisco, Cal.

over the management of the growing operation from Looff and Friedle by 1926, formally changing its name to Whitney's At the Beach in 1928, and less formally, Playland. (Although the park was also popularly known as Playland at the Beach from the days of the Whitneys, it was never the legal name.) Unlike many amusement parks elsewhere in the country, Playland thrived during the Depression, expanding to cover nearly three city blocks by 1934. The Whitneys gradually bought all of the concessions, including the food vendors and rides, snapping up the roller coaster in 1936 and the merry-go-round in 1942. The purchase of the Cliff House in 1937 placed most of the beach real estate firmly in Whitney hands.

Throughout the war years, Playland remained a popular destination. To encourage visitors to explore the whole midway, not just the best-known attractions,

the Whitneys came up with the idea of "booster tickets": a ticket bought for a popular ride, like the Bob Sled Dipper, included a coupon for a less-popular ride for only a few pennies more. But by 1950, the Shoot the Chutes was dismantled, and five years later, the Big Dipper, one of the park's earliest roller coasters, followed it to the scrap heap. When George Whitney, the man who put Playland on the national map, died in 1958, his son, George, Jr., struggled to keep the amusement park a San Francisco destination.

In the early 1960s, a Whitney family dispute moved Playland into the hands of Robert Fraser, who sold it to developer Jeremy Ets-Hokin in 1971. Ets-Hokin tore it down a year later. Fortunately, the Looff Hippodrome was saved, finding a home first in Long Beach and then, in 1998, in San Francisco's own Yerba Buena Gardens, where it continues to spin today.

Playland promotional photo and Playland tickets, 1950s. Cliff House Collection

THE COMPETITION

THE CLIFF HOUSE HAS never been without competition at the beach, and never more so than during the Whitney era. But most of the competition at that time was also operated by the Whitneys, who knew that a trip to the beach usually gave visitors a good appetite.

In 1936, waffle aficionados watched as the Waffle Shop went up on the Great Highway between Cabrillo and Balboa streets. Some onlookers were old enough to remember Boston the Waffle Man, who sold delicious "indented cakes" from a cottage at the corner of Fulton Street and the Great Highway. When the old, shingled waffle parlor became a casualty of the expansion of Playland, those who mourned its loss later welcomed the new Waffle Shop into the oceanside community.

Nearby, at the Pie Shop, diners could sit down to a complete pie meal, with a chicken turnover for

Full parking lot at Ocean Beach on December 17, 1936. Courtesy of the San Francisco History Center, San Francisco Public Library

a main and pie à la mode for dessert. Three giant ovens were used to turn out a menu that typically listed chicken, beef, apple, and apricot turnovers and fourteen different pies. There was also ice cream served plain, in sodas, in sundaes, or between two cookies, in Playland's own It's-It ice cream sandwich, all fashioned from ice cream made in the Whitneys own plant. On weekends during World War II, the bakers hand kneaded some seven hundred pounds of dough for the hundreds of pies they turned out to keep the crowds happy.

On an equally busy weekend, the Hot House, famous for its house-made enchiladas, chiles rellenos, tamales, tostadas, and other Mexican and Spanish dishes, regularly served as many as twelve hundred tamales. The perennially crowded space, with its tile floors, colorful pottery, and sunny Mexico atmosphere, was demolished along with the rest of Playland in 1972, but reopened in a nearby storefront on Balboa Street shortly after, where it remained for a few years before a Chinese restaurant took its place.

The "It" Stand, known for its "broiled steer meat hamburgers cooked without grease" and its "electric grilled hot dogs," was another busy Playland spot. Although not the only stand serving burgers on the oceanfront, it was one of the best and typically jammed with customers. The White Castle chain, born in the Midwest, had popularized the hamburger after World War I, and the Whitneys sold plenty of America's favorite fast-food sandwich at their many concessions, using more than twenty-five thousand pounds of ground beef for their patties on a good weekend.

The Sea Lion Café sold burgers, too, but it was renowned for its clam chowder and for its Sunday breakfasts, especially before the Cliff House reopened in 1937. One of the early eateries on the beach's restaurant row, it was seriously in need of repairs when it was bought by the Whitneys in 1929, who promptly renovated it, creating a bright, attractive restaurant that seated fifty diners and sold takeaway hot dogs and hamburgers from an open front.

Tait's at the Beach was another early member of the restaurant community. The building, which stood on the Great Highway between Ulloa and Vicente streets, had a checkered history. According to historian Woody LaBounty, in the 1850s, it was a roadhouse named Brooks Folly, after a lawyer who had it constructed from materials salvaged from a shipwreck, and for the balance of the nineteenth century, it experienced a largely notorious career under various names. At the turn of the century, it was purchased by Alexander and Ida Russell, a wealthy couple who made it their home, furnishing it elegantly, installing a Japanese garden, and hosting lectures on Eastern theologies.

Following the sudden death of Mrs. Russell—she was given morphine to lessen the pain during a carbolic acid–laced treatment to remove wrinkles from her neck, a deadly combination—Mr. Russell sold his home to restaurateur John Tait in 1919, who had opened the newly built Cliff House in 1909. Tait quickly turned the Russell mansion into the lively Tait's at the Beach, known for its food, music, and fun: "*the* place to go for socialites and celebrities and those who enjoyed mingling with same." Prohibition and the Depression combined to put Tait's out of business by 1931 (even though John Tait was known to serve a drink or two during the 1920s, it didn't save Tait's), and others who attempted to run a business in the old Russell mansion failed (or were closed down by the police). The building burned to the ground in 1940.

Tait's at the Beach was indeed the talk of the oceanfront in the early 1920s, a role that Whitneys' Topsy's Roost assumed in the mid-1930s. Topsy's was housed in the old Ocean Beach Pavilion, which in its heyday had been famous for its giant pipe organ, busy dance floor, and big concerts, and its menu featured the "world's most delicious fried chicken," along with waffled-fried potatoes, corn pone and honey, and other southern dishes. Private "roosts" (booths) made to look like rickety chicken coops lined the mezzanine and the dance floor, faux fowl decorated the walls and rafters, and chicken footprints covered the tabletops. More than a thousand diners and three hundred dancers could be accommodated, and on many nights, Topsy's was packed. But what set Topsy's apart was the "transportation" from the mezzanine to the dance floor: children's playground slides were used by waiters with their trays full of dinner plates and by guests looking to dance or eat on the lower floor. In 1936, local columnist Carl T. Nunan was enthusiastic in his praise of the scene: "How different the swingy captivating tunes of Ellis Kimball's orchestra compared with the sour notes of the wheezy, asthmatic organ that gave itchy feet to the waxed-floor hoofers who once graced the dance floor of the old [Ocean Beach Pavilion]. The best music, the best eats and the most colorful and unique restaurant in the entire west, Topsy's Roost."

That popularity eventually faded, and Topsy's Roost closed not long after the war ended. The building had a number of occupants after Topsy's demise, and was finally torn down in the early 1970s.

Interior of Topsy's Roost, Chutes at the Beach. Topsy's was described as "The largest, the most unusual, the most popular place of its kind in California." Postcard, circa 1936. Cliff House Collection

The Show Boat and Levee—Topsy's Roost—Chutes at the Beach—San Francisco—Whitney Bros., Props.

WHITNEY BROS' FAMOUS
PLACES TO DINE
AT THE BEACH

The HOT HOUSE
SPECIALIZING IN ENCHILADAS · TAMALES · TOSTADAS · CHILE RELLENOS AND OTHER DELICIOUS MEXICAN AND SPANISH DISHES · PREPARED BY EXPERTS AND SERVED IN THE DELIGHTFUL ATMOSPHERE OF SUNNY MEXICO

The "IT" STAND
FAMOUS FOR PLATE BROILED STEER MEAT HAMBURGERS COOKED WITHOUT GREASE · AND ELECTRIC GRILLED HOT DOGS CONTAINING VITAMIN "D" · MADE ESPECIALLY FOR OUR USE · GOOD COFFEE ALWAYS

The PIE SHOP
HOMEMADE PIES & CAKES TURNOVERS · SANDWICHES · FRESH FROZEN ICE CREAM AND FOUNTAIN SPECIALS · ALL ICE CREAM, PIES & CAKES SERVED IN WHITNEY BROS. RESTAURANTS AND STANDS ARE MADE HERE

The SEA LION Cafe
BREAKFASTS · LUNCHES · DINNERS · STEAKS · CHOPS · HAM AND EGGS · WAFFLES · HOT OR COLD SANDWICHES · HOME MADE PIES · SPECIAL SUNDAY DINNERS · THE SEA LION IS A POPULAR PLACE FOR SUNDAY BREAKFASTS

The WAFFLE SHOP
SPECIALIZING IN CREAM WAFFLES · STRAWBERRY AND PECAN WAFFLES HOT CAKES WITH LITTLE PIG SAUSAGES, BACON OR HAM · STEER BEEF HAMBURGERS · ELECTRIC GRILLED HOT DOGS · CHOW MEIN · PIES & CAKES

TOPSY'S ROOST
FEATURING THE WORLD'S MOST DELICIOUS FRIED CHICKEN · BAKED HAM CHICKEN PIE · CORN PONES · HOT BISCUITS · WAFFLE FRIED POTATOES · AND OTHER DELICIOUS SOUTHERN DISHES · DANCING · PARTIES & BANQUETS

The CLIFF HOUSE
SAN FRANCISCO'S FINEST AND MOST HISTORIC DINING PLACE · SPECIAL SUNDAY MORNING BREAKFASTS · LUNCHEONS · DINNERS · CUISINE UNEXCELLED · BEAUTIFUL MARINE DINING ROOM · NATIVE REDWOOD BAR AND COCKTAIL LOUNGE

PLAYLAND AT THE BEACH · S.F.

GOOD THINGS TO DRINK

COCKTAILS		MIXED DRINKS	
Martini	.30	Gin Rickey	
Manhattan	.30	Sloe Gin Rickey	
Old Fashioned	.30	Tom Collins	
Honolulu	.35	Bourbon Highball	
Pink Lady	.35	Whiskey Sour	
Daiquiry	.35	Scotch Highball (Dom.)	
Side Car	.35	Scotch Highball (Imp.)	
Bacardi	.35	Singapore Sling	
Topsy Southern	.35	Mint Julep	

STRAIGHT		FIZZES	
Bourbon Whiskey	.25	Gin Fizz	
Bourbon (6 years old)	.30	Sloe Gin Fizz	
Bourbon (18 years old)	.40	Silver Fizz	
Rye Whiskey	.30	Golden Fizz	
Scotch Whiskey (Dom.)	.25	Royal Fizz	
Scotch (Imported)	.35	New Orleans	
Fleischmann's Gin	.25	Waldorf	

LIQUEURS — CORDIALS			
Creme de Menthe	.30	Apricot Nectar	
Creme de Cocoa	.30	Brandy (Calif.)	
Benedictine (Imp.)	.40	Brandy (Imp.)	

CALIFORNIA WINES PER GLASS — 20c
Port .. Claret .. Angelica .. Sherry .. Chablis .. Burgur

CALIFORNIA BOTTLED WINES

Dry	½ Bot.	Bot.	Sweet, etc.	½ Bot.	B
Burgundy	.45	.85	Port	.75	I
Claret	.45	.85	Sherry	.75	I
Cabernet	.45	.85	Angelica	.75	I
Sauterne	.45	.85	Muscatel	.75	I
Riesling	.45	.85	Burgundy Carb.	1.75	3
Sonoma RUBIO	.45	.85	Moselle Carb.	1.75	3
Tipo R Tipo W	.75	1.25	Champagne	2.25	3

BEVERAGES

Bottled Beers (Local)	.25	Ginger Ales	
Bottled Beers (Eastern)	.35	Lime Rickey	
Mineral Water	.50	Orange Rickey	

DANCING

Places to Dine at the Beach, promotional booklet, 1930s. Cliff House Collection

Topsy's Roost - S.F.

Playland at the Beach

Menu

Eat with your fingers ~ Topsy Style

Souvenir Menu ~ Take Me Home

Cocktails

Oyster	.25
Crab	.25
Fruit	.25

Topsy's Specials

HALF

FRIED SPRING CHICKEN	.50
CHICKEN TAGLIARINI	.50
CHICKEN PIE ALABAM	.50
HAM AND EGGS TOPSY	.50
N. Y. SIRLOIN STEAK	.75
CRAB LOUIE	.50
CHICKEN SALAD	.50
Combination Salad	.25
Hearts of Lettuce	.25
Sliced Tomatoes	.25

HOT

Biscuits and Honey	.15
Corn Pones and Honey	.15
Waffle Fried Potatoes	.15
Chicken Broth	.15
Crisp Celery Hearts	.15
Jumbo Olives	.15

DESSERTS

Mammy's Apple Pie	.15	Apple Pie a la Mode	.30
Whitney Bros. Ice Cream	.15	Fruit Jello or Cobbler	.15

DRINKS

Coffee	.10	Pot of Tea	.15	Milk	.10
Bottled Beers—Local	.25		Eastern Beers	.35	

TOPSY'S SPECIAL SANDWICHES

Sugar Cured Ham	.25	Smoked Liverwurst	.25
Club Sandwich	.50	Sliced Chicken	.50
American or Swiss Cheese			.25
Chicken Salad Sandwich			.35

Colored views of Topsy's Roost—Set of 5 post cards 10c. We pay postage if you address cards and drop in Topsy's mail boxes. Ask waiter.

RULES OF THE ROOST

LIQUOR SERVICE CHARGE

As we pay a high license fee for the privilege of serving liquor, in case patrons bring liquor with them, or wine, a corkage charge of 25c will be made for each member of the party. This applies to all members of the party regardless of how many consume the liquor, except minors who are not in any case permitted to buy or consume liquor on the premises.

Bringing in of Ginger Ale, Rickey, Beer, etc., is strictly prohibited. We charge our full list price for such beverages brought in by patrons.

See Separate Menu for
TOPSY'S SPECIAL $1.00 DINNERS

Served during following hours only: Saturdays, 5:00 p. m. to 8:00 p. m.; Sundays, noon to 9:00 p. m.; other days 5:00 p. m. to 9:00 p. m.

TOPSY SEZ:

Minimum Service Saturday nights and Holidays $1.00 per person after 9 p. m. Minimum charge at all other times 50c per person. No cover charge at any time. All sales subject to State Sales Tax. Checks of $2.50 or more subject to 3% Federal Tax.

Examine check before paying. Kindly report any inattention or overcharge to the floor manager.

Please do not smoke on the dance floor as it is dangerous to others. Dance soliciting is not permitted.

We are not responsible for lost articles left in booths. Use check room on main floor near entrance.

Please remember our delicious Fried Chicken, Hot Biscuits, Waffle Fried Potatoes, etc., are prepared to order. This takes a little time. Enjoy our music and dancing. Your patience will be rewarded. Eat with your fingers, enjoy that chicken, and have a good time.

Phone SKyline 3423 for Reservations or Party Arrangements.

Topsy's Roost is open from noon to 1 a. m. Sundays, and from 5 p. m. to 1 a. m. week days.

We close Mondays . . . Except Holidays

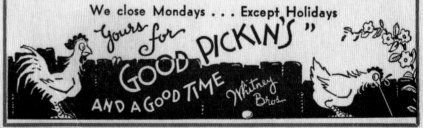

Yours for "GOOD PICKIN'S" AND A GOOD TIME Whitney Bros.

Topsy's Roost menu, circa 1936. Cliff House Collection

A STARRING ROLE

THE WESTERN EDGE of San Francisco has made it to the big screen in a number of noteworthy films: Orson Welles walked past the Fun House at Playland in the 1948 *Lady from Shanghai* (an earlier scene with Welles and Rita Hayworth in the mirror maze inside the Fun House was shot on a Hollywood set); Anne Hathaway took her royal grandmother, Julie Andrews, to the Musée Mécanique in the 2001 *The Princess Diaries*, sadistic killer Eli Wallach turned up outside and inside Sutro Baths—the ice rink, the promenade, the monumental staircase all visible—and outside the Cliff House in the 1958 *The Lineup*, a film noir valentine to San Francisco; and a scene of a meeting inside the Cliff House appeared in Erich Von Stroheim's 1925 masterpiece *Greed*. In the early 1970s, the interior of the Cliff House also made it to the small screen, appearing in an episode of the *Streets of San Francisco*.

But the film that showed the Cliff House off best was *Alexander's Ragtime Band*, released in 1938. The story opens in 1915 and stars Tyrone Power, Jean Hersholt, Don Ameche, and Alice Faye. A memorable scene in the movie includes views of Seal Rocks in the moonlight, a row of neon signs looking south down Ocean Beach, and the Cliff House's neoclassical exterior and chandelier-rich interior. At the time it was produced, *Alexander's Ragtime Band* was, at $2,275,000, the costliest film every made by Twentieth Century Fox Film Corporation. A sizable chunk of the bill went into re-creating the interior of the 1909 Cliff House on a Hollywood sound stage, an amount rumored to be $100,000, including the cost of special ordering seven glass chandeliers from Czechoslovakia.

In April 1938, before the film opened nationally, the *San Francisco Call Bulletin* reported on the San Francisco visit of Jean Hersholt, with the actor observing, "This will be . . . the second time I've appeared at the Cliff House in a picture. The first was in 1923 when I played in the actual building for a scene in . . . *Greed*. . . . Almost 15 years to the day I walked again onto the same set, only this time in Hollywood."

In the same article, Tyrone Power reminisced about being in the Cliff House as a child with his father, Tyrone, Sr., a stage and screen actor: "I recall visiting with my father . . . when he was appearing at one of the city's theaters. Dad took me with him to dine at the Cliff House. As I was then rather a small boy, he lifted me to the windowsill, so that I might look out at the seals playing on the rocks."

During the early 1980s, a Cliff House cocktail waitress waited on a young man who seemed intrigued by the photograph on the wall next to his table. He finally remarked to her that he had never expected to sit down in a place as famous as the Cliff House beneath a picture of his father, Tyrone Power. The young man was Tyrone Power, Jr., born in January 1959, little more than two months after his father's premature death from a massive heart attack.

In the early 1980s, bandleader and comedian Phil Harris experienced an echo of Power's experience. While enjoying lunch at the Cliff House, he realized he was seated beneath a photograph of his wife, singer and actress Alice Faye, Power's costar in the Oscar-winning movie that had given the Cliff House its own starring role.

CLIFF HOUSE ★

SAN FRANCISCO, CALIFORNIA

Whitney Bros., Proprietors

AFTERNOO...
AN...
COCKTA...

Cliff House

San Francisco

...nday Breakfast

Cocktails and Wines

COCKTAILS

Martini	60
Manhattan	60
Old Fashioned	60
Gimlet	65
Side Car	65
Bacardi	65
Daiquiri	65
Alexander	65
Pink Lady	65

MIXED DRINKS

Gin Fizz	65
Silver Fizz	65
Royal Fizz	65
Golden Fizz	65
New Orleans Fizz	**60**
Gin Rickey	65
Tom Collins	65
Singapore Sling	65
Sloe Gin Fizz	65
Egg Nog	65

BRANDIES · COGNACS

Hennessy	85
Monnet	85
Courvoisier	85
Christian Brothers	60

LIQUEURS · CORDIALS

Creme de Menthe	60
Creme de Cacao	60
Benedictine, D.O.M.	85
Drambuie	85
Grand Marnier	85
King Alphonso	60

		Half Bottle	Bottle
CALIFORNIA DINNER WINES (WHITE)	**SAUTERNE, RIESLING, CHABLIS**		
	Beaulieu Vineyards	1.25	2.25
	Wente Brothers	1.25	2.25
	Almaden	1.25	2.25
	Beringer Brothers	1.25	2.25
CALIFORNIA DINNER WINES (RED)	**BURGUNDY AND CABERNET**		
	Almaden	1.25	2.25
	Wente Brothers	1.25	2.25
	Beaulieu Vineyards	1.25	2.25
	Beringer Brothers	1.25	2.25
CALIFORNIA ROSÉ WINE	Almaden Grenache Rosé	1.25	2.25
CALIFORNIA CHAMPAGNE	Korbel Sec	3.50	6.50
	Paul Masson, Extra Dry	3.50	6.50
IMPORTED CHAMPAGNE	Piper Heidsieck	5.00	10.00
	Mumm's, Extra Dry	5.00	10.00
SPARKLING BURGUNDY	Korbel Rouge	3.50	6.50
	Paul Masson	3.50	6.50
IMPORTED WHITE AND RED STILL WINES	Chateau Rieussec, 1933		4.50
	Chablis, Grand Cru Vaudesir, 1947		4.50
	Liebfraumilch	2.50	4.50
	Margaux, 1952		4.00
	St. Julien, 1950		4.50
	Batard Montrachet, 1933	2.50	
	Eschenauer, 1940		4.50

About California Wines

The correct wine at any time is the wine you enjoy most. Fine California wines are the perfect compliment to fine foods. Wine with a meal produces a feeling of serenity and well-being, and adds to the pleasure of good eating. The first California wines were made by the Spanish Padres more than two centuries ago. Over the years the prestige of these great wines has grown until today they are recognized as being among the finest in the world.

A CENTURY OLD SA...

The C... CLIF... AT SEA... BL...

THE ORIGINAL CLIFF HOUSE — BUILT IN 1858

THE THIRD CLIFF HOUSE — FINISHED IN 1896

sea foods

Morro Bay Abalone, Saute	2.45
Hangtown Fry	2.35
Pacific Ocean Halibut Steak	2.50
Farallone Island Salmon Steak	2.50
Fried Pacific Coast Crab Legs, Tartar Sauce	**2.95**
Oysters Kirkpatrick	2.35
Broiled Swordfish Steak	2.50
Fried Eastern Scallops	2.50
Prawns, Newberg	2.50
Fried Filet of Sole	1.75
Idaho Brook Trout	2.50

desserts

Assorted Pies	.35
Our Four Layer Cakes	.35
Ice Cream	.35
Sherbet	.35
Parfait	.65
Sundae	.50
Baked Alaska	1.25
Fruit Jello	.25
French Pancakes	1.25
Cherries Jubilee (for two)	3.20
Fried Cream in Blue Flame	1.00

appetizers

Pacific Coast Crab Legs, Supreme	1.50
Assorted Hors d'Oeuvres	1.50
Canape of Caviar	2.50
Canape of Anchovies	1.35
Fresh Crab or Shrimp Cocktail, Supreme	**.90**
Fresh California Fruit Cup, Supreme	.85

egg dishes

Eggs with Ham, Bacon or Sausage	1.55
Spanish Omelette	1.55
Chicken Liver Omelette	1.70
Fresh Mushroom Omelette	1.70
Cheese Omelette	1.55
Ham Omelette	1.55
Plain Omelette	1.20
Eggs, Benedict	1.95

cheese

Bleu	.50
Liederkranz	.55
Monterey Jack	.40
American Cheddar	.40

soups

French Onion Soup au Gratin	.50
Beef Consomme	.50
Cream of Tomato	.50
Clam Chowder	.50

vegetables

Fresh Leaf Spinach	.50
Garden Peas	.50
Buttered String Beans	.50
New Carrots	.50
Cauliflower	.60
Broccoli	.50

potatoes

French Fried	.50
Hashed Browned	.50
Au Gratin	.50

beverages

Coffee, Cup	.20
Tea	.20
Chocolate	.25
Sanka Coffee	.30
Milk	.15

Cliff House menu, 1950s.
Cliff House Collection

A Divided Service of a Single Order will be Twenty-five Cents Extra.　　　Minimum Service Per Person 75c

Today's Luncheon

Served from 12 noon to 3:00 p.m.

MONDAY, JUNE 15, 1959

Cliff House Lobster Tail Salad, Choice of Dressing

A La Carte 2.35
Complete Luncheon . . $2.95

New York Cut Steak a la Minute

A La Carte $3.25
Complete Luncheon . . $3.85

Hot Turkey or Beef Sandwich, Open Faced, Potatoes and Vegetable

A La Carte $1.95
Complete Luncheon . . $2.55

LUNCHEON APPETIZERS
Fresh Crab or Shrimp Cocktail 60¢

Price of Entree determines price of your Complete Luncheon

Choice of one

Chilled Orange, Tomato or Pineapple Juice
Mixed Green Salad
Chicken Noodle or Onion Soup

Choice of one:

Today's Special Sea Shore Mixed Grill 2.30
Prawns, Oysters, Scallops and Fillet of Sole with
French Fried Potatoes, Tartar Sauce
Stuffed Green Peppers, Spanish Sauce 1.95
Braised Turkey Wings in Burgundy Sauce 1.75
Pork Spareribs with Sauerkraut 1.75
Veal Scallopini a la Marsala 2.30
Old Fashioned Beef Stew 2.30
Fresh Crab Meat or Shrimp Louis 2.40

Buttered Carrots   Snowflake Potatoes

Choice of one:

Ice Cream (assorted flavors)   Sherbet   Jell-O   Cheese Cake
Baked Apple   Assorted Pies or Layer Cake

Choice of one: Coffee, Tea or Milk

FROM OUR Salad Bar

FRESH CRAB OR SHRIMP LOUIS . . 1.95

CLIFF COURT SALAD 1.95
With diced Chicken and
Asparagus Spears

CLIFF HOUSE SALAD BOWL 1.95
With Avocados, Anchovies,
and Asparagus Tips

CHEF HEINZ'S FRESH CALIFORNIA
FRUIT SALAD 2.45

GREEN GODDESS SALAD 1.95
With Julienne Breast of Chicken
or Crab Meat

GOLDEN GATE SALAD 1.95
With Breast of Chicken Julienne

ASSORTED COLD MEATS, GARNI . . 2.35

SLICED COLD BAKED HAM AND
TURKEY PLATE 2.85

MIXED GREEN SALAD BOWL 1.20

CHEF HEINZ'S CLIFF HOUSE Specialties

Pacific Crab Legs, Cliff House (under glass) 2.95
Filet of Sole, Marguery 2.45
Breast of Chicken, Sous Cloche (under glass) 2.95
Sirloin Steak a la Minute 3.50
Broiled Australian Lobster Tail 3.25
Spring Chicken, Saute Sec 2.85

A CALIFORNIA DELICACY
Tender Morro Bay Abalone,
Saute Meuniere . . . 2.45

Roast Prime Rib of Beef, au jus 3.25
Wiener Schnitzel, a la Holstein 2.95
Special Seafood Platter 2.70
Calf's Sweet Breads, Saute 2.70
Cream Chicken a la King on Toast . . . 2.45

FROM THE Broiler

Chateaubriand, Assiette . 10.80
(for two)

Planked Sirloin Steak . . 9.50
(for two)

Sirloin Steak a la Minute 3.50
New York Cut Steak (one pound) . 4.25
Filet Mignon (one pound) 4.75
Broiled Lamb Chops (2) 3.50
Half Spring Chicken 2.70

sandwiches

Club Sandwich 1.75
Dagwood Sandwich 1.75
Monte Cristo 1.50
Sliced Chicken 1.20

Chef's Special Chicken Sandwich
with Creamed Mushroom
Sauce 1.95

Baked Ham 1.20
Denver Sandwich (open faced) . . 1.50
Melted Cheese on Toast 1.20
American or Swiss Cheese 90

Children's menu, 1950s. Cliff House Collection

CLIFF HOUSE

CLIFF HOUSE

KIDDIES' MENU

FOOD for SMALL FRY

SOUP du JOUR
BROILED FRENCH LAMB CHOP
on TOAST with VEGETABLE and
POTATOES · ROLLS and BUTTER
ICE CREAM, SHERBET
or FRUIT JELLO
MILK or HOT CHOCOLATE
1.95

SOUP du JOUR
CREAMED CHICKEN on TOAST
with MASHED POTATOES and
BUTTERED PEAS · ROLLS and BUTTER
ICE CREAM, SHERBET
or FRUIT JELLO
MILK or HOT
CHOCOLATE
1.60

SOUP du JOUR · or FRUIT JUICE
CHICKEN SANDWICH
with
POTATO CHIPS
ICE CREAM, SHERBET
or FRUIT JELLO
MILK or HOT CHOCOLATE
1.30

SOUP du JOUR or FRUIT JUICE
HAMBURGER PATTY on TOAST
with POTATO CHIPS
ICE CREAM, SHERBET
or FRUIT JELLO
MILK or HOT CHOCOLATE
1.20

World Famous
CLIFF HOUSE

AT SEAL ROCKS—
BY THE BLUE PACIFIC

CORN DOGS

A LONGTIME OCEANFRONT favorite, these dressed-up hot dogs were originally sold at Playland under the brand name Pronto Pup, and later at the Pronto Pup stand in the gift-shop building that stood next door to the Cliff House until 2003. The recipe is included here for the many aficionados of this dubious delicacy, and especially for the firefighters who worked at the nearby fire station on Geary Boulevard during the days of the Pronto Pup stand. Their frequent trips down to the beach to pick up a batch of corn dogs for lunch were legendary.

8 hot dogs
8 wooden sticks, each about 5 inches long,
    such as a Popsicle stick
2 cups yellow cornmeal
2 cups all-purpose flour
½ cup sugar
2½ teaspoons baking powder

1 cup whole milk
2 eggs
¼ cup honey
¼ cup canola or corn oil
Canola oil for deep-frying
Yellow mustard for serving

SKEWER EACH HOT DOG onto a wooden stick, leaving enough of the stick uncovered to grasp the end easily with tongs. In a large, deep bowl, stir together the cornmeal, flour, sugar, and baking powder. In a second bowl, stir together the milk, eggs, honey, and oil. Add the wet ingredients to the dry ingredients and mix until evenly combined, but do not overbeat. The batter is best if used immediately, so make it just before you are ready to begin frying.

Pour the oil to a depth of about 4 inches into a deep pan 10 inches in diameter and heat to 350 degrees F on a deep-frying thermometer. When the oil is ready, grasp the end of a stick with tongs, dip the hot dog into the batter, rotating it to coat it evenly, and then slip the coated hot dog into the hot oil. Repeat with a second hot dog. Fry, turning the hot dogs over occasionally to ensure even browning, until the coating is chestnut brown and crisp, about 3 minutes. Using the tongs, remove the hot dogs from the oil, brush with the mustard, and repeat with the remaining hot dogs, frying 2 at a time. Serve piping hot.

Appetizer Variation: The Cliff House kitchen occasionally gets requests for an appetizer version of this Ocean Beach classic. To make the appetizers, cut the hot dogs crosswise into ½-inch-thick rounds, then cut each round in half vertically, to form 2 half-moons. Using 3-inch wooden skewers, slip a half-moon onto each skewer. Dip the half-moons into the batter and then fry in the hot oil as directed. Brush with mustard and serve at once.

Serves 4

LAZY MAN'S CIOPPINO

SOME EXPERTS BELIEVE cioppino was created by Sicilian immigrant fishermen who reportedly threw unsold seafood into a big pot at the end of the day, and then shouted for their fellow wharf mates to "chip in" their unsold catch as well. Others insist it was invented by Giuseppe Buzzaro, formerly of Genoa, and that the name evolved from *ciuppin*, Genoese dialect for a seafood stew. And still others contend it is a San Francisco adaptation of *cacciucco*, the famed seafood stew of Tuscany. Whatever its origin, it has long been a favorite with Cliff House diners. Serve it in big bowls with sourdough bread and a glass of Sonoma Sauvignon Blanc.

3 tablespoons olive oil
1 large white onion, diced
3 celery ribs, diced
1 large red bell pepper, seeded and diced
1 leek, white part only, diced
5 cloves garlic, minced
1 fennel bulb, trimmed and diced
1 tablespoon dried basil
1 teaspoon dried thyme
1 teaspoon dried tarragon
1 teaspoon paprika
1 teaspoon freshly ground black pepper

2 glasses dry white wine
1 tablespoon Pernod (optional)
1 can (6 ounces) tomato paste
1 can (28 ounces) diced tomatoes, with juice
1 can (28 ounces) tomato sauce
3 bottles (8 ounces each) clam juice
2 cups water
1 pound large shrimp (16/20 count), peeled and deveined
1 pound Manila clams, scrubbed
1 pound rock cod fillets, cut into 1-inch pieces
8 ounces sea scallops, cut in half horizontally
8 ounces fresh-cooked Dungeness crabmeat, picked over

IN A LARGE, deep pot, heat the olive oil over high heat. Add the onion and celery and sauté until the onion is translucent, about 3 minutes. Add the bell pepper, leek, garlic, and fennel and sauté for 2 minutes. Add all of the dried herbs, the paprika, and the black pepper and stir well. Pour in 1 glass of the wine and the Pernod, if using, and add the tomato paste, diced tomatoes with their juice, tomato sauce, clam juice, and water. Stir well and bring to a simmer. Reduce the heat to low and simmer gently, uncovered, for 30 minutes to blend the flavors. Meanwhile, sip the second glass of wine.

Add the shrimp and clams to the pot, discarding any clams that failed to close to the touch, and cook for 2 minutes. Add the cod and scallops and cook until the cod is opaque throughout and all of the clams have opened, about 2 minutes longer. Add the crabmeat and cook just until heated through. Ladle into large bowls, discarding any clams that failed to open, and serve at once.

Serves 8

HERB-ROASTED CORNISH HEN

WITH BABY SPINACH, CANDIED WALNUTS, AND PERSIMMON SALAD

WHEN SHORTY ROBERTS reopened the Cliff House after World War I, he hired a French chef to prepare a roasted, stuffed "squab chicken" that featured a different stuffing every night. The term *squab chicken* is a bit of a mystery today: was the chef using a squab (fledgling pigeon) or a poussin (baby chicken)? This contemporary take on that decades-old tradition dispenses with the stuffing in favor of a lighter salad and uses Cornish hens in place of the harder-to-find poussins or squabs. The dish is still occasionally featured today on our specials menu.

HERB BUTTER
Leaves from 4 fresh thyme sprigs, finely chopped
Leaves from 4 fresh parsley sprigs, finely chopped
Leaves from 4 fresh tarragon sprigs, finely chopped
1 shallot, finely diced
2 cloves garlic, finely minced
Grated zest of 1 lemon
1 teaspoon kosher salt
½ cup (4 ounces) butter, at room temperature

4 Cornish hens, 16 to 18 ounces each

SALAD
1 Fuyu persimmon
1 pomegranate
4 ounces baby spinach
½ cup candied walnuts (homemade or purchased)

VINAIGRETTE
1 tablespoon red wine vinegar
1 tablespoon balsamic vinegar
1 teaspoon sugar
½ teaspoon salt
¼ teaspoon freshly ground black pepper
¼ cup walnut oil
¼ cup olive oil

PREHEAT THE OVEN to 425 degrees F. To make the herb butter, in a small bowl, work the herbs, shallot, garlic, lemon zest, and salt evenly into the butter.

Use one-fourth of the herb butter for each hen. Using your fingers, separate the skin from the flesh on the breast of 1 hen, and spread some of the butter evenly over the flesh, being careful not to tear the skin. Rub the remaining butter over the skin on the breast and legs. Repeat with the remaining hens and butter. Place the birds, breast side up, in a roasting pan.

Place in the oven and roast for 15 minutes. Baste the birds with the pan juices, reduce the temperature to 350 degrees F, and continue to roast for 30 minutes.

While the hens are roasting, make the salad. Peel the persimmon and cut lengthwise into 8 thin slices. Set aside. Cut the pomegranate in half horizontally. With one hand, hold a pomegranate half, cut side down, over a large bowl, keeping your hand below the bowl rim. With a large spoon, firmly strike the top and sides of the pomegranate half repeatedly. The seeds will drop into the bowl. (You may need to ease out any reluctant seeds with your fingers.) Repeat with the other pomegranate half. In a bowl, mix together the persimmon slices, pomegranate seeds, spinach, and walnuts. Set aside.

To make the vinaigrette, in a small bowl, whisk together both vinegars and the sugar, salt, and pepper until the sugar dissolves. Whisk in both oils.

When ready, remove the birds from the oven and let rest for 5 minutes. Split each hen in half lengthwise. Pour the vinaigrette over the salad and toss.

Arrange each split hen on a warmed dinner plate. Place a mound of the salad alongside. Serve at once.

Serves 4

CRABMEAT MONZA

EARLY IN THE TWENTIETH CENTURY, this dish was served in a number of San Francisco restaurants, including the dining room of the Hotel St. Francis, the venerable Tadich Grill, and, of course, the Cliff House, where it appeared on a menu as early as 1912.

PASTRY SHELLS
1 egg
3 tablespoons water
4 frozen puff pastry rectangles, each 3 by 5 inches

FILLING
3 tablespoons butter
12 large white button mushrooms, trimmed and quartered
½ cup dry sherry

3 tablespoons all-purpose flour
1 cup heavy cream
1 cup water
1 teaspoon paprika
Pinch of cayenne pepper
Pinch of ground nutmeg
1 teaspoon Dijon mustard
1½ pounds fresh-cooked Dungeness
   crabmeat, picked over

TO PREPARE the pastry shells, preheat the oven to 350 degrees F. In a small bowl, lightly beat together the egg and water to make an egg wash. Set aside. Leave the frozen pastry rectangles at room temperature for 10 to 15 minutes, to allow them to thaw partially. Then, using a sharp knife, lightly score a second rectangle on each pastry rectangle, making it ½ inch smaller on all sides and being careful not to cut all the way through the pastry. Brush the pastry rectangles with the egg wash and place them, well spaced, on a baking sheet. Reserve the remaining egg wash.

Bake the pastry shells until puffed and golden brown, about 15 minutes. Remove the shells from the oven and let them cool until they can be handled, then gently lift off the smaller rectangle from each shell. Set the pastry shells aside on the baking sheet, and reserve the tops. Leave the oven on.

To make the filling, in a sauté pan, melt the butter over high heat. When the butter foams, add the mushrooms and sauté for 1 minute. Add the sherry and cook, stirring, until the mushrooms are tender, about 2 minutes. Sprinkle the flour over the mushrooms and cook, stirring, for 1 minute. Pour in the cream and water, stirring to combine, and bring the mixture to a simmer, stirring constantly. Add the paprika, cayenne, and nutmeg and simmer, stirring often, until the sauce thickens, 2 to 3 minutes. Taste the sauce to make sure all the raw flour flavor has cooked away. If it hasn't, cook for a minute longer. Stir in the mustard and then add the crabmeat and stir gently to heat through, leaving as many large pieces of crab intact as possible. Stir in the reserved egg wash for extra richness.

Reheat the pastry shells in the oven for about 30 seconds, then transfer the shells to individual plates. Spoon the warm crab mixture into the pastry shells, dividing it evenly. Cap with the reserved tops and serve at once.

Serves 4

HOT BUTTERED RUM

AMERICANS HAVE BEEN sipping this cold-weather drink since colonial times, when campaigning politicians reportedly handed it out to warm up their constituents before they headed off to the voting booth. When the Whitneys reopened the Cliff House in 1937, this old-fashioned rum concoction was one of the most popular beverages on the bar menu.

BUTTER MIX
½ cup (4 ounces) butter, at room temperature
I cup lightly packed dark brown sugar
I½ teaspoons ground cinnamon
½ teaspoon ground nutmeg
½ teaspoon ground cloves
¼ teaspoon ground allspice

About ½ cup butter mix
32 ounces (4 cups) boiling water
9 ounces (I cup plus 2 tablespoons) light or dark rum
6 cinnamon sticks

TO MAKE the butter mix, combine all of the ingredients in a metal bowl and, using the back of a large spoon, blend together until thoroughly combined. If the mixture is too stiff to mix evenly, briefly place the bowl over very low heat until the mixture softens slightly. Do not leave it on the heat too long, as you don't want the butter to melt. You will only need about ½ cup of the mix for this recipe.

Transfer the balance of the mix to a tightly covered container and refrigerate. It will keep for up to 2 weeks.

Have ready 6 warmed 10-ounce mugs. Place 1 heaping tablespoon of the butter mix in each mug. Then add 6 ounces (¾ cup) boiling water and 1½ ounces (3 tablespoons) rum to each mug and stir well. Slip a cinnamon stick into each mug and serve at once.

Serves 6

PART FOUR

THE UNCERTAIN YEARS

PART FOUR
THE
UNCERTAIN
YEARS

Cliff House and adjacent gift shop, circa 1965. Cliff House Collection

PAGE 146

Cliff House menu cover, 1978. The cover mistakenly adds more than a decade to the true opening year of the first Cliff House. Cliff House Collection

DURING THE YEARS George Whitney, Sr. was getting the Sky Tram up and running, tearing down aging rides at Playland, and trying to turn Sutro Baths into a profitable operation, George, Jr. was in Southern California helping Walt Disney develop his new amusement park. Disney put him in charge of organizing the ride lines and maximizing crowd flow, tasks for which his years of experience at Playland had prepared him well.

But when George, Sr. unexpectedly took ill and died in 1958, George, Jr. returned to San Francisco to assume his father's role in the family business. Everything seemed to need attention, and for the next few years, he slowly chipped away at the mountain of tasks. In a June 1963 article in the *San Francisco Examiner*, Whitney described the state of the eleven-acre Playland and its possible future, observing that the city's rising property values meant that the rides, restaurants, shooting galleries, Fun House, and other draws would inevitably be replaced by homes and retail spaces. Because the park was still drawing crowds as large as twenty-five thousand on warm weekends, he insisted he would keep it open for another five to seven years, maybe longer, then listed a number of immediate improvements he was planning: a new $250,000 roller coaster; at least three new smaller rides,

in addition to the Space-Copter and Bubble Bounce he had already installed that year; restaurant upgrades that would recapture the "reputation they had at one time for quality and service"; much-needed paint on many of the structures and rides; and more and better lighting. His idea was to re-create the amusement park of the past with the economics and engineering of the present.

But any improvements to the park would not be made by George Whitney. The early 1960s were years of discord between Whitney and his mother, Eva, who could not agree on the fate of their empire. In the end, she sold her controlling interest in Playland to developer Robert Fraser, a sale that put Fraser in charge of the park.

With Playland in new hands, George Whitney began to focus his attention on operating the Cliff House and Sutro Baths, which he owned with his sister, but soon sold the abandoned pool areas of the baths to Fraser, who eventually bought the ice rink and museum as well. Whitney and his sister were left with only the Cliff House, the north annex, the large gift shop called the Seal Rocks Pavilion, and several small buildings on the adjacent property housing modest restaurants and coffee shops. Whitney finally bought out his sister.

HISTORY ALMOST REPEATS ITSELF

OLD-TIMERS OFTEN talked about how the Cliff House had been hexed since its beginnings in gaslight San Francisco. George Whitney knew the history, too: a dynamite explosion shattered the north wing in 1887, a raging fire razed the whole building in 1894; and only fifteen years later, another unstoppable blaze destroyed the chateaulike Cliff House of 1896. So, everyone was imagining the worst on November 12, 1963, when fire threatened the same rocky promontory.

Beginning at about five-thirty in the afternoon, the five-alarm fire raged for more than three hours before it was brought under control. Some fifteen thousand onlookers swarmed into the area and watched as more than three hundred firefighters fought the flames, their work made more difficult by strong winds, low water pressure, and limited access because of the sheer cliff on the seaward side. When the smoke finally cleared, the Cliff House

Cliff House and Seal Rocks (center) and Sutro Baths (far right), circa 1965. Cliff House Collection

and the small restaurants next to Sutro Baths were still standing, but the buildings between them—Seal Rocks Pavilion, its gift shop and basement filled with antique treasures, and a smaller building with two snack stands and an exhibit of ship models—were reduced to glowing embers. The loss was estimated at $1,000,000. The blaze, which the fire chief suggested was likely due to faulty wiring in the pavilion, had come close to the Cliff House, with some sources putting the flames no more than thirty feet away. But the building remained unscathed.

Just three years later, in June 1966, the famed landmark was threatened with fire again. When Whitney sold Sutro Baths to Robert Fraser, he agreed to operate the ice rink and museum for two years until Fraser had his plans for a two-hundred-unit apartment complex ready to go. With his investors set, Fraser shut down the business, emptied the building of its contents, and called a demolition company. The workers were just beginning to dismantle the building when a fire broke out. It burned the natatorium to its foundations, taking with it the Cliff Chalet coffee shop next door, which my husband, Dan, owned at the time. As in the past, billowing dark smoke rose from the western edge of the city, drawing thousands to watch as the historic baths were reduced to ash. More than a quarter of a century later, Whitney described the Sutro Baths fire as "suspicious," suggesting it may have been started by the night watchman for the demolition company. His suspicion echoed what had been said the night of the blaze by locals, who had heard that the company, which was behind schedule on the work, had hired a night watchman who had been linked to an equally suspicious fire at his previous job.

NEW FACES AND FACELIFTS

ONCE AGAIN, the Cliff House escaped the flames, and people still came to eat, to drink, and to watch the sea lions stretch and bark on Seal Rocks. But they did not come in the numbers they had in the past. The Foster's chain, which had been operating the restaurant for fifteen years, ended its tenure in April 1968, and Whitney assumed the daily operation of the landmark.

Down the road, Playland was changing, too. The Pie Shop was still selling fourteen different kinds of pie, the

Seal Rocks Pavilion shortly before it was destroyed by fire in 1963. Cliff House Collection

Hot House was still fueling locals with enchiladas and tamales, and the midway still promised peep shows, a roller coaster, and mechanical fortunetelling gypsies, but the crowds had thinned noticeably. Nearby, the building that had once housed the famed Topsy's Roost had gone through many changes. It had been a rental hall called the Surf Club; a slot-car racing center; a rock ballroom known as Family Dog on the Great Highway, which hosted such era icons as the Grateful Dead; and the Friends and Relations Hall, where the rock opera *Tommy* was performed.

In January 1971, nostalgia went on the auction block: for eleven days, the Cliff House was the site of the sale of George Whitney, Sr.'s collection of relics from Sutro Baths and the Cliff House. A flyer advertised just some of the many treasures: a 1905 Franklin automobile, Japanese suits of armor, the Last Supper in 3-D, models of the twenty-one California missions, posters from both world wars, mummies from Peru and Egypt, and old Cliff House commodes. The large crowd that gathered on the first day of the sale was a mix of serious shoppers, such as the preserved-corpse aficionado from

Alexandria, Virginia, who managed to buy up all of the Peruvian mummies, and folks who either remembered Sutro Baths or who wanted a glimpse of what the place must have been like. People could be seen carrying out everything from theater playbills and vintage spinning wheels to an old time-card rack. Tank suits from Sutro Baths at $4.00 each were among the best sellers. (Today, the same suits sell for as much as $1,000 apiece.)

Oakland resident P. E. De Bath passed up a tank suit in favor of a more unique item: a life-sized—and lifelike—self-portrait of Japanese artist Ito Hamashi dating from the 1870s and affectionately known as "Mr. Ito." The artist had crafted his own uncanny likeness in wood by posing in front of a series of adjustable mirrors. It included more than two thousand individual pieces of wood that were dovetailed and glued together, along with hair from the artist's own body, which he individually inserted into holes he had drilled into the wood. The finished, somewhat emaciated-looking figure was dressed in a skimpy brocade loin cloth.

The statue had arrived in the United States in 1895, and was later displayed in the Sequoia Room of the Cliff House. The small, wiry De Bath, an old showman who at seventy was still performing part-time as Popo the Clown at Oakland's Children's Fairyland, paid $2,500 dollars for "Mr. Ito," explaining that it had been part of his life from 1927 to 1940, when they had toured the Far East together with a traveling circus. The sculpture was hidden away during the war years because of strong anti-Japanese sentiment in the United States, and then disappeared entirely after the De Bath purchase.

Once the sale was over, the crowds were gone, too, and the Cliff House continued on its downward spiral. In October 1972, Millie Robbins, writing in the *San Francisco Chronicle*, painted a particularly unflattering portrait: "Every day, rain or shine, hundreds of tourists alight from sightseeing buses for a look at our 'world-famous' Cliff House. How many of them, we wonder, are disillusioned and disappointed. One undistinguished building is weather-beaten and shoddy. Its once fine dining room has been closed for

Only known photograph that shows one of five Italian ceramic ladies prior to removal from the Sutro Baths restroom. Two of the ladies are on display at the Cliff House today. The present whereabouts of the lady in the photograph is unknown. Courtesy of the San Francisco History Center, San Francisco Public Library

Sutro's and the Cliff Chalet
just prior to the fire, 1966.
Courtesy of Frank and
Ruth Mitchell

Cliff Chalet, 1966. Cliff
House Collection

Sandwiches

ROYAL CHUCK-BURGER
King-Size Portion of U. S. Choice
Steer Beef Ground Daily, on Our
Delicious French Roll, with Lettuce,
Tomato, Dill Pickle, Bermuda Onion
and French Fried Potatoes
$1.25

HAMBURGER
Generous Portion of Choice Ground
Beef—Crisp Lettuce, Pickle, Onions
75c
with Cheese 85c
French Fried Potatoes 30c

HOT ROAST CROSS RIB OF BEEF or HOT ROAST TURKEY SANDWICH
Served with Mushroom Gravy,
Potatoes and Vegetable
$1.45

JUICY STEAK SANDWICH
Tender Choice Top Sirloin Steak
Served Open-Face on Toast,
Garni of Vine Ripened California
Tomatoes, French Fried Potatoes
$2.05

...uicy Ground Beef Patty Served on a Toasted Bun, Covered with
...le Chili Beans, Topped with Raw Onions

...OF CHICKEN SALAD SANDWICH, with Lettuce and Tomato . . .95
...95   Tuna Salad 75
...ato   95   Grilled Nippy Cheese 75
...85   Grilled Ham 65

Side Order of French Fries 30 85

Dieter's Delight
LOW CALORIE PLATE
A Ground Sirloin Patty with Creamy Cottage Cheese,
California Fruit Salad and Sliced Tomato,
Served with Melba Toast
$1.25

...hilled Salads
With Choice of Dressing

. . .1.35
4. Fruit Salad
Cottage Cheese or Sherbet Center 1.35
. . .1.35
5. Shrimp or Crab Louis
Our Own Special Dressing 1.85
. . .1.35
6. Small Dinner Salad
Mixed Greens and Tomato 45

AMBROSIAL DELIGHTS FROM OUR

Fountain

Sundaes
Swiss Chocolate, Hawaiian Pineapple,
Crushed Strawberry 65
Ice Cream Soda 45
Orange Whip 55
Orange Juice and Orange Sherbet
Whipped Frosty Like a Shake
Creamy Rich Milk Shakes 50
...Malt 55
...arkling Frosty Root Beer
...or Coke Float 45
...r Banana Split 85
...Whole Fresh Banana and Three Scoops of
...Richest Ice Cream Covered with Delicious
...gs. Topped with Gobs of Whipped Cream,
Nuts, and a Cherry
...or Sherbet 30

Danny's Cliff Chalet
menu, 1966. Cliff
House Collection

Aerial view of the Sutro Baths fire, June 20, 1966. Courtesy of the Golden Gate
National Recreation Area Archives

Aftermath of the Sutro Baths fire, June 26, 1966. Courtesy of the San Francisco
History Center, San Francisco Public Library

three years—'for redecoration.' Some pieces of its heavy china are displayed 'for sale' in the drab windows of the gift shop—also closed." No one was surprised when George Whitney announced the following February that he had decided to close the Cliff House forever.

But Whitney would have to retract that statement just a few weeks later, when word leaked that he had leased the Cliff House to the We Four group, who owned The Pub, a popular spot on Geary Boulevard, and who, despite the name, numbered five: Tony Kent, Jerry Dal Bozzo, David Verschoor, Stuart Goldberg, and Thomas La Rusch. According to Kent, Whitney contacted the group "because he realized it would take youthful thinking and a youthful operation to make the place successful."

Kent and his partners quickly set to work, inside and outside. The lower portion of the building's exterior was painted a deep blue, while on the upper portion a pair of twenty-three-year-old artists created a seascape mural that extended onto part of the gift shop next door. The gigantic mural took just three days to paint, with one artist on the scaffold, a paint sprayer in one hand and a walkie-talkie in the other, and the second artist, also armed with a walkie-talkie, guiding the paint sprayer

from the ground. Indoors, the bar at the north end of the building was refurnished with overstuffed furniture, faux Tiffany lamps, and potted plants—the classic 1970s look. The plan was to use one large room for Sunday brunch and banquets, and turn the main dining room into an art space for local artisans, such as glassblowers and potters, to exhibit their work. The gift shop, which Whitney leased separately, was also slated for a makeover. New lessee Alan Young was eager to trade out cable car—emblazoned mugs and the like for items that would appeal to both San Franciscans and tourists. Young's goal was to sell the work of Northern California artists, but he promised to be realistic, too, and set aside a corner for the familiar souvenirs of San Francisco, explaining "a lot of people want them."

In late April, the We Four debuted the "new" Cliff House with a cocktail dance in the former dining room. Many of the city's leading citizens turned out for the affair, such as former Secretary of the Navy Paul Fay, Jr., author Curt Gentry, and vintner and property mogul John Traina. The launch made the society column of the *San Francisco Chronicle*, and the new operators hoped to continue to draw the people who came that night and plenty of others.

"Blue" Cliff House, circa 1973. Cliff House Collection

A CHANCE ENCOUNTER

THE WE FOUR never got the promised brunch or banquet trade going. In fact, anyone who went to the Cliff House with an appetite had to content themselves with a sandwich or a snack in the bar, the only food service available in the once-famed dinner spot. But a chance encounter between John Hountalas, the brother of my husband, Dan, and George Whitney in March 1973 soon changed the dining scene at the Cliff House.

The Hountalas family had been part of the Ocean Beach community since 1906. When Dan and John's father, Michael, arrived from Greece in 1919, he rented space in the car barn at the terminus of the streetcar line that carried bathers to Sutro Baths and set up a tobacco and candy stand. He soon added a grill for hamburgers and hot dogs, a cooler for soft drinks, and a counter with about twenty stools for diners. In 1941, six-year-old Dan sold hot roasted peanuts from a little red wagon stationed just outside the car barn. (That same wagon had provided visitors to Ocean Beach with a steady supply of hot roasted peanuts for about thirty-five years before it

was given to the young entrepreneur.) In February 1949, an early-morning three-alarm fire destroyed the car barn and my father-in-law's snack stand along with it. Only the wagon was saved.

In 1952, my father-in-law acquired the Golden Gate View coffee shop, joining a thriving lineup of Greek American–owned diners, snack shops, and restaurants adjacent to the Cliff House. In 1958, Dan and his father took over the operation of the Cliff Café next door to the Golden Gate View, and then merged the two businesses into the Cliff Chalet coffee shop. When the Cliff Chalet burned to the ground in the same 1966 fire that wiped out Sutro Baths, Dan became the national sales manager for a large grocery wholesaler. We met in 1970, when I was working for one of his company's clients, and married two years later.

When my brother-in-law John ran into Whitney that March day, Whitney mentioned that he wanted to see the Cliff House filled with diners again. Dan and I had been married just six months and going into the restaurant business was not in our immediate plans. But the Cliff House and everything near it had always been a big part of Dan's life. When he was just two years

Streetcar terminal, December 23, 1937. Courtesy of the San Francisco History Center, San Francisco Public Library

Streetcar terminal fire, February 12, 1949. Courtesy of the San Francisco History Center, San Francisco Public Library

old, Dr. Emma Sutro Merritt, who was then living on Sutro Heights, treated him for a minor illness. And a few years later, when Dan wasn't selling peanuts in front of his father's stand, he was busy exploring every nook and cranny of the Cliff House not far down the road. When his mother needed crabs for dinner, his father would go diving for them from Seal Rocks, slip the catch into a gunnysack, and Dan would retrieve the sack full of crabs, dog paddling that night's dinner back to shore. More and more, Dan's indelible connections to the Cliff House made leasing it sound like the right thing to do and a great opportunity—at least to me. But it took plenty of talking before John and I were able to convince Dan that he wanted to be back in the restaurant business.

Dan and I met with Whitney and signed a lease for the old upstairs banquet room that had been part of the 1950 remodel. In June 1973, we opened Upstairs at the Cliff House, a breakfast and lunch spot that quickly became known for its large selection of three-egg omelets. The following June, with liquor license in hand, we debuted the Ben Butler Bar at the south end of the building, naming it for a Seal Rocks's sea lion that had enjoyed fame in the nineteenth century. By June 1975, the We Four had abandoned its stake in the Cliff House and Dan and I had taken over the bar, rechristening it the Phineas T. Barnacle Bar, and had opened the Seafood and Beverage Company in the main dining room. On September 11, 1975, we celebrated the debut of the dining room with a gala that boasted not only a Hollywood atmosphere,

Cliff House coaster, 1950s. Cliff House Collection

A most unusual sight from the Cliff House observation terrace—the Marin Headlands under a blanket of snow, circa 1975. Courtesy of Dennis O'Rourke

View from Ocean Beach of the Cliff House, Seal Rocks, and the Marin Headlands under snow, circa 1975. Courtesy of Dennis O'Rourke

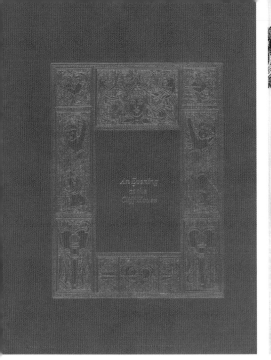

but also a number of Hollywood stars, including Jane Withers, George Montgomery, Giselle Mackenzie, Dean Jones, and Adam West. Dinner was a menu of Cliff House classics, including seafood cocktail, lobster thermidor, roast sirloin of beef with sauce bordelaise, and baked Alaska. There was an art auction and a fireworks display, with proceeds going to the fund for the restoration of the old north windmill in Golden Gate Park.

In 1974, as we were expanding our role inside the Cliff House, the National Park Service (NPS) began negotiations for the purchase of the building and its 3.7-acre site from George Whitney. Robert Fraser had been unable to go forward with his plans for the Sutro Baths site after the 1966 fire, primarily due to public sentiment against it, and had sold the land to the NPS in 1973. The NPS had also purchased the 2.8-acre site next to the Cliff House, and both properties were incorporated into the Golden Gate National Recreation Area, a federal project that would eventually grow to include a large

collection of noncontiguous areas stretching from Marin County in the north to San Mateo County in the south. The Cliff House was an important piece in this slim stretch of the puzzle, and it would take until July 1977 to complete the sale, with Whitney receiving nearly $3.8 million for the property. The government assured us that we could remain tenants, though only on a year-to-year basis. That same year, Dan and I incorporated our business, christening our company Peanut Wagon Inc., after his childhood business venture.

At the time of the sale, Whitney sold a number of his treasures to us, including two six-foot Italian porcelain tile figures of women that once graced the walls of Sutro Baths; a life-sized redwood grizzly bear, the former mascot for a shipping line; and a ten-foot-tall cowboy statue that once welcomed visitors to Frontierland at Playland. (Today, the bear and the cowboy greet visitors at the entrance to the Cliff House, and one of the porcelain ladies is displayed on the upper level and the other

Distinguished Persons of Hospitality

An Evening at the Cliff House

*Thursday, September eleventh, nineteen hundred and seventy-five
in the one hundred twenty-first year of the Cliff House*

The Premiere Evening Menu
*the eleventh day of September
nineteen hundred and seventy five*

Hors D'oeurves
Sparkling Champagne
San Francisco Seafood Cocktail
Roast Sirloin of Beef, Sauce Bordelaise
or
Lobster Thermidor
Rice Saute   Fresh Fruit
Crisp Greens
With Herbed French Dressing
Sourdough French Bread
"Seward's Folly"
Coffee

Amaretto
"With Love"

The Cliff House Seafood & Beverage Company
San Francisco, California

View from Sutro Heights, circa, 1980. Photo by McKinney, Courtesy of Smith Novelty Company. Cliff House Collection

on the lower level, near Sutro's Bar.) We also purchased Whitney's collection of more than one hundred and fifty original photographs of celebrities who had visited the Cliff House during 1930s, 1940s, and 1950s. These now adorn the walls in the Bistro. Since the 1970s, we have steadily added to the collection. Today, Sharon Stone, Robin Williams, Grace Slick, the Smothers Brothers, Herb Caen, and Nicolas Cage (who dined weekly at the Cliff House on steamed clams during production on the 1996 film *The Rock*) are displayed alongside Ginger Rogers, John Wayne, and Judy Garland. In 2004, I discovered nine original Cliff House celebrity photographs that had gone astray on eBay, among them Clark Gable, Carole Lombard, and Susan Hayward. My bids brought them back to their rightful place in the Bistro lineup.

It would take time for the NPS to decide the fate of the Cliff House—restoration or demolition?—but by January 1979, it had decided the fate of the seascape mural contributed by the We Four: it would be painted out. Families had begun to drift back for the views and the food, and the government thought a facelift would keep

them coming until a decision on the building could be made. The new paint job—off-white with brown trim—and repairs to the exterior were budgeted at $100,000, and the public seemed to approve of the new look.

THE LONG HAUL

THE PAINT JOB was an easy decision. Deciding on a plan for the Cliff House that everyone—the NPS, the city, neighborhood groups, historic preservationists—could agree on would take more than twenty years. In the meantime, life went on at the Cliff House. In 1977, we initiated Coast Guard Appreciation Day in honor of a branch of the service we felt had seldom received the recognition it deserved. Sea rescues had long been a necessity of Ocean Beach life, and in 1871, the Life-Saving Service was formed. Six years later, the Coast Guard Golden Gate Life Boat Station was opened at the foot of Fulton Street, and in 1915, the Life-Saving Service and the Coast Guard merged, operating together out of the Fulton Street building until it was closed in 1951. But the importance of the

Lifeboat riding the breakers, with the 1896 Cliff House in the background. The Life-Saving Service, founded in 1871, merged with the Coast Guard in 1915. Cliff House Collection

Life-Saving Station in the shadow of one of two giant windmills that pumped water into Golden Gate Park, circa 1910. Cliff House Collection

Lifeboat, Ocean Beach, circa 1910. Courtesy of the San Francisco History Center, San Francisco Public Library

Cliff House at sunset, 1980. Cliff House Collection

Coast Guard to our area remains vital to this day, and the annual Cliff House lunch lets these men and women know that we continue to be grateful for their work.

In 1982, we refurbished the interiors of the Cliff House at a cost of about $200,00, including the addition of a banquet room on the lower level. At Upstairs at the Cliff House, we continued to serve the popular omelet, sandwich, and salad menu in the daytime and introduced a new dinner menu. These changes brought more customers, as did a variety of events, planned and unplanned. In mid-June 1983, San Franciscans gathered at the Cliff House to watch a 1903 Packard Model F pull away from the seashore on a transcontinental journey that would end in New York two months later, traveling the same route taken by another 1903 Model F exactly eighty years earlier. In 1986, a severe earthquake in Alaska sent the threat of high, fast-moving waves washing over the California coast. Residents of low-lying areas were urged to flee to higher ground and everyone else was warned to stay away from the shoreline. Thrill-seekers rushed to the beach for a view of the giant waves, only to be stopped by the police, who closed off access to the coast. But a number of enterprising souls slipped through the barricades and took up good ocean-view positions at the Cliff House. Many indulged in some "liquid courage" as they watched and waited. Finally, after two-foot waves lapped harmlessly at the Cliff House sea-wall for more than an hour, the tsunami threat was called off, and the crowds headed inland, with several Cliff House workers wondering why customers who had thought there would be no tomorrow didn't tip better today.

The following year, the Cliff House donated two horses to the San Francisco Police Department's mounted patrol unit, one of which we named Cliff House—Cliff, for short. We ran a contest for local kids to name the second of the two mounts, with Wavy Davy the winning moniker. In August 1987, *Back to the Beach*, a sequel to the popular beach-party movies of the 1960s, opened starring Annette Funicello and Frankie Avalon with troublesome teens of their own. Both stars went on a promotional junket that dropped them off at the Cliff House, to the delight of a large crowd of fans. In February 1989, a single California sea otter was spotted

The Cliff House from Ocean Beach, prior to the restoration. Photo by Ed Schuster, Cliff House Collection

from the Cliff House terrace, the first sighting near San Francisco Bay in more than a century of this once widely hunted and now protected marine mammal.

When the Loma Prieta earthquake shook the city in October, the Cliff House lost only a few bar glasses and never lost power or water. Residents from the city's hardest hit neighborhoods soon heard that the Cliff House was a welcome oasis in the chaos and made their way to the beach for a hot meal. Not far behind were hardworking emergency personnel from the fire and police departments, who knew free sandwiches awaited them.

The Cliff House was not as lucky in December 1995, when a series of ferocious storms struck the Bay Area, leaving a wake of destruction in its path: downed power lines, shattered trees, streets littered with debris, and a forty-foot sinkhole in the pricey Sea Cliff neighborhood. We lost more than three hundred square feet of window glass, including six five-by-ten-foot panes that dated from 1909. We also saw a pair of four-hundred-pound ventilation fans lifted off the roof and planted in front of the main entrance, and a

large section of the roof was ripped away and left hanging sideways. Fortunately, before the winds did their damage, all of the customers had been evacuated, the building had been closed, and only a night watchman and a manager remained inside. A day later, we welcomed customers back to all areas of the Cliff House except for the main dining room. The building had sustained $750,000 in damage, and would not be fully reopened for about two months. That gave us time to take many of the water-damaged celebrity photographs in the dining room to the conservation department at the nearby Legion of Honor museum for restoration. Some, sadly, could not be saved.

That wet and windy December storm wasn't the only tempest brewing in 1995. Since the late 1980s, the GGNRA had been seriously edging toward a resolution on what to do with the Sutro Historic District, the area bounded by Sutro Heights Park, the Pacific Ocean, and El Camino Del Mar. At the heart of the district sat the Cliff House, and almost no one lacked an opinion on what should be done to it.

Storm damaged exterior, December 1995.
Cliff House Collection

Acrylic sheeting goes up to cover blown-out windows, December 1995.
Cliff House Collection

The Cliff House from Sutro Heights, prior to the restoration. Photo by Ed Schuster, Cliff House Collection

UPSTAIRS

AT THE

Cliff House

SINCE 1850

WHERE SAN FRANCISCO BEGINS ®

SEAL ROCKS

&

OCEAN BEACH

&

GOLDEN GATE

OMELETTES

OMELETTES ARE SERVED WITH ROAST POTATOES • FRESH FRUIT GARNISH • AND TOASTED ENGLISH MUFFINS

#1 DENVER Ham, Bell Pepper & Onion $8.45

#2 FRESH MUSHROOM & CHEESE Swiss, Cheddar or Jack $7.95

#3 RATATOUILLE Eggplant, Zucchini, Tomato, Green Pepper & Onion $7.95

#4 ARTICHOKE HEARTS, TOMATO, ONION & SWISS CHEESE $8.25

#5 CHEESE Swiss, Cheddar or Jack $7.45

#6 BACON, TOMATO & MUSHROOM $8.45

#7 BACON, MUSHROOM & SWISS CHEESE $8.45

#8 BACON & CHEESE Swiss, Cheddar or Jack $8.25

#9 "BAUERNFRÜHSTÜCK" Ham, Potatoes, Onions & Cheddar $8.95

#10 "FARMERS" Sausage, Bacon, Potatoes & Tomato $8.95

#11 HAM & CHEESE Choice of Swiss, Cheddar or Jack $8.25

#12 "JOE'S SPECIAL" Ground Beef, Spinach, Onion & Parmesan $8.25

#13 "SEAFOOD" Shrimp, Scallops, Mushrooms, Scallions & Cheese $12.25

#14 SPINACH, BACON, ONION & CHEDDAR $8.45

#15 SPINACH, MUSHROOMS & CHEDDAR $8.45

#16 BACON, TOMATO, GUACAMOLE & CHEESE Swiss, Cheddar or Jack $9.75

#17 TOMATO, ONION, MUSHROOMS, SPINACH & CHEDDAR $8.95

#18 "JOHNSON'S" Dungeness Crab, Guacamole & Sour Cream $14.95

#19 SPINACH, TOMATO & FETA $8.25

#20 "EL RANCHO OLÉ" Green Chilies, Onion, Mushrooms, Tomato & Cheddar $8.45

☆ ALL AMERICAN ☆
BREAKFAST

CINNAMON-RAISIN FRENCH TOAST
Maple-Orange Syrup, Crisp Bacon
& Fresh Fruit
$8.45

MEXICO CALIENTE
Scrambled Eggs with Spicy Sausage
Rolled in Flour Tortilla with Salsa & Refried Beans
$9.25

GOLDEN WAFFLE
Maple-Pecan Butter Sauce, Crisp Bacon
& Fresh Fruit
$8.45

GRANOLA PARFAIT
Layered Fresh Fruit, Yogurt & Granola
Served in a Parfait Glass
$7.45

POACHED EGGS ON SALMON & CRAB CAKES
Spicy Tomato Saffron Sauce
& Fresh Fruit
$12.95

TRADITIONAL LOX & BAGEL
A Toasted Bagel with Lemon Pepper Smoked Salmon
Sliced Onions, Capers & Cream Cheese
$9.45

TWO SCRAMBLED OR FRIED EGGS
Choice of Breakfast Sausages, Smoked Cured Ham
or Bacon Served with Roast Potatoes
& Toasted English Muffins
$8.25

Adolph Sutro
(1830-1898)
San Francisco Mayor
(1895-1897)
Purchased Several Miles
of Shoreline Along Ocean Beach
(1881)
Built the Second Cliff House
& Sutro Baths
(1896)

Plan of Sutro Heights, Cliff House & Seal Rocks (1894)

SALADS

CAESAR SALAD
The Classic Caesar $6.75
With Bay Shrimp $8.45

ORIENTAL CHICKEN SALAD
Shredded Breast of Chicken with Lettuce, Rice Noodles
& Sesame Seeds $10.95

SUTRO SHRIMP LOUIS
A Traditional San Francisco Favorite $16.45

GARDEN GREENS SALAD
Choice of Ranch, Thousand Island or Blue Cheese
Dressing $5.45

Postcard of the First Cliff House as Viewed from Sutro Heights (Built in 1863) & Destroyed by Fire on Christmas Day 1894)

COLD SANDWICHES

ALL SANDWICHES ARE SERVED WITH GREEN SALAD

CLUB HOUSE
Toasted Triple Decker on Sourdough with Bacon, Ham,
Turkey, Cheddar & Sliced Tomatoes
$8.95

OCEAN BEACH
Chilled Bay Shrimp Salad topped with Sliced Tomato
& Avocado Served Open-faced on Dark Rye Bread
$9.75

THE B.L.T. UPDATE
Crisp Bacon, Sliced Tomato, Lettuce & Avocado
on Toasted Sourdough Bread
$8.45

HOT SANDWICHES

ALL SANDWICHES ARE SERVED WITH GREEN SALAD

THE "SUNSET"
Grilled Marinated Chicken Breast on French Bun with
Lettuce, Tomato & Sliced Red Onion
$9.75

VEGETABLE TREAT
Grilled Eggplant & Zucchini on Toasted Sourdough
Bread with Roasted Bell Peppers & Melted Jack Cheese
$7.75

THE "UPSTAIRS" BURGER
Served with Grilled Onion, Mushrooms & Jack Cheese
$9.45

Beverages

HOUSE WINE BY THE GLASS $4.25

PREMIUM WINES AVAILABLE-PLEASE ASK YOUR SERVER FOR LIST

BEER
Draft $2.95
Pint $4.25
Domestic Bottle $3.00
Imported Bottle $3.75

FRESH BREWED COFFEE
Regular & Decaf $2.00

ESPRESSO DRINKS
Caffe Latte/Cappuccino/Caffè Mocha $2.95
Espresso $2.45
Double Espresso $3.25

HOT TEA & ICED TEA $2.00

HOT CHOCOLATE $2.45

FRESH ORANGE JUICE $2.75

SOFT DRINKS $1.95

ICED LEMONADE $1.95

MILK $1.95

PARTIES OF 8 OR MORE 17% ADDED—NOT RESPONSIBLE FOR LOST ITEMS

SALES TAX WILL BE ADDED TO ALL ITEMS SOLD

THE SOUP POT

CLIFF HOUSE CLASSIC
New England Clam Chowder
Loaded with Clams!

CUP $4.25
BOWL $5.75

SIDE ORDERS

Bacon $1.75
Sausage $1.75
Toast or Muffin $1.95
Potatoes $1.95
Bagel $2.25

Historic Photographs Used Courtesy of Marilyn Blaisdell. Menu Design by Barbara Latolice Graphic Design, Sausalito, CA.

POTENTIAL PRIVATE PARTY PEOPLE — NEWS — GIFTS, GLORIOUS GIFTS...

TRY OUR TERRACE ROOM!

NESTLED TWO LEVELS BELOW YOU IS
OUR TERRACE ROOM,
A PRIVATE BANQUET FACILITY WHICH
PROVIDES THE SAME SENSATIONAL
SEASCAPE VIEWS YOU ARE ENJOYING
RIGHT NOW AND IS IDEAL FOR
PRIVATE PARTIES,
MEETINGS, BANQUETS & RECEPTIONS.

A WIDE RANGE OF MENU ITEMS ARE
AVAILABLE, FROM HORS D'OEUVRES
TO BUFFET SERVICE
TO FULL COURSE MEALS.
OUR BANQUET MANAGER WILL BE
HAPPY TO FILL YOU IN ON THE DETAILS
AND SHOW YOU THE ROOM;
JUST CALL 666-4017.

OUR STAFF LOOKS FORWARD
TO MAKING YOUR PARTY OR
MEETING A GREAT SUCCESS!

THE CLIFF HOUSE IS ... A WHIZ AT FIZZ!

THE CLIFF HOUSE ALREADY HAS A WELL DESERVED
REPUTATION AS ONE OF THE ALL TIME GREAT
IRISH COFFEE PURVEYORS IN THE CITY.
BUT DID YOU KNOW THAT WE ARE
UNEQUIVOCALLY #1 WHEN IT COMES TO SERVING
THE-CONSUMED-MOSTLY-WITH-SUNDAY BRUNCH
"RAMOS FIZZ"? C'EST VRAI!

NOW IF PERCHANCE YOU WOULD LIKE TO TRY
IT OUT ON THE HOME FOLKS, DO IT THIS WAY:
1 PART - EGG WHITE
1 PART - GIN
1 PART - SWEET & SOUR
1 PART - CREAM
SUGAR TO TASTE
ADD CRUSHED ICE
DASH OF ORANGE JUICE
5 DROPLETS, PARFUMERIE FUNEL ORANGE
FLOWER WATER

SHAKE THROUGHLY, AND PROCEED TO SERVE
TO SOME DELIGHTED FRIENDS OR GUESTS.

(P.S. BETTER MAKE A SECOND BATCH RIGHTAWAY!)

CLIFF HOUSE GIFT SHOP

WE HOPE YOU HAVE ENJOYED YOUR VISIT
HERE, AND THAT YOU JUST MIGHT WANT TO
TAKE SOMETHING HOME WITH THE NAME OF
"CLIFF HOUSE" ON IT ...
WE KNOW JUST THE PLACE TO FIND IT!

WE HAVE A WIDE VARIETY OF ATTRACTIVE
POSTCARDS, TASTEFUL MEMORABILIA, AND
LOTS OF OTHER QUALITY GIFT ITEMS FOR
EVERY (AND ANY) OCCASION.

BE SURE AND CHECK OUT OUR RANGE OF
CLIFF HOUSE SIGNATURE MERCHANDISE...
SWEATSHIRTS, T-SHIRTS, CAPS, MUGS,
ETC., ETC.

SINCE 1850
Cliff House
WHERE SAN FRANCISCO BEGINS

NAME·THE·STARS

· "OFF THE CLIFF HOUSE WALL" OF STARS ·

CLIFF HOUSE HAS BEEN CARRYING ON A TRADITION OF ASSURING CELEBRITIES PRIVACY FOR OVER 130 YEARS. IN APPRECIATION, HUNDREDS HAVE SAID "THANKS" BY SENDING AUTOGRAPHED PICTURES. OTHERS, LIKE MANY SONS AND DAUGHTERS OF CINEMA STARS RETURN WITH FAMILY MEMBERS, SHOWING OFF THEIR PARENTS' PHOTOS.

· STARS "IQ"UIZ ANSWERS ·

Cliff House menu, 1990. Cliff House Collection

GEORGE WHITNEY, SR. was a great showman, and Floyd Jennings and Gene Turtle had the perfect show for him: a camera obscura. It would not be the first camera obscura in San Francisco. Woodward's Gardens, an early amusement park and museum complex, and the towering 1896 Cliff House had each housed one. But both were long gone, and Whitney, Jennings, and Turtle agreed the city was ready for a new one. The small free-standing building debuted in 1946, on the observation deck directly behind the Cliff House.

The origin of the camera obscura, an optical device that projects an image of what surrounds it onto a view-able surface, dates to the tenth century. By the thir-teenth century, it was used to observe solar eclipses safely, and later it served as an important early stage in the evolution of photography. By the late-nineteenth and early-twentieth centuries, the camera obscura had become a popular addition to many parks and museums around the United States and elsewhere. Whitney saw it as a natural extension of the attractions at Playland.

Visitors paid an entrance fee, then proceeded into a small, barely lit room, where they were treated to a panoramic view of Ocean Beach and the roiling sea. The principle was simple: light and images entered "the camera" through a copper turret outfitted with a front-surfaced mirror and passed through concave and convex lenses that focused the images onto a large parabolic disk. The turret slowly rotated, delivering the visitors a complete 360-degree view of the exterior surroundings— distant shores, circling birds, sleepy sea lions, breaking waves, sometimes a sailboat—in roughly six minutes.

A little more than a decade later, Whitney decided the camera's housing needed a eye-catching facelift, so Jennings and Turtle gave it the profile of a classic 1950s box camera, complete with a pair of black spools at the front to resemble film-advance knobs. The rest of the exterior was painted bright yellow and "Giant Camera" was printed in huge let-ters on one side.

When the National Park Service (NPS) bought the Cliff House in 1977, the oversized curiosity was part of the deal. Arguing that it obstructed the public's view of the ocean, especially Seal Rocks, the NPS announced that it would be razing the camera obscura in October 1980. Armed with a petition signed by thou-sands of local residents, the San Francisco Board of Supervisors fought back, and William Whalen, general superintendent of the Golden Gate National Recreation Area (GGNRA), proved a sympathetic ear, carrying the city's request to save the Giant Camera to the NPS. A last-minute reprieve left it operational through 1983 because of "the public sentiment expressed in favor of it." The immediate response of the Board of Supervisors was to nominate the camera for the National Register of Historic Places, but the nomination was turned down because the structure failed to "meet the criteria for exceptional significance of properties less than 50 years old."

Nearly twenty years would pass before the camera obscura was threatened again. During that time, the NPS, which had made little progress on its plan for the Sutro Historic District, regularly renewed the lease on the camera building. Then, in June 1999, park officials issued an eviction notice to the building's lessee so the camera could be removed and the NPS could go for-ward with its decision to restore the 1909 Cliff House. As in 1980, the Board of Supervisors, fueled by strong public support, jumped into action, and by the end of 2000, the federal government's plan to move the Giant Camera was dropped. Once again, the board nominated the camera for the National Register of Historic Places, and on May 23, 2001, it was added to the register for "its engineering significance."

According to Joseph Durrance, who has carefully documented the history of the Cliff House's camera obscura and was an important member of the 1999 cam-paign to save it, the Giant Camera is now the "oldest freestanding camera obscura still in its original loca-tion in the United States." Following its remodel in 1957, Jennings and Turtle built two additional freestanding cameras in settings of dramatic natural beauty, one at Colorado Springs, Colorado, and one in Chattanooga, Tennessee. Unlike their San Francisco landmark, both were dismantled and have since disappeared.

Camera obscura overlooking Seal Rocks, prior to the restoration. Photo by Ed Schuster, Cliff House Collection

A VISIT TO THE PAST

DROP IN A COIN and the six-foot-tall papier-mâché redhead known as Laffing Sal will release an ear-splitting bellow from her gap-toothed smile. From 1940 until 1972, she rose (actually it was her "twin sister"; the current Sal was the dutiful understudy, in case the original automaton broke down) over the entrance of the Fun House at Playland, where her wild and wooly cackle ricocheted throughout the park. Slip a coin into the Rock-Ola baseball game and watch the batter connect with a pitch, sending the ball sailing into an outfield defended by the 1937 Yankees. For yet another coin, you can squeeze the handle on the Love Meter to find out your sex appeal, keeping the fingers crossed on your other hand that you are "tempting" rather than "overrated." In the mood for band music? Feed the Engelhardt Piano Orchestration and it will strike up a piano, flute pipes, a cymbal, and a tambourine all at the same time. Want your fortune read? Choose your teller from among a mechanical Gypsy, a mechanical wizard, and a Royal typewriter that taps it out while you watch.

These mechanical treasures are just a handful of the hundreds in the Musée Mécanique. From 1972 until 2002, this world-class collection of antique arcade games, with its animated dioramas, flip-card movies, mechanical musical instruments, and more, was housed in the basement of the Cliff House, a claustrophobic catacomb at the end of a narrow stairway. All of the pieces were acquired by the late Edward Zelinsky, a fifth-generation San Franciscan who began collecting at the age of eleven or twelve in the 1930s. In the years after World War II, Zelinsky became friends with George Whitney, Sr., whose interest in arcade games and similar ephemera matched Zelinsky's. They met for lunch once a month, where they traded ideas along with music boxes, player pianos, and even a steam motorcycle on one occasion. Many of the pieces in the Zelinsky museum once enchanted visitors to Sutro Baths (which had its own Musée Mécanique) and Playland, including the modestly bawdy "Have a Look at the Sultan's Harem" peep show from the Fun House.

The museum was moved from its basement home in September 2002, to clear the way for the restoration of the Cliff House, with assurances that the National Park Service would secure the collection a permanent home. With general manager Dan Zelinsky, Edward's son, at the helm, the museum was relocated to Pier 45, where it remains until a venue is ready. According to local historian Woody LaBounty, the museum continues on a month-to-month lease from the city's Port Commission and faces an uncertain future.

THE CLIFF HOUSE CRAB LOUIS

SPELLED EITHER Crab Louis or Crab Louie, but always pronounced LOO-ey, this iconic salad boasts countless versions and nearly as many originators. Most culinary scholars and historians agree that it first appeared early in the twentieth century, though no one agrees on who created it, or which state can rightfully claim it. Helen Evans Brown, in her highly respected 1952 *West Coast Cook Book,* doesn't mention the name of its inventor, but she does place it on the menu of San Francisco's Solari's Restaurant by 1914, and chef Victor Hirtzler, who ran the kitchen at the Hotel St. Francis from 1904 until 1926, included a recipe for it in his 1910 cookbook. Cliff House diners were ordering Crab Louis around that time, but since the 1970s, we have been serving our own variation on the classic, adding citrus fruit, avocado, olives, and cucumbers to the traditional combination of crabmeat, tomatoes, hard-cooked eggs, and iceberg lettuce. In the 1990s, we replaced our version with a classic Crab Louis and were immediately besieged by phone calls, e-mails, and letters imploring us to bring back the Cliff House recipe. We did, and vowed never to tamper with it again.

LOUIS DRESSING
1 cup mayonnaise
½ cup chili sauce
2 tablespoons finely chopped green bell pepper
1 tablespoon minced green onion, white part only
2 teaspoons fresh lemon juice
1 teaspoon Worcestershire sauce
Salt and freshly ground pepper

1 grapefruit
1 large orange
½ head iceberg lettuce, cut into 4 equal wedges
1 pound fresh-cooked Dungeness crabmeat, picked over
12 cucumber slices
2 tomatoes, quartered lengthwise
12 black olives
4 eggs, hard cooked, peeled, and halved lengthwise
1 lemon, cut into 8 wedges
1 avocado, halved, pitted, and peeled
1 tablespoon chopped fresh chives
1½ cups Louis dressing

TO MAKE the dressing, in a bowl, combine all of the ingredients and mix well. Cover tightly and refrigerate until well chilled, at least 4 hours. You will need 1½ cups dressing for this recipe. Store any leftover dressing in a covered container in the refrigerator for up to 1 week.

Using a sharp knife, cut a slice off the top and bottom of the grapefruit, to expose the flesh. Stand the grapefruit upright on the cutting board. Following the contour of the fruit, cut downward, removing the peel and pith in thick strips, then cut the fruit crosswise into 4 rounds. Repeat with the orange. Set the grapefruit and orange rounds aside.

Have ready 4 plates, each 8 to 10 inches in diameter.

Place 1 lettuce wedge in the center of each plate, and top each wedge with one-fourth of the crabmeat. Viewing each plate as if it is a clock face, arrange, in the following order, 3 cucumber slices, 2 tomato wedges, and 3 black olives at 2 o'clock. At 6 o'clock, position 2 egg halves and 2 lemon wedges. At 9 o'clock, place 1 grapefruit slice and 1 orange slice. Halve each avocado half lengthwise, and then thinly slice each quarter lengthwise, leaving the slices attached at one end. Fan the slices of each avocado quarter and place on top of the crabmeat. Garnish the salads with the chives.

Divide the dressing evenly among 4 small bowls, and set a bowl alongside each salad. Serve at once.

Serves 4

CLIFF HOUSE CLAM CHOWDER

CLAM CHOWDER HAS appeared on Cliff House menus since the mid-1890s, and even then the debate over which one was best, New England white or Manhattan red, was probably heard in the dining room. That question was settled when Dan and I began operating the Cliff House in the 1970s. We serve a New England-style white chowder that evolved from a recipe developed by Dan's family in their restaurants near the Cliff House.

---

4 bottles (8 ounces each) clam juice
4 cups water
2 cups (1 large or 2 medium) peeled and diced
   russet potatoes
½ cup (4 ounces) butter
½ cup olive oil
2 cups (about 1 large) diced white onion
1 cup (about 2 ribs) diced celery
½ cup (about 1 small) seeded and diced green bell pepper

¼ teaspoon dried basil
¼ teaspoon dried thyme
Pinch of dried tarragon
¼ cup dry white wine
¾ cup all-purpose flour
2 cups heavy cream
1 bay leaf
Salt and freshly ground black pepper
4 cans (6½ ounces each) chopped clams, drained

IN A SAUCEPAN, combine the clam juice, water, and potatoes and bring to a boil. Cook until the potatoes are just tender when tested with a fork, 8 to 10 minutes. Do not overcook. Remove from the heat and drain the potatoes, reserving the cooking liquid and the potatoes separately. Set aside.

In a large pot, melt the butter with the olive oil over medium heat. Add the onion and celery and sauté briefly. Add the bell pepper and sauté until just barely beginning to soften, 1 to 2 minutes. It is important that the vegetables remain fairly crisp as this point, as they will continue to cook in the chowder. Add all of the dried herbs and sauté for a few seconds to toast them slightly. Pour in the wine and cook for about 1 minute to cook off most of the alcohol. Reduce the heat to low and add the flour, a little at a time, while stirring constantly. When all of the flour has been incorporated,

cook the mixture, stirring constantly, for 2 to 3 minutes to blend thoroughly.

Slowly add the reserved warm potato cooking liquid, continuing to stir. The mixture will begin to thicken the moment you start adding the liquid. Next, slowly add the cream, again stirring constantly. Add the bay leaf and season to taste with salt and pepper. Increase the heat to medium and allow the mixture to come to a boil, stirring constantly to prevent scorching. Reduce the heat to low and cook for 5 to 10 minutes to cook away the raw taste of the flour. The soup will be fairly thick. If you prefer a thinner soup, add water or milk to thin to the desired consistency.

Add the cooked potatoes and the clams and simmer gently until heated through. Be careful not to overcook them. Discard the bay leaf, and season to taste with salt and pepper. Ladle into warmed bowls and serve at once.

Serves 10 generously

BEN BUTLER CRAB SANDWICH

THIS OPEN-FACED sandwich was introduced at the Cliff House in the 1970s, to celebrate the memory of a great sea lion who ruled the "rocks" in the late 1800s. He was named after Benjamin Franklin Butler, also known as Beast Butler, an unpopular Civil War general who, in his role as military governor of occupied New Orleans, called for treating any lady who insulted an officer or soldier "a woman of the town plying her avocation"—in other words, like a prostitute. The only thing our popular Ben Butler shared with the mean-spirited general was his name. Accompany his eponymous sandwich with a small green salad.

I jar (4 ounces) diced pimientos
I cup mayonnaise
½ cup chopped green onion, including green tops
I teaspoon dry mustard

I teaspoon Tabasco sauce
I pound fresh-cooked Dungeness crabmeat, picked over
8 slices sourdough bread, toasted and kept warm
8 slices sharp Cheddar cheese

PREHEAT THE BROILER. Open the jar of pimientos, drain, and scoop out half of the pimientos into a bowl. Cover the remaining pimientos with water, cap tightly, and refrigerate for another use. They will keep for up to 1 week. Add the mayonnaise, green onions, mustard, and Tabasco sauce and stir until well mixed. Carefully fold in the crabmeat, distributing it evenly and keeping the large pieces intact.

Divide the crab mixture evenly among the toasted bread slices, and place the slices on a baking sheet. Slip under the broiler until the crabmeat is just hot, about 1 minute. Remove from the broiler, top each sandwich with a slice of the cheese, and return the sandwiches to the broiler just until the cheese melts.

Transfer the sandwiches to plates, arranging 2 sandwiches on each plate, and serve at once.

Serves 4

POPOVERS

WHEN I WAS growing up on the East Coast, my mother prepared popovers for breakfast as a special treat on holiday mornings. In 1978, we started serving Sunday brunch at the Cliff House, and it seemed natural to include this East Coast tradition on the menu. But the popovers proved so popular, we now offer them every day, served with butter, jam, and honey, in the Bistro restaurant. They are also our most sought-after recipe.

BATTER
2 cups whole milk
5 eggs
2 teaspoons sugar
½ teaspoon salt
2 cups all-purpose flour
2 tablespoons canola or corn oil

FOR PREPARING PANS
¼ cup all-purpose flour
¼ cup canola or corn oil

TO MAKE THE BATTER, in a large bowl, combine the milk, eggs, sugar, and salt and stir to mix well. Add the flour and stir until thoroughly combined. Add the oil and continue to stir for another minute. The batter can be made up to 2 days in advance, covered tightly, and refrigerated. In fact, allowing the batter to rest for a while yields a lighter, better popover. Also, because the batter will keep for 2 days, you can bake half of it for one meal and the rest of it for another meal. If a layer of foam appears on the surface of the batter during the rest period, briefly stir the batter again just before using.

Place two 12-cup popover pans (or standard muffin pans) in the oven and preheat the oven to 350 degrees F.

While the oven is heating, in a small bowl, stir together the flour and oil for preparing the pans. When the oven is ready, remove the hot pans and, using a pastry brush, brush the cups with the flour-oil mixture, coating the surface thoroughly and pouring off any excess oil. Immediately fill each cup two-thirds full (about 3 tablespoons) with the batter.

Bake the popovers for 35 to 40 minutes. They are ready when they have risen and are puffy and the batter's egg yellow color has turned an even brown. Do not open the oven door during baking or remove the popovers from the oven before they are done. If you do, they will quickly collapse. Remove from the pans and serve piping hot.

Makes 24

SEWARD'S FOLLY

BETTER KNOWN AS baked Alaska, this longstanding dessert favorite has been on the menu for most special-occasion dinners at the Cliff House since the 1970s. When the Cliff House restoration was completed in 2004, we decided to retire this showy classic. Many longtime customers still request it.

STRAWBERRIES
2 pints strawberries
⅓ cup sugar, or to taste

MERINGUE
3 egg whites, preferably pasteurized
¼ teaspoon cream of tartar
2 tablespoons sugar

6 slices pound cake (homemade or purchased),
   about ½ inch thick
6 scoops premium vanilla ice cream
1 eggshell half
About 1 ounce 151 proof rum

TO PREPARE the strawberries, hull and slice them and place in a bowl. Add the sugar, stir gently to mix well, and let stand for 2 hours at room temperature.

To make the meringue, in a bowl, using an electric mixer, whip the egg whites on high speed for 15 seconds. Add the cream of tartar and continue to whip for 1 minute. While continuing to whip, gradually add the sugar and whip until stiff peaks form.

Place the pound cake slices in a single layer in the bottom of a 6-by-10-inch oval baking dish. They should fit snugly. Place a scoop of ice cream on top of each cake slice. Spoon the strawberries evenly over the ice cream and cake. Gently spoon the meringue over the strawberries, evenly covering the entire surface of the dessert. Using a kitchen torch (see note), quickly brown the sides of the meringue (the flaming rum, added next, should

brown the top). Nest the eggshell half in the center of the meringue, and fill it halfway with the rum.

Carry the dish to the table, being careful not to spill the rum. Then, just before serving, ignite the rum with a long-handled match and, using 2 long-handled spoons to ensure a good grip, lift the eggshell and pour the flaming rum evenly over the top of the meringue. When the flames die, serve at once.

Note: If you do not have a kitchen torch, preheat the oven to 500 degrees F. Spoon the meringue over the assembled dessert as directed, and place the eggshell in the center of the meringue, but do not add the rum. Place in the oven until the meringue is golden brown, then remove from the oven, add the rum to the eggshell, and proceed as directed.

Serves 6

RAMOS FIZZ

FOR MANY SUNDAY-MORNING regulars at the Cliff House, brunch isn't brunch without a Ramos Fizz. For thirty years, the Cliff House was featured on the label of Parfumerie Funel–brand orange flower water, which declared that we used its product exclusively—"none to equal it"—for our Ramos Fizz. The brand is no longer available, but any good-quality orange flower water will work. We do suggest using Gordon's gin for this recipe. We've tried many brands, but Gordon's has a distinct floral aroma that no other gin can match in a fizz.

5 ounces Gordon's gin
5 ounces sweet and sour mix
5 ounces half-and-half
5 ounces egg white, preferably pasteurized
1 ounce fresh orange juice

6 sugar cubes
3 or 4 drops orange flower water
2 cups ice cubes
Ground nutmeg for garnish

IN A BLENDER, combine all of the ingredients except the garnish, cover tightly, and, holding the lid firmly in place, process on medium-high speed until the mixture is smooth and frothy. Divide evenly among 6 glasses, sprinkle the tops with nutmeg, and serve at once.

Serves 6

BLOODY MARY

DUBBED "AMERICA'S LIFESAVER," this elixir is a must at a Cliff House Sunday brunch. We experimented with a number of tomato juices, and Sacramento brand was the hands-down winner and is the only brand we recommend. You will need only half of the 46-ounce can of juice for this recipe. Drink the balance as is, or use it to make another batch of mix.

BLOODY MARY MIX

1 can (46 ounces) Sacramento tomato juice
16 ounces (2 cups) chili sauce (see note)
1 bottle (8 ounces) clam juice
1 teaspoon Worcestershire sauce
½ teaspoon Tabasco sauce
½ teaspoon prepared horseradish
½ teaspoon freshly ground black pepper
¼ teaspoon salt

Ice cubes
Vodka, 1½ ounces per drink
Celery ribs

TO MAKE THE MIX, open the can of tomato juice, pour half of it (23 ounces, or 3 cups minus 2 tablespoons) into a tall pitcher, and reserve the balance for another use. Add the chili sauce, clam juice, Worcestershire sauce, Tabasco sauce, horseradish, pepper, and salt and stir until thoroughly combined. The mix will keep, tightly covered, in the refrigerator for up to 5 days.

To make each drink, fill a tall, 16-ounce glass with ice cubes. Add 1½ ounces vodka and fill the glass to the top with the mix (about 6 ounces, or ¾ cup). Slip a celery rib into the glass and serve at once.

Note: Chili sauce usually comes in 12-ounce bottles. You will need about 1⅓ bottles to make the mix.

Makes enough mix for 8 drinks

PART FIVE

THE CLIFF HOUSE TODAY

PART FIVE
THE CLIFF HOUSE TODAY

ALLAN TEMKO, ARCHITECTURE CRITIC for the *San Francisco Chronicle*, didn't have a kind word to say about the Cliff House and its neighbors in a October 9, 1989 article: "Decades of neglect, decay and vulgarity have turned the Cliff House—once a glory of the West—into a crumbling tourist trap. . . . Two strange leftovers from the sideshow days of Playland disfigure the lower terrace: a collection of slot machines and coin-activated toys called the 'Musee Mechanique' [sic] and an ill-housed 'Camera Obscura.' They are tawdry enough for Pier 39." His solution? "What is left of the decomposing main building of 1909, a very ordinary design by the . . . [Reid Brothers], obviously should be pulled down and replaced by a superb new building that will be seismically safe. Only a preservationist geek would wish to save the present structure as a historic landmark." As for the souvenir shop and Pronto Pup stand next door and Louis' Restaurant just up the road? "Tawdrier still . . . [and they] should all be destroyed and mercifully forgotten."

The "very ordinary design" that Temko so thoroughly disparaged was actually no longer even visible. The neoclassical detail that had characterized the Reids' modestly scaled 1909 building had been either stripped away or masked by an accretion of twentieth-century additions. That meant that proponents of restoring the historic structure typically pulled out old photographs to support their position that the building was far more

Upstairs at the Cliff House, January 17, 2003. Photo by Ed Schuster, Cliff House Collection

Seafood and Beverage Company, January 29, 2003. Photo by Ed Schuster, Cliff House Collection

Phineas T. Barnacle Bar, January 15, 2003. Photo by Ed Schuster,
Cliff House Collection

Ben Butler Bar, January 17, 2003. Photo by Ed Schuster,
Cliff House Collection

Seafood and Beverage Company, January 17, 2003. Photo by Ed Schuster, Cliff House Collection

architecturally interesting and appropriate than Temko and many of his fellow critics claimed.

At the same time that Temko was goading the preservationists with his denunciation of the "decomposing" Cliff House, San Francisco architect James Ream was also riling them, by volunteering a design that would replace the structure with a trio of large glass-and-steel cupolas reminiscent of Kew Gardens. The round glass vaults would be linked by walkways and terraces, and together the spaces would accommodate a first-class restaurant, cafés, a sandwich shop, a national park information center, a gift shop, and even the "tawdry" museum and camera obscura.

Ream's free blueprints, which needed an angel with $15 million to see them realized, gained lukewarm approval from the public and no approval from the National Park Service (NPS), which was prohibited from considering any plans for a new building without holding a series of public meetings. Also, according to the general management plan drawn up by the NPS in 1980, the matter of a new structure would be possible only after the 1909 building was deemed unsound: "If sufficient historic fabric and structural integrity is not present to allow restoration of the 1909 Cliff House, it may be removed and replaced with a modern structure."

In the summer of 1992, the NPS unveiled preliminary plans for a nearly $20 million revitalization of the Sutro Historic District by the prestigious San Francisco landscape architecture firm of EDAW. They called for a two-story visitor center with a "grand staircase" down to the Sutro Baths ruins, moving the camera obscura and the Musée Mécanique into the visitor center and replacing them with a combination observation and

A last view of Seal Rocks from the Seafood and Beverage Company, January 29, 2003. Photo by Ed Schuster, Cliff House Collection

weather tower, and a new neoclassical façade for the Cliff House. The plans also included the restoration of the "waterworks" that once pumped seawater into the swimming pools at the baths, the erection of a fifty-five-foot steel catwalk between the Cliff House and the waterworks for visitors who wanted a close-up view of the surf, the construction of a walkway along the western edge of the baths with a network of footpaths, and the replanting of trees and shrubs. The most unusual feature would be the holographic projection of the once-palatial Sutro Baths onto the fog-shrouded ruins. Not in the plan was Louis' Restaurant (formerly Louis' Sandwich Shop), which would be forced to move from its original 1937 location "to open up a grand view of the ocean." In 1949, the restaurant had escaped a fire that burned down the nearby streetcar barn. Seventeen years later, it escaped the flames that reduced Sutro Baths to ashes, sustaining only smoke damage and broken windows. A third escape attempt, this time in the form of a Help Save Louis' campaign, came within days of the release of the EDAW plans.

The wheels of government revolved slowly, and it took nearly a year to set a date for a hearing on the proposed changes. About ten days before the hearing, harsh criticism of the plan to restore the 1909 Cliff House hit the media. Surprisingly, it came from two prominent organizations that usually champion historic preservation, San Francisco Beautiful (SFB) and the local chapter of the American Institute of Architects (AIA),

whose presidents sent letters to Brian O'Neill, superintendent of the Golden Gate National Recreation Area (GGNRA). Gerald D. Adams, in the May 17, 1993 *San Francisco Examiner*, reported that SFB president Robert Friese set a relatively polite tone, writing, "This important site is capable of a much more appealing and creative structure." AIA president James Follett was less diplomatic, stating, "The 1909 Cliff House was little more than a rectangular box devoid of any visual grace. The return of [that] form would be an immense disservice to this unique site." And James Ream, whose glass cupolas had never been given a chance by the NPS, was pricklier still, comparing the restoration of the 1909 structure to "building a Motel 6 on Union Square." All three men called for the GGNRA to establish a national design competition for a new Cliff House and visitor center, with Follett asserting that "for a site of such immense possibilities, only the best is good enough."

O'Neill remained unmoved, and the GGNRA announced it was going ahead with the restoration for two reasons. First, extensive investigations had found that although the interior of the building had been almost totally changed over the decades, approximately 80 percent of the Reids' 1909 "structural system and exterior appearance" remained unaltered. Second, the NPS had to act in accordance with the provisions of the National Historic Preservation Act, which required it to save any structure of historic quality, a quality that the GGNRA insisted had been established.

A LAST LOOK AT THE OLD BEFORE MAKING
WAY FOR THE NEW. FOR A SITE OF
SUCH IMMENSE POSSIBILITIES, ONLY THE BEST IS GOOD ENOUGH.

REINVENTING A LANDMARK

THE GGNRA'S DECISION did not end the Cliff House controversy, and architects, preservationists, neighborhood activists, and government officials continued to bicker over its fate. In the meantime, Dan and I hired Page & Turnbull, a leading local preservation architecture firm that had restored a number of historic sites in the city, including the 1909 Garden Court in the Palace Hotel and the 1910 Geary Theater, to create a design that would both preserve the Reid Brothers' original neoclassical building and add architecturally harmonious elements to bring it up to contemporary structural standards. The lead architect on our project was Mark Hulbert, and when he moved to another local firm, C. David Robinson Architects, we moved with him.

In October 1998, Dan and I finally signed a new twenty-year contract with the NPS to continue our operation of the Cliff House food and beverage concessions. At the time of the signing, we were told that our design would be presented to the GGNRA advisory commission for review within twelve months and then would be subject to a period of public comment.

Another four years would pass—years of reviewing and bickering, reviewing and bickering. Finally, in 2002, our design was accepted and the financing of the restoration was set. The estimated cost of the project was $14 million, with the federal government funding $1.9 million of the total. Dan and I were responsible for the balance, which we raised through bank loans and by mortgaging properties we owned. In January 2003, work on the "new" Cliff House began.

First, the old north annex, housing the gift shop and Pronto Pup, and the north addition to the Cliff House itself were knocked down and replaced with the Sutro Wing, a three-story steel building that borrowed design elements from the old Sutro Baths and included glass on two sides with views of Seal Rocks and the Marin Headlands. Next, the 1909 building was restored, which involved tearing down a 1950 addition at the south end of the building, stripping away the façade down to the original raw concrete, and extensive seismic work. The latter produced an interesting discovery: There was only one footing on the entire foundation, which meant that

North end of the 1909 structure is revealed during demolition, 2003.
Photo by Nibbi Bros.

North end of the 1909 structure fully exposed, 2003.
Photo by Nibbi Bros.

Demolition reveals there were no footings on the foundation of the 1909 structure, May 7, 2003. Photos by Nibbi Bros.

Without footings, the 1909 structure was cantilevered, but the building fared well in two major earthquakes. Photo by Nibbi Bros.

the building was actually cantilevered. Some local historians have speculated that because the structure went up not long after the 1906 earthquake, when hundreds of buildings were rising all over town, the overworked city inspectors gave most construction sites, including the Cliff House, only a quick look before signing off on them. Despite its balancing act, the building reportedly never moved during two major earthquakes, in 1957 and 1989. Updating the slapdash 1909 foundation added another $1 million to the budget and many weeks to the schedule.

The NPS requirement that the restoration duplicate the aesthetic features with the same materials the Reid Brothers had used also proved more costly than

Demolition of the south end of the building begins, May 12, 2004.
Photo by Nibbi Bros.

Demolition continues, May 12, 2004.
Photo by Nibbi Bros.

Demolition of the south end halfway completed, May 12, 2004.
Photo by Nibbi Bros.

1909 south exterior is revealed, May 12, 2004.
Photo by Nibbi Bros.

Steel framework for the new Sutro Wing, June 24, 2003.
Photo by Nibbi Bros.

View from the Sutro Baths ruins of the new Sutro Wing, September 12, 2003.
Photo by Nibbi Bros.

View of the 1909 exterior and Ocean Beach, May 12, 2004.
Photo by Nibbi Bros.

Restoration of the 1909 façade, May 3, 2004.
Photo by Nibbi Bros.

Dan Hountalas aboard a U.S. Coast Guard helicopter surveying construction
progress, August 18, 2003. Photo by Nibbi Bros.

Restoration of 1909 exterior with view of the Sutro Baths ruins, September 12, 2003.
Photo by Nibbi Bros.

Surviving portion of a beautifully frescoed 1909 interior wall is discovered, May 12, 2004. Now on display in the entryway. Photo by Nibbi Bros.

It took seven strong workers to maneuver her into position, September 3, 2004. Photo by Nibbi Bros.

One of the two fully restored Italian ceramic ladies is readied for her new place of honor in the Cliff House entryway, September 3, 2004. Photo by Nibbi Bros.

The second Italian ceramic lady, also fully restored, is displayed downstairs in Sutro's, September 9, 2004. Photo by Nibbi Bros.

Redwood bear, acquired from George Whitney, greets visitors, October 6, 2004. Photo by Ed Schuster, Cliff House Collection

originally planned. The contractor turned to a Chicago company for a custom concrete mix that matched the nearly century-old exterior surface. Once the façade and the foundation of the 1909 building were finished, a clear-glass atrium was erected to connect the building to the Sutro Wing and to serve as the main entrance. Finally, a trio of public observation decks were built on the ocean side. And when the dust finally settled, the once-endangered Louis' Restaurant was still standing in its original 1937 location.

At the time work started, the Cliff House had nearly two hundred employees, was open seven days a week for breakfast, lunch, and dinner, and served more than

View of Seal Rocks from Sutro's, September 17, 2004. Photo by Ed Schuster, Cliff House Collection

twenty-five thousand meals a month. We were able to keep only the Upstairs at the Cliff House restaurant, the Ben Butler Bar, and the lobby gift shop open during the restoration. That meant we had to lay off over half of our employees; however, those workers were offered the first available positions when the project was finished. Even when we closed down completely for four and a half months beginning in May 2004, we kept on fifteen employees to plan for the reopening. Others who had been accumulating vacation time at our suggestion took time off with pay and returned well rested.

The price tag ballooned beyond the original estimate to $18 million, which was covered in part by the NPS,

The Bistro, September 29, 2004. Photo by Ed Schuster, Cliff House Collection

Another view of the Bistro, September 29, 2004. Photo by Ed Schuster, Cliff House Collection

and the construction time grew from eighteen months to twenty-two months. But the extra money and delays were quickly forgotten when the project, which proved to be a successful example of a public-private partnership, was completed in October 2004.

The extensive seismic work on the 1909 building delayed the completion of its restoration, so we introduced the new bars and restaurants in phases, with Sutro's and Sutro's Bar, both in the Sutro Wing, debuting in September, and the Bistro, the Zinc Bar, and the Terrace Room, all in the original building, opening in October. On October 19, following a ribbon-cutting ceremony

Camera obscura, January 15, 2003. Photo by Ed Schuster, Cliff House Collection

attended by a gaggle of city dignitaries, hundreds of San Franciscans crowded into the beautifully restored landmark for the food and for the views—views that remain as breathtaking today as they were in 1863 on opening day of the first long, low, clapboard Cliff House.

Sutro Baths ruins, March 30, 2005. Photo by Ed Schuster, Cliff House Collection

October 19, 2004, opening day ribbon-cutting ceremony with Mayor Gavin Newsom (center) in attendance, Dan Hountalas doing the honors, and the author, Mary Germain Hountalas (far right). Photo by Nibbi Bros.

Aerial view after completion of the restoration, 2004. Photo by Nibbi Bros.

The "new" Cliff House from Ocean Beach, March 31, 2005. Photo by Ed Schuster, Cliff House Collection

THE CLIFF HOUSE GOES GREEN

THE ORIGINAL CLIFF HOUSE was built in the mid-nineteenth century and even the current Cliff House dates to 1909, but the newly restored building's garbage program is entirely twenty-first century. Food waste is composted; all menus, bottles, and cans are recycled; and used cooking oil is trucked away for conversion to biofuel. The kitchen staff uses unbleached paper towels, and garbage bins are kept clean with a daily rinse, rather than lined with plastic or even biodegradable bags. By instituting all of these environmentally savvy actions, the Cliff House has reduced its garbage collection by nearly 80 percent.

Of course, garbage collection will never disappear entirely, and we know that. We have even shown our appreciation for the diligent trash collectors of San Francisco by honoring one of its longtime workers. Just before the 2004 reopening, John Guaraglia, a seventy-four-year-old retired trash collector, watched as a plaque bearing his name was installed on the door of our brand-new trash room. Guaraglia's father began picking up trash at the newly built Cliff House in 1909, and John joined him on his route when he was only twelve years old. The day of the dedication, many of Guaraglia's fellow Sunset Scavenger retirees turned up to show their support for one of their own—a group of workers who have spent their lives disposing of everyone else's discards.

But going green is not only about trying to reduce the amount of garbage we generate. It is also about the food we serve. The kitchen focuses on purchasing locally grown and produced foods that are also organic, when possible. But if it is a choice between buying from local suppliers and buying organic items trucked in from a thousand miles away, the local products win, with general manager Ralph Burgin explaining that "it just doesn't make a lot of sense, environmentally speaking, to truck products in from far away"—a twenty-first-century answer for a bright green nineteenth-century landmark.

The kitchen staff also does what it can to help the less fortunate in the community. Each week, they pack up as much as they can for Food Runners, a volunteer organization that picks up excess perishable and prepared food from restaurants, caterers, and the like and delivers it to shelters and neighborhood programs that feed the needy.

SCALLOP CEVICHE

BE SURE TO USE only the best-quality dry-pack scallops for this appetizer, which is regularly featured in our Sutro's restaurant. Because the citrus juice "cooks" the scallops, changing their texture much like heat does, the shellfish must be perfectly fresh.

MOROCCAN SPICE OIL
2 teaspoons paprika
2 teaspoons ground cardamom
1 teaspoon ground coriander
1 teaspoon ground turmeric
1 teaspoon ground cumin
1 teaspoon cayenne pepper
Grated zest of 2 lemons
4 cloves garlic
1 tablespoon kosher salt
1¼ cups olive oil

CEVICHE
1 pound dry-pack sea scallops, cut into small dice
Juice of 1 lemon
Juice of 1 lime
2 tablespoons extra-virgin olive oil

FOR SERVING
1 tablespoon finely diced avocado
1 teaspoon finely sliced fresh chives
Sea salt
Moroccan spice oil for drizzling

TO MAKE THE SPICE OIL, in a small sauté pan, toast the paprika, cardamom, coriander, turmeric, cumin, and cayenne over medium-high heat until they release their aroma, about 2 minutes. Remove from the heat and transfer to a blender. Add the lemon zest, garlic, and salt to the blender. With the motor running, add about ¼ cup of the olive oil, or as needed to form a thick paste. Add the remaining 1 cup oil to the paste and continue to process to thin the paste to a pourable oil, forming an infusion of spices. You will need only a small amount of the spice oil for this recipe. Store the remainder in a tightly covered container in the refrigerator for use in other dishes. It will keep for up to 1 year.

To make the ceviche, in a bowl, combine the scallops, lemon juice, lime juice, and olive oil, and stir gently. Cover and refrigerate for 1 hour.

Remove the ceviche from the refrigerator, stir gently again, and divide evenly among 4 plates, each about 6 inches in diameter. Top with the avocado and chives, dividing them evenly, and then with a sprinkle of salt. Drizzle with the spice oil and serve at once.

Serves 4 as an appetizer

SUTRO CRAB CAKES

THE FAMED WEST Coast Dungeness crab has been on Cliff House menus since the days of Captain Junius Foster, and crab cakes are one of the best ways to show off the big, meaty crustacean. We accompany our version with a salsa of white peaches and corn during the summer and early fall months, and an avocado dressing the rest of the year.

2 tablespoons butter
5 tablespoons canola oil, plus more as needed
I carrot, peeled and finely diced
2 shallots, finely diced
2 celery ribs, finely diced
Grated zest of I lemon
I tablespoon minced garlic
I tablespoon minced fresh thyme
I teaspoon cayenne pepper

I tablespoon Old Bay seasoning
½ teaspoon paprika
I cup mayonnaise
I cup panko (Japanese bread crumbs)
2 pounds fresh-cooked Dungeness crabmeat, picked over
2 teaspoons kosher salt
Sweet Corn and White Peach Salsa or Avocado Green
    Goddess Dressing (opposite)

IN A SAUTÉ PAN, melt the butter with 3 tablespoons of the canola oil over medium heat. Add the carrot, shallots, celery, lemon zest, garlic, and thyme and cook, stirring occasionally, until the vegetables are tender, 2 to 3 minutes. Add the cayenne, Old Bay seasoning, and paprika, mix thoroughly, and remove from the heat. Transfer to a large bowl and let cool completely.

Add the mayonnaise, panko, crabmeat, and salt to the cooled vegetables and mix gently until well combined. Let the mixture rest at room temperature for 20 minutes, so the panko can soak up some of the moisture. Use a 2-ounce scoop to portion the mixture, and shape each scoop into a cake 2 inches in diameter and 1 inch thick. You should have 16 cakes. Refrigerate the cakes until you are ready to cook them.

Make either the salsa or the dressing and set aside.

To cook the crab cakes, in a large sauté pan, heat the remaining 2 tablespoons canola oil over medium heat. When the oil is hot, working in batches to avoid crowding, add the crab cakes and cook, turning once, until golden brown on both sides and heated through, about 2 minutes on each side. Remove from the pan and keep warm. Cook the remaining crab cakes the same way, adding more oil to the pan as needed to prevent sticking.

To serve, divide the crab cakes among warmed plates and serve with the salsa or dressing. Serve at once.

Serves 8 as an appetizer or 4 as a main course

SWEET CORN
AND WHITE PEACH SALSA

3 tablespoons butter
Kernels cut from 3 ears corn
Kosher salt

2 large white peaches, pitted and diced
2 tablespoons sugar
1 tablespoon finely sliced fresh chives

IN A SAUTÉ PAN, melt the butter over medium heat. Add the corn kernels and sauté until just tender, about 2 minutes. Season to taste with salt, remove from the heat, and transfer to a small bowl. Set aside to cool completely.

Meanwhile, place the peaches in a bowl, sprinkle with the sugar, and set aside at room temperature for about 5 minutes. The sugar will draw the natural juices from the peaches, creating a little juice for the salsa. When the corn is cool, add it and the chives to the peaches, then season with salt to taste. You should have about 3 cups. You won't need all of the salsa for serving the crab cakes. Cover and refrigerate the remainder and use as a dip for raw vegetables or chips.

AVOCADO GREEN
GODDESS DRESSING

2 avocados, halved, pitted, peeled, and chopped
Leaves from 1 bunch fresh basil
Leaves from 1 bunch fresh tarragon
Leaves from 1 bunch fresh parsley
Leaves from ½ bunch fresh dill

2 cloves garlic
2 cups mayonnaise
2 teaspoons kosher salt
⅛ teaspoon cayenne pepper

IN A BLENDER, combine the avocados, all of the fresh herbs, and the garlic and process until smooth. Add the mayonnaise, salt, and cayenne and process again until smooth. Taste and adjust the seasoning with salt and cayenne. You should have about 3 cups. You won't need all of the dressing for serving the crab cakes. Cover and refrigerate the remainder and use as salad dressing.

STEAMED MUSSELS
WITH ANCHOR STEAM BEER

THIS RECIPE HONORS another San Francisco landmark with a history nearly as long as that of the Cliff House: Anchor Brewing Company and its Anchor Steam beer, which dates from 1896. If you cannot find Anchor Steam where you live, you can substitute any high-quality full-flavored beer.

HARISSA
1 carrot, peeled
5 cloves garlic
2 shallots
1 jalapeño chile
1 red bell pepper
1 yellow bell pepper
1 celery rib
1 tablespoon coriander seeds

1 tablespoon cardamom seeds
1 tablespoon caraway seeds
1 tablespoon cumin seeds
¼ cup paprika
2 tablespoons chile flakes

MUSSELS
5 tablespoons unsalted butter
5 tablespoons canola oil

2 onions, sliced
1 teaspoon sugar
2 tablespoons minced garlic
2 pounds mussels, scrubbed and debearded
1 cup Anchor Steam beer
¼ cup harissa
Salt and freshly ground black pepper
¼ cup coarsely chopped fresh chives

TO MAKE THE HARISSA, preheat the broiler. Arrange the carrot, garlic, shallots, chile, bell peppers, and celery on a rimmed baking sheet. Place under the broiler and broil, turning the vegetables as needed, until nicely charred on all sides, 3 to 5 minutes. Some vegetables may char more quickly than others, so remove each one as it ready. (Or, use a charcoal or gas grill.)

Remove the vegetables from the broiler and let cool until they can be handled. Halve and seed the bell peppers and chile. Chop all of the vegetables and transfer to a blender. Add the coriander, cardamom, caraway, cumin, paprika, and chile flakes and process until the mixture is smooth. You will need only ¼ cup harissa for the mussels. Transfer the remainder to a tightly covered container and store in the refrigerator for use in other dishes. It will keep for up to 2 weeks.

To prepare the mussels, in a large sauté pan, melt 2 tablespoons of the butter with 2 tablespoons of the oil over medium heat. Add the onions, sprinkle with the sugar, and cook, stirring occasionally, until the onions

are soft and chestnut brown, about 10 minutes. Remove from the heat and transfer the onions to a bowl.

Return the pan to medium heat and add the remaining 3 tablespoons each butter and oil. Add the garlic and sauté until golden brown, about 1 minute. Add the mussels, discarding any that failed to close to the touch, and sauté until some of the mussels begin to open, about 2 minutes. Deglaze the pan with the beer and cook, stirring, for 1 minute to release any browned bits from the pan bottom. Mix in the reserved onions, raise the heat to medium-high, and cook until all of the mussels have opened. Mix in the harissa, then remove from the heat. Using a slotted spoon, divide the mussels evenly between 2 deep individual serving bowls, discarding any that failed to open. Leave the liquid in the pan.

Return the pan to medium-high heat and reduce the liquid until it has a medium soup consistency. Season to taste with salt and pepper and pour evenly over the mussels. Garnish with the chives and serve at once.

Serves 2

ROASTED BEET SALAD
WITH CITRUS-HORSERADISH VINAIGRETTE

SEASONALITY IS THE primary factor in determining which salads will be made each week for the Terrace Room Champagne brunch, which is just one of the reasons why Sunday brunch at the Cliff House is a "can't miss" experience. This combination of roasted beets with a brightly flavored vinaigrette is one of our most requested wintertime salads.

8 red beets, unpeeled
1 teaspoon kosher salt
¼ teaspoon freshly ground black pepper
¼ cup olive oil
1 cup dry white wine
1 cup fresh orange juice
2 fresh thyme sprigs

CITRUS-HORSERADISH VINAIGRETTE
¼ cup reduced beet cooking liquid
¼ cup fresh orange juice
2 tablespoons sherry vinegar
1 teaspoon prepared horseradish
1 teaspoon salt
Pinch of sugar
¼ cup extra-virgin olive oil

8 ounces fresh goat cheese, crumbled
Chopped fresh chives for garnish

PREHEAT THE OVEN to 350 degrees F. Place the beets in a roasting pan just large enough to hold them in a single layer, and sprinkle with the salt and pepper. Drizzle the olive oil evenly over the beets, then rub the beets with the oil to coat evenly. Add the wine, orange juice, and thyme to the pan, place over high heat, and bring to a boil. When you see steam rising, remove the pan from the heat, cover tightly with aluminum foil, place in the oven, and roast until the beets are fork-tender, about 1 hour.

Remove the beets from the pan and set aside. Strain the liquid in the pan through a fine-mesh sieve into a small saucepan, place over high heat, and reduce to ¼ cup. Set aside to cool. Trim and peel the hot beets, holding them with a paper towel to protect your fingers from the heat. (Beets are easier to peel when they are hot.) Cut the beets into wedges or rounds, as desired, then let cool completely and divide evenly among 8 salad plates.

To make the vinaigrette, in a small bowl, whisk together the reduced beet liquid, orange juice, vinegar, horseradish, salt, and sugar until well combined. Slowly whisk in the olive oil.

Pour the vinaigrette over the beets, dividing it evenly. Garnish the salads evenly with the goat cheese and chives and serve at once.

Serves 8

OCEAN BEACH

THIS IS OUR Cliff House variation on the ever-popular Sex on the Beach cocktail. In our version, the traditional orange juice is traded for pineapple juice.

Ice cubes
1½ ounces vodka
½ ounce peach schnapps

3 ounces pineapple juice
1 ounce cranberry juice

FILL A 12-OUNCE highball glass with ice cubes. Pour in the vodka and peach schnapps, and then stir in the pineapple juice. Float the cranberry juice on top. Add a tall straw and serve at once.

Serves 1

HPNOTIQ BREEZE

JAIME WONG, assistant general manager of the Cliff House, created this variation on the Bay Breeze, a combination of vodka or rum and cranberry and pineapple juices. Wong replaces the vodka with Hpnotiq, a French fruit liqueur made from Cognac, vodka, and tropical fruit juices, but then, not wanting to disappoint vodka fans who expect more of a punch, he uses cranberry vodka instead of cranberry juice.

Ice cubes
2 ounces Hpnotiq liqueur
1 ounce cranberry vodka

2 ounces pineapple juice
Lemon twist for garnish

FILL A COCKTAIL SHAKER two-thirds full with ice cubes and add the liqueur, cranberry vodka, and pineapple juice. Cover and shake well, then strain into a martini glass. Garnish with a lemon twist. Serve at once.

Serves 1

SIMPLY PUT,

THE CLIFF HOUSE IS THE PLACE TO BE.

SELECTED BIBLIOGRAPHY

Barker, Malcolm E., comp. *More San Francisco Memoirs 1852-1899*. San Francisco: Londonborn Publications, 1996.

Berglund, Barbara. *Making San Francisco American*. Lawrence, Kansas: University of Kansas Press, 2007.

Blaisdell, Marilyn. *San Francisciana: Photographs of the Cliff House*. San Francisco: Marilyn Blaisdell, 2005.

Brown, Helen Evans. *West Coast Cook Book*. Boston: Little, Brown and Company, 1952.

Edwords, Clarence Edgar. *Bohemian San Francisco*. San Francisco: Paul Elder and Company Publishers, 1914.

Hansen, Gladys. *San Francisco Almanac*. San Francisco: Chronicle Books, 1975.

Land and Community Associates. "Sutro Historic District Cultural Landscape Report." Prepared for National Park Service, September 1993.

Manning, Kathleen, and Jim Dickson. *San Francisco's Ocean Beach*. Charleston, SC: Arcadia Publishing, 2003.

Admission tickets, 1909. From the collection of Glenn D. Koch

Martini, John A. "Sutro Baths, A Developmental History." Prepared by Architectural Resource Group for National Park Service, February 2008.

Muscatine, Doris. *A Cook's Tour of San Francisco*. New York: Charles Scribner's Sons, 1963.

Neville, Amelia Ransome. *The Fantastic City: Memoirs of the Social and Romantic Life of Old San Francisco*. Manchester, NH: Ayer Company Publishing, 1975. First published 1932 Houghton Mifflin, Boston.

O'Brien, Robert. *This Is San Francisco*. New York: Whittlesey House, 1948.

Okamoto, Ariel Rubissow. *A Day at the Seaside*. San Francisco: Golden Gate National Parks Association, 1998.

Richards, Rand. *Historic San Francisco*. San Francisco: Heritage House Publishers, 2003.

Soyster, Cynthia. "Adolph Sutro, My Great-Grandfather." Address to the Daughters of California Pioneers, San Francisco, CA, December 5, 1998.

Smith, James R. *San Francisco's Lost Landmarks*. Sanger, CA: Word Dancer Press, 2005.

Stewart, Jr., Robert E., and Mary Frances Stewart. *Adolph Sutro, A Biography*. Berkeley: Howell-North Books, 1962.

Talavera Berger, Frances de, and John Parke Custis. *Sumptuous Dining in Gaslight San Francisco 1875-1915*. Garden City, NY: Doubleday & Company, 1985.

Taylor, Bayard. *Eldorado, or Adventures in the Path of Empire, Comprising a Voyage to California, Via Panama, Life in San Francisco and Monterey, Pictures of the Gold Region, and Experiences of Mexican Travel*. New York: Time-Life, 1983. Facsimile reprint from 1850.

Wiley, Peter Booth. *National Trust Guide San Francisco*. New York: John Wiley & Sons, Inc., 2000.

Newspaper and periodical archives 1860–2008: *Californian, Daily Alta California, New York Times, Reno Evening Gazette, San Francisco Bulletin, San Francisco Call, San Francisco Call Bulletin, San Francisco Chronicle, San Francisco Daily Morning Call, San Francisco Examiner, San Francisco News, Scribner's Monthly*, and Western Neighborhood Projects newsletter.

Web sites: www.cliffhouseproject.com, www.outsidelands.org, www.sfgenealogy.com, www.sfmuseum.org, and www.sfpl.lib.ca.us.

Souvenir booklet, 1940s. Cliff House Collection

ACKNOWLEDGMENTS

Many people have contributed to the realization of this book, and I am deeply indebted to all of them.

Gary Stark, who developed and maintains www.cliffhouseproject.com, a wonderful Web site dedicated to the Cliff House, offered not only many rare images from his extensive collection, but also spent valuable time reading early drafts of the manuscript for accuracy.

John Martini, a retired National Park Service ranger and historian, also took time to read the manuscript and to clear up a number of murky historical facts. In addition, he led me to rare early photographs in the San Francisco Department of Public Works collection at the San Francisco Public Library.

Dennis O'Rourke, whom I met through a number of pitched bidding battles for Cliff House memorabilia on eBay, provided his own images and hundreds of old photographs and postcards.

Jim Bell, a longtime friend and business associate, not only gave me full access to his large collection of photographs, but also restored one of the Cliff House Collection's most unusual photographs of Adolph Sutro's 1896 structure.

San Franciscan Ed Schuster carefully chronicled the twenty-two-month restoration of the Cliff House, and then presented me with a complete collection of his photographs. Nibbi Brothers Construction, led by project manager Alex Boren, also provided an invaluable photographic history of the restoration, including a detailed record of the difficulties encountered. Many images from both of these generous sources grace these pages.

I also want to thank Frank and Ruth Mitchell, who developed at their own expense several new images from their treasured negatives; Bob Schlesinger, another eBay regular, who scanned many of his acquisitions for me; Glenn Koch, who permitted the use of his rare original 1909 Grand Opening menu; Zoe Heimdal, of www.sanfranciscomemories.com, who allowed the reproduction of a key image; and Marilyn Blaisdell, who made possible the addition of an original menu for President Theodore Roosevelt's 1903 luncheon to the Cliff House Collection.

For their help with researching images, I want to thank the following individuals and institutions: supervising librarian Kathleen A. Correia, in the California History Section of the California State Library, Sacramento; photo curator Christina Moretta and her staff, of the San Francisco History Center of the San Francisco Public Library; reference archivist Amanda Williford, of the Golden Gate National Recreation Area Archives; and program coordinator Carol Boyce, of the Buffalo Bill Historical Center in Cody, Wyoming.

Cliff House staff members Kevin Weber, Art Bradley, Brian O'Connor, and Jaime Wong spent many hours working on the recipes in the book, and Art was also indispensable in getting me up to speed on various new computer functions I was forced to master. I am grateful to all of them for their dedication.

I am also grateful to Susie Biehler, who persistently encouraged me to undertake this book project. She also introduced me to Amy Rennert, who proved not only an excellent literary agent but also lead me to the perfect writing partner, Sharon Silva—together we made a great team.

Special thanks to Ten Speed editor Veronica Randall, who though faced with a tight schedule and far more images to choose from than book pages, handled a difficult task with confidence and humor, and to Ian Shimkoviak and Alan Hebel of The Book Designers for the handsome design.

Finally, thank you to my husband, Dan, for patiently enduring life with me during this long project and for providing me with the support and encouragement I needed to see it through.

Equestrienne and friends on Ocean Beach with the 1909 Cliff House in the background. From the collection of Glenn D. Koch

INDEX